Death in Avignon

Death in Avignon

A PENELOPE KITE NOVEL

SERENA KENT

HARPER

An Imprint of HarperCollins*Publishers*

HarperCollins books may be purchased for educational, business, or sales promotional use. For information, please email the Special Markets Department at SPsales@harpercollins.com.

FIRST EDITION

Library of Congress Cataloging-in-Publication Data

Names: Kent, Serena, author.
Title: Death in Avignon : a penelope kite novel / Serena Kent.
Description: First edition. | New York, NY : Harper, [2019] | Series: Penelope Kite ; book 2
Identifiers: LCCN 2019007889 (print) | LCCN 2019008569 (ebook) | ISBN 9780062869906 (E-book) | ISBN 9780062869883 (Paperback) | ISBN 9780062869890 (Library)
Subjects: | GSAFD: Mystery fiction.
Classification: LCC PR6111.E594 (ebook) | LCC PR6111.E594 D425 2019 (print) |
DDC 823/.92—dc23
LC record available at https://lccn.loc.gov/2019007889

20 21 22 23 24 LSC 10 9 8 7 6 5 4 3 2 1

Death in Avignon

1

IT WAS A GLORIOUS LATE October morning. Under a sapphire sky, the Luberon ridge rippled down into the valley and the warmth of summer lingered. An immense cathedral quiet seemed to stretch to the distant hills.

On the terrace of Le Chant d'Eau, Penelope Kite breathed in deeply and drew the bow across the strings of her cello. The first note came out as a growl, followed by a low rumble. As her bowing became more confident, the tone gained in purity.

The music calmed her. Not that her jitteriness today was a bad thing. Nothing like those first weeks in St Merlot, when she had been a woman in volcanic form, erupting in the heat of August. It was amazing how much she had achieved in such a short time. The ramshackle old farmhouse had been replastered and repainted. The electrical rewiring had been completed. She had recently taken delivery of a large woodburning stove, and soon she would have two new bathrooms.

Even more satisfyingly, she had made friends. And, after much anticipation, tonight was the night she was going out to dinner with the mayor of St Merlot, the knee-tremblingly handsome and charming Laurent Millais. Third-time lucky, she hoped. Frustratingly, something always seemed to get in the way.

But so far, so good. He had called to confirm. The plan was to drop in first to the opening of an art exhibition in Avignon, and then have dinner at La Coquillade at Gargas. Just the two

of them. La Coquillade was a very smart restaurant and boutique hotel surrounded by olive groves, pools, and vineyards
and renowned for its romantic atmosphere. Penelope felt a surge
of excitement, then slapped herself down. Laurent was merely
keeping his word that he'd take her out to celebrate the solving of
two murders that had disrupted her first months in the Luberon.
No need to make a show of herself.

She should try to concentrate on the music.

❧

SHE WAS tackling a particularly fiendish passage when the familiar sound of scattering stones on the track announced an
unscheduled arrival. The car clattered down the drive, spitting
gravel, then skidded to a halt with the squeal of a braking system
pushed well beyond its comfort zone.

Penelope knew immediately who it was. She rested her bow
and waited for the click of stiletto heels on the flagstones.

"*Coucou*, Penny!"

"*Bonjour*, Clémence."

Clémence Valencourt appeared on the terrace in beautifully
tailored cropped black trousers, with a tight white silky top that
showed not even a suspicion of middle-aged bulge, a look Penelope could only aspire to. Copious loops of costume pearls
and gilt topped off with what looked like—and probably was—a
genuine Chanel jacket. The petite Parisienne smiled, revealing
perfect white teeth. "That was very good, Penny. I recognise it—
Rachmaninov? Continue, please!"

"Well. If you don't mind, I should just finish this section. It's
a tricky bit and I've nearly mastered it."

"*Impeccable.* You finish, and I will listen as I make us some
coffee."

Penelope ran through the difficult section a few more times until the smell of coffee became too compelling to ignore.

Clémence brought two cups outside and they sat companionably at the white café table under an olive tree in a galvanised steel planter. Sheer bliss, thought Penelope, as she tipped her head back in the sunshine. It was such a pleasure that the air was still warm enough to be able to sit outside, even in the middle of autumn.

"Penny, I did not realise how well you played. You have many surprises for us, *n'est-ce pas?*"

Penelope accepted the compliment—for indeed it was one—from this chic, cultured woman who had become an unexpected ally. "Well, I used to be so much better, but I am getting there. It just takes time. But this *is* my time, the chance I longed for to take up some of my interests again. Music. Gardening. Maybe even some painting, though I haven't done any of that since I got married."

"Yes, Penny, we all benefit, *sans* husband."

Penelope was itching to quiz her about M. Valencourt, who was away so often, but Clémence continued without drawing breath.

"And you are an artist as well? *Mon dieu*, what talent has arrived in St Merlot!"

Penelope was never quite sure when the Frenchwoman was sending her up. "I wouldn't say I was an artist—but I have always wanted to learn to paint properly, and here seems to be the perfect place."

"Yes, Penny, it is the light. Artists have come to Provence for centuries."

Penelope hesitated, knowing that it was best she say something now, and not let Clémence find out from someone else. "Laurent is taking me to an exhibition this evening."

Clémence stiffened a little. She looked up at Penelope from behind a wing of perfectly coiffed blond hair, her eyes wide. "This evening . . . at Avignon?"

As an upmarket property broker, Clémence spread her net wide. "I believe so. He wants to support a friend—and the press will be there. He does enjoy being mentioned in *La Provence*, doesn't he?"

"He's becoming quite vain about publicity, it's true. It will be the opening of the new exhibition at the Gilles de Bourdan Gallery. I hear that Nicolas Versanne is showing some of his new paintings. Nicolas and Claudine Versanne—you met them at Laurent's dinner party, remember? Claudine is director of the Museum of the Ochre Paints at Roussillon. What a good idea to ask you to come, too."

"'Come, *too*?'" Penelope smelt a rat. "Are you going?"

"I might drop in."

Penelope felt the cosy tête-à-tête with the gorgeous mayor receding into the middle distance. She was never quite sure about the current status of Clémence's sophisticated relationship with him. There had been a fling earlier in the year, and possibly others in the past, but that seemed to be over. And Penelope's own feelings on the matter were complex, to say the least.

"It's only the evening out he promised me weeks ago, you know, after all the . . . unpleasantness in the village. We were going to go last week, but one of his friends had a crisis and he had to cancel. It's very sweet that he's keeping his word."

"I should introduce you to my musician friends," said Clémence, apparently not willing to be outdone as far as expanding Penelope's social circle was concerned. "They play together in a group, and they are always looking for new players. They perform from time to time around the Luberon. Perhaps you might be interested in joining them?"

Penelope had always loved playing for an audience. As a closet show-off she found the exhilaration of performance addictive, and it was one of her main regrets about her staid and conventional life in England that she had given up playing in public. The idea of performing with a group in France intrigued her.

"Well, I'd love to meet them and hear them play."

"In fact, Penny, they are giving a concert in Viens in a few weeks' time. Why don't you come along with me then?"

Viens was the village fifteen kilometres away where the Valencourts lived in some splendour. Their palatial house boasted curving marble staircases, medieval stone carvings, and walls bearing aristocratic escutcheons. So far, Penelope had not been introduced to M. Valencourt. Come to think of it, she didn't even know his first name. Maybe he would be there. Penelope couldn't help her curiosity, but Clémence had a habit of waving away any direct inquiries.

"That is very kind of you. I would love to do that," said Penelope.

Sometimes she couldn't imagine why she had been so wary of Clémence's brittle exterior. Her heart was in the right place. It had just taken a couple of local murders to locate it—an option admittedly not available to all. "By the way," Clémence said, pulling a pretty frown. "What *are* you wearing?"

Penelope looked down at her old Laura Ashley dress and cardigan. The comfortable canvas shoes and the bare, slightly goosepimply legs that she was intending to shave later. "I wasn't expecting visitors."

Her former estate agent gave her a pained look that implied any Frenchwoman worth her salt would be visitor-ready at all times.

Penelope was used to this by now. Their fledgling relationship was founded on the difference between a Frenchwoman and an Englishwoman, both *d'un certain âge*. It went without saying that the Englishwoman knew her place as the underdog in matters of fashion. But she was learning new tricks fast. Why, it had been weeks since a single croissant had passed Penelope's lips for breakfast, let alone two.

She listened respectfully as Clémence advised her that a well-cut little black dress was always acceptable attire at an art world gathering. In exchange, Penelope gave her opinion when Clémence asked her view on advertising property in the British press. And she put the date of the concert in Viens in her diary.

※

WHEN CLÉMENCE had left, Penelope went back to her Rachmaninov. But it failed to catch fire or to calm her conflicting emotions. Much as she had come to like her, seeing Clémence still made her feel inadequate. There were so many necessary improvements to implement, both to the crumbling old farmhouse and to her person.

This time last year she had been a bored middle-aged divorcée in Esher, taken for granted by the family and missing work after her boss retired, and she decided to leave, too. True, it had been a nightmare in Provence at first, what with the dead body in the swimming pool, but she had discovered layers of St Merlot's history that she might never otherwise have known. Not an ideal way to become known as a *femme fatale*, maybe, but she had made some interesting friends in the process, not least the mayor.

The thought of him sent her scurrying upstairs to assess the possibilities of finding a well-cut black dress in her cupboard.

❦

THE PILE of discarded clothes grew.

After more fruitless tussling, she slumped onto the bed and switched on her iPad. She bypassed the predictably depressing news stories in the *Daily Telegraph* online after a cursory glance at the headlines, but couldn't stop herself reading some nonsense about what milestone birthdays should mean for your wardrobe. Penelope didn't like the sound of that "should." That was another reason she was happy to have left Surrey: all the bossy expectations of the English middle classes. Do this. Do that. Go to this restaurant. Eat kale. Read this book. And now, wear these clothes.

There was nothing more than common sense for those who had recently turned fifty. Style icon Inès de la Fressange urged her to aim for sensuality rather than sexiness, "as it was stronger." This gnomic utterance was accompanied by a list of items to jettison, which included glittery blousons, embroidered and studded skinny jeans, and very high stilettos—none of which Penelope had ever been remotely tempted to buy in the first place.

Downstairs, she made herself a cup of strong British tea and wondered why she felt like a teenage girl steadying herself for a first date, especially when any effort would be pointless. Laurent Millais was way out of her league.

2

ON THE DOT OF SIX, Laurent arrived in his blue Mercedes. It matched his eyes, a felicity that Penelope suspected was far from coincidental.

"You look very elegant," he said.

In the end, she had gone for stark (and slimming) simplicity: a loose black silk top over black cropped trousers and high heels. "Thank you. So do you."

He was devastatingly attractive in a casual black linen suit and pale blue shirt. His floppy, honey-coloured hair was still sun-streaked from the long Provençal summer. On an Englishman of the same age it would have looked too long, but it was perfect for Laurent Millais, showcasing his wonderful cheekbones, classical straight nose, and smooth, tanned complexion.

He bent down to kiss her three times on the cheeks, left-right-left. Penelope hoped she wouldn't let herself down by going red and having a hot flush as his lips lightly brushed her skin. She breathed in his lemony wild herb cologne.

"I shall drive like an English gentleman, not so fast," he said as he opened the passenger door for her. "I know you don't like to race around the bends like we all do."

"That would be most considerate."

True to his word, they had a pleasantly sedate drive down to the main road along the valley floor with none of the nervy clutching for the door handle and pressing down on an imaginary brake that was a feature of any ride with Clémence. As they bowled along a nearly empty road past apricot orchards that flamed with scarlet leaves and dormant lavender fields of pale grey corduroy, Laurent chatted of this and that: village matters concerning St Merlot's knottier problems, such as the recent disappointing quality of the wild boar pâté supplied by the *Epicerie-Fruiterie* and whether the boules used by the pétanque team should be paid for by the mairie.

"Of course, it is merely a gesture of support," he continued. "I doubt that the money we give the players ever gets further than the bar. None of them have any intention of replacing boules that have served them so well for decades."

"What's happening with the Priory development?" asked Penelope.

Laurent was part of a consortium involved in turning an abandoned medieval nunnery, Le Prieuré des Gentilles Merlotiennes, into a spa hotel. The idea was to use as many natural, locally grown herbs as possible in the lotions and potions they used. Penelope had even been asked to consider planting lavender on part of her land to add to the supplies. She couldn't wait to get started and take her cut in aromatherapy sessions.

"It's all moving in the right direction," said Laurent. "The permissions are now in place, and contracts are being signed with the building firm. The architect hopes that work will start soon, so long as the weather holds."

In the clear sky of an October evening in Provence, the setting sun was still above the horizon. They were heading into its rosy caress.

"You mean when a few clouds gather in your endlessly blue skies here," said Penelope. It was a source of great amusement to her, the way the southern French cast baffled looks up at the heavens whenever the sky clouded over and the temperature dropped, and muttered darkly, "*C'est pas normale.*"

"You wait. You have not seen a Luberon winter yet, have you?"

"No, but it can't possibly be as bad as a wet, cold, and grey English one, when the dismal damp just goes on and on, and everyone's coats start to grow moss."

"Moss, really?"

"Oh, yes," said Penelope gravely. "We have to get our coats specially treated." She waited until his shudder subsided, then smiled. "No, not really! But it feels like it. It's a kind of damp heaviness that weighs you down. At least the sun shines here, even when it's cold."

"That's true. But you wait until the mistral starts. A howling wind all day and all night, rushing down the Rhône to the south. It can send people mad."

They shot forward smoothly onto a stretch of dual carriage-way. Olive groves and tall cypress trees stood serenely against a spectacular mountain backdrop as they sped west along the valley towards the grandeur of Avignon.

"It won't make any difference to me, then, will it? You all think I'm mad anyway."

"Not mad, just different."

Penelope hoped there might be a chance to explore that avenue further, but Laurent had moved on to the subject of Avignon. "Out of season, Penny, it is gorgeous, you will love it. In the summer, it is terrible. Thick with tourists, hot, students on every corner pretending to be Bob Dylan or Marcel Marceau miming a tree."

"Only during the festival, surely." Penelope had arrived in Provence too late for the famous Avignon Festival (somewhat like

Edinburgh, she guessed, but without the dour Scottish masonry and the grey rain).

"You might be surprised. Everyone likes to play up to the city's artistic reputation."

"I can't wait," said Penelope.

⚜

THE GILLES de Bourdan Gallery was on the Rue des Teinturiers, a picturesque cobblestone street shaded by trees inside the mighty city walls. A small canal ran along its length, and the area's industrial heritage was marked by a series of waterwheels once used by the dyers who had made the street their own. Penelope got a kick from walking into the gallery with Laurent, noticing the looks of envy from other women. But the moment quickly passed. He was approached by so many people that he disappeared into a scrum from which Penelope felt like a rugby ball being gradually worked to the back. She accepted a glass of rosé from a bespectacled young waiter with a long, plaited beard and looked around for the canapés.

The exhibition was in a modern, purpose-built extension to the rear of the gallery. This light and airy space was divided into four rooms, each dedicated to a different artist, one of whom was Nicolas Versanne. According to the catalogue, the works on show ranged "from the conceptual to the figurative, providing us with a narrative of diverse interpretations, from black to white, from despair to elation." Penelope suppressed a snort of amusement. Why did the French always make everything sound so pretentious?

She looked around for Nicolas and his wife, Claudine, remembering how pleasant they had been at Laurent's dinner party. The exhibition was already busy, the crowd a mixture of well-dressed middle-aged people, younger guests in black, and a considerable number of self-consciously artistic figures in eccentric clothes. One woman wore a leopard-print catsuit under a fuchsia cloak. Which might have worked if she had been on the right side of seventy. Another elderly blonde in a white miniskirt held a long-haired pug to her breast. Penelope wondered for a moment whether she was Brigitte Bardot. Plenty to look at, she thought, even if she was wandering around on her own. She would have hours of chat with Laurent later over dinner. It was a very pleasant prospect.

She entered Room One and found herself staring at a line of green bottles hanging on a string, each dripping red dye onto the floor beneath. Facing the array was a large tuba with smoke issuing from its horn. She looked, thoroughly confused, at the title. *The Price of War.* The price of this baffling piece by installation artist Nina Chiroubles was thirty thousand euros. Penelope was further perplexed by a pile of used cans (*The West*, twenty-five thousand euros) and moved on to another 3D exhibit on the wall. Upon closer examination it turned out to be the gallery's defibrillator.

A woman (not much younger than Penelope) wearing purple leggings and a mini-skirt and sporting turquoise hair in a cockatoo style had backed a small, worried-looking man into a corner. She poked a black-varnished fingernail at him. The words "struggle" and "progressive" compounded his ordeal.

So much conceptual art was a big fat fraud, thought Penelope, heading for the door and hoping against hope that beyond it might await a work of art that retained some grip on reality.

The next room was full of large canvases, signed "Scarpio" in fluorescent yellow. Almost all were black. They varied in size from a small square of black in a golden and ornate frame to a large unframed black canvas that towered over her. She peered at the title. *Study in Black VI.* A snip at ten thousand euros. Looking around at the crowd, who seemed to be giving this room rather less attention, she noticed an emaciated man with long, improbably dark lank hair, wrinkles like crevasses, and dark glasses. He was wearing black jeans and a black T-shirt and jacket.

Either this was the artist or Keith Richards had just flown in, thought Penelope as she exited swiftly past a medium-sized canvas that was coloured a refreshing slate grey. The next room was much, much busier.

As she entered, the unmistakable plummy tones of a British expat, speaking in English, boomed out over the crowd. "People always want to know where the inspiration comes from! What does that matter? I have spent my life justifying my reasoning. It's the painting that emerges that is important!"

Instinctively, Penelope turned away. She had been avoiding other expats for the past few months, preferring to immerse herself in local life. There was something all too familiar about this Englishman, his thick blond hair running to grey, his smooth tanned face, and a broad build that would once have been athletic. He stood supremely confidently before a gaggle of women. "Well, what do you think?"

He was talking to her. His acolytes stopped talking and looked round. They were all well-dressed ladies with unnaturally plump lips and unlined foreheads. If they could have raised their eyebrows they would probably have done so.

Penelope smiled weakly and wondered whether there was any chance she could get away by pretending not to understand.

"Don't be shy! How super of you to come and see my show."

The dashing artist bore down upon her like a yacht in full sail. He was wearing a baggy cream suit, a pink shirt, and a cravat patterned with vintage racing cars. She found herself shaking a firm and energetic hand.

"Pleased to meet you, Mr . . . Mr . . ."

"Roland Galbraith Doncaster. Call me Don, everyone does. And correct me if I'm wrong, but *you* are Penelope Kite!"

He gave her no time to deny it.

"I've heard about you and your baptism of fire here! You've made quite the splash, haven't you! Though maybe 'splash' is inappropriate!" He chortled at his own joke. "You must come over one day and tell me all about it. You're the talk of the expatriate community. We've all been wondering when we would run into you—and here you are!"

"How on earth did you know who I—?"

He pulled out a large handkerchief and mopped his brow. "Claudine said you liked art and you might be persuaded along. Glad to see you've made it. Thought you might not come. After all, this is real art, art with guts—none of that old-lady watercolour stuff. No offence!"

Don Doncaster flashed a warm smile at her, and Penelope could see why he was surrounded by this simpering crowd of admirers. He had a certain charisma, though it might only have been that supreme confidence, a type Penelope had known and learned to be wary of over the years.

She steeled herself and made an attempt at conversation.

"So, this is your room, is it?"

Only now did she focus on the art. And as she took in the paintings, the harsh and unavoidable truth could not be ignored. They were dreadful. In fact, the only guts Penelope could discern were those it took to own up to having created them. The paint was trowelled on so thickly that flowers and plates of fruit stood proud in messy, sticky relief. Sunflowers glared truculently. Bright purple spears of lavender. A melon lay disembowelled. It was all quite ghastly.

"My humble daubings." He narrowed his eyes to judge her

reaction. A veil of terrible false modesty clung to his smile. "And doing rather well this evening, if I do say so myself. Managed to sell most of them already so I'm afraid there's not much left for you."

A titter of self-conscious laughter from the groupies.

"What a shame," said Penelope. "Oh, well . . ."

He was clearly in his element, leaning nonchalantly against a table and devouring the large bowl of green olives next to him, switching attention from one fan to the next. One woman in her forties took a selfie with him in front of a vast garish painting of a poppy field from which a dog's head protruded in life-sized plaster relief. Penelope was rooted to the spot by the spectacle, taking in all the details to recount later to her friend Frankie, who would find it hilarious.

"Darling, do have one of these, they are simply heavenly." Penelope realised he was holding out the bowl to her. "Pure Provençal fabulosity. Olives stuffed with almond. I must have them! Getting to be quite the diva these days. Even being imitated now, don't ya know! Guard against, guard against!"

Penelope declined politely. "I must go and see the last room. I haven't been there yet."

"Oh, I am sure you will enjoy those. They are a little abstract for my taste, but there's no denying his quality. Mixes all his own pigments—can't think why!" He popped an olive into his mouth. "Mmm, mmm, mmm. Delicioso! Go on, have one!"

"No really, I—"

"Dear lady, if you are going to live in this area, you simply must try these little miracles. I insist; it's non-negotiable!" He pressed the bowl on her and gave her another dazzling smile.

Even though Penelope did not actually like green olives much, she had no choice but to take one. When he turned away to address one of his admirers, Penelope dropped it into her handbag.

She was just sidling out of the room when she was engulfed in the aroma of expensive cigars as Don's hand clamped onto her forearm. Against her will, she found herself pulled towards the paintings. Close up, they were even worse. Penelope was forced to contemplate a gruesome purple church in a meadow with two lambs gambolling in the foreground, eyes wide with fright.

"So, Mr . . . Don. You are a figurative artist."

"Seems to be what the public want. And we must always give the public what they want, don't you think. If they want social comment, they can go and see Nina's work. If they want Provence, I will give them sunflowers and lavender."

Penelope escaped his grasp and made for the door. "Excuse me. I've just seen my friend, back soon."

She bumped straight into Laurent.

"There you are, Penny! I'm sorry we got separated."

"I can see why you didn't venture in there," she said, cocking her head back at the room. "Shocking waste of good paint."

"Come on, let's go and find the room with Nicolas's work," said Laurent. "Your faith will be restored, I promise."

⁂

IN THE corner of the room, Nicolas Versanne was giving his full attention to a couple in their sixties. With his designer glasses and neat dark hair glinting with silver, the artist might have been mistaken for a successful architect or businessman. Like Laurent, he had a very attractive aura of confidence that needed no bombast.

It was clear that this room was the heart of the exhibition. Nicolas's paintings were abstract: rich vibrant colours were exquisitely juxtaposed, then overlaid with deep indigos, sultry purples, and black to create subtle shapes and shadows that seemed both to hide and reveal a true subject. She found herself seeing landscapes and figures that on closer inspection were not there. The effect was magical. As she gazed at them, her mind joined the dots, then rejoined them in a different way. The colours, chosen deliberately to vibrate against one another, sent a frisson down her spine.

Penelope studied a small painting that suggested a street corner at dusk with deep, subtle shades of midnight blue, grey, and mauve. She was not alone in admiring it. The small man in a dark suit she had seen being harangued by Nina Chiroubles in the installation room was alongside her, his lean foxy face and goatee composed around a faint smile as he scribbled some words in a dog-eared notepad.

Hearing Nicolas and Laurent greeting each other affectionately, she turned around.

"You remember Penny—Penelope Kite—from my dinner party, don't you?" Laurent extended an arm towards her.

"Of course!" said Nicolas. "I'm delighted to see you again, and thank you for coming!"

They kissed three times, and right on cue his wife, Claudine, materialised, a French Audrey Hepburn in her exquisite little black dress. She, too, greeted Penelope warmly.

"Congratulations, Nicolas. Your work is simply stunning," said Penelope.

From the small man came a sigh, then more scribbling. Nicolas looked over with a fleeting glance of irritation and then steered the group away.

"Who is that?" whispered Penelope.

"Emile Sablon."

They watched the thin black-suited figure retreat from a canvas, then bend over his notepad like a question mark.

"The art critic for *La Provence*. Used to work on *Le Monde*, and holds himself in extremely high regard. Typical Parisian."

Penelope's eyes followed the man as he slid out of the room towards Don Doncaster's space. He paused at the doorway, gave a loud theatrical sigh, and plunged in.

"He's really going to enjoy Don's stuff," murmured Penelope, before re-addressing herself to Nicolas. "Well, I think your work is marvellous."

"It pleases you?"

"Yes, very much." She stopped herself just in time from saying that she didn't want to be rude about the other rooms, but was relieved to see some real art. "I'm very drawn to the smaller canvases. There is so much depth to them, and I love the subtlety of the colours."

Claudine beamed. She had obviously said the right thing. "I have been helping Nicolas to experiment with using replicated antique paints from the museum. They are all made from natural materials, from plants to rocks that are pulverised into dust. The quality of the resulting colour is very special. The way it can catch the light is quite different from modern mass-produced oil and acrylic paint. My favourite is the one over there—it looks different from whichever way you approach it. Let me show you."

Penelope was guided to an observation spot. She wondered if Claudine knew she was having dinner with Laurent later, and whether that had made a difference to how readily she had apparently been accepted by this group of friends.

A loud crash from one of the other rooms made them jump.

Penelope's first thought was that one of the pieces of installation art had fallen and shattered on the stone floor. Shouts quickly followed, and a couple of screams.

She and Claudine joined the general rush to the door to see what had happened. In the Doncaster room, all was confusion. A tall man in a black suit rushed past them, parting the crowd, and demanded that everyone back away. "Give him some air," he shouted.

A hush descended with the appearance of this man's commanding presence. As the guests pulled back, the cause of the commotion was clearly visible. There on the floor lay the inert figure of Don Doncaster, head cradled in the arms of an overwrought middle-aged woman attempting to give him the kiss of life with more relish than strictly necessary. She was shoved out of the way by another woman who attempted to pull him up to perform the Heimlich manoeuvre. Then she, too, was cast to one side as a svelte young man in a tweed suit several generations too old for him rushed in, bearing the defibrillator Penelope had seen earlier.

Don's cravat was ripped off, then his shirt, at which point there were a few gasps from his female support group. The pads were applied. The whining machine charged itself up and gave a loud clap. The artist shivered under the electric shock.

It looked bad. The chest remained still after three attempts. Suddenly Don's back arched violently. The first-aider put his ear to Don's chest, motioning for silence.

"There is a beat! Weak, but it is there."

He commanded all the onlookers to clear the room. Penelope paused by the door for a last look at the scene. Don's well-polished brown brogues contrasted sickeningly with his grey, clammy complexion and dishevelled hair.

At the entrance to the gallery and outside on the cobbled street, a large crowd milled around anxiously. The art critic hovered by the door, as if wondering whether he ought to be making the most of a bad news story. A few women sobbed in each other's arms. The installation artist Nina Chiroubles pushed her way into the entrance. Penelope spied Claudine in one corner on the phone, whispering urgently. Nicolas stood talking grimly with the youth in the tweed suit.

Snatches of conversation flew back and forth.

"They're saying he started choking. Then he went red and fell forward. What a terrible thing to happen."

"Yes, poor man."

"What if he dies?" someone else said. "Do you think his paintings will rise in value? They usually do, don't they?"

A loud, heavily accented Spanish voice—speaking in English—cut in behind her.

"Therre h'are of course some arrtists whose death leaves a hole in the warp and the weft of our cuulltural tapestry. Such artists will rise in value as the time goes by. But I would not count Mr Doncaster in that group. He fulfils a need, that is all."

Penelope turned to identify the source of the voice. Standing a few paces away was Keith Richards's double, the genius behind the sequence of black works. It really did not seem right to be discussing his fellow artist like this, and Penelope shot him a black look she was sure he would have no trouble interpreting.

She stepped away smartly and looked around for Laurent.

Clémence materialised at her side. "What's going on? I've only just arrived."

Penelope started to explain. All deliberations were cut short by the wail of a siren, growing louder. Seconds later, an ambulance pulled up. Paramedics rushed in.

From where she was standing by the entrance, Penelope could see the tall man who initially took charge come to the doorway of the Doncaster room, where he was immediately besieged by curious onlookers. "Is that M. de Bourdan?" Penelope whispered

to Clémence. It seemed safe to assume that he was the epony-
mous owner of the gallery.

"Yes."

"What a shame—his wonderful party. Let's hope the medics
get Don back on his feet and there's no lasting damage."

Laurent was speaking to the gallery owner as a stretcher
bearing the unconscious artist was rushed past into the ambulance. The siren restarted, ripping into the evening air, and
Don Doncaster was borne away.

Penelope saw Laurent pull out his mobile for a brief, intense
conversation. When he came over to Penelope, his expression
was sober. As the only holder of public office, he felt obliged to
accompany the sick man to the hospital in Avignon.

"Of course you must," she said, sensibly.

Yet again, there would be no dinner à deux.

3

"ONE MOMENT HE WAS ROARING like a lion to his pride—and the next he was flat on the floor," mused Penelope the next morning.

M. Charpet took off his beret and scratched his head. Her gardener hadn't even got as far as the plum trees he was intending to clear of dead wood and suckers before he had heard the story. His walrus moustache drooped and the moist brown eyes were appropriately grave. "*Mais, c'est terrible, madame . . .*"

"It was, M. Charpet. Quite surreal, in the middle of all those appalling jaunty pictures, too. And I don't know why, but I had the dreadful thought that it might all be some kind of publicity stunt."

"Publicity stunt?" The old man screwed up his farsighted eyes. "So you did not like this man?"

Penelope started to deny it—she didn't know Don Doncaster, after all. Then she sighed as she recognised the truth in Henri Charpet's words. "It was only a first impression, and I wouldn't say I didn't like him. No, it was more that I thought he was a certain type of expat with an unnecessarily high opinion of himself. In fact he was quite charming. It was just . . ."

The gardener nodded sagely, patiently waiting for her to explain. He crinkled his walnut face and lit one of his pungent cigarettes. Penelope never stopped marvelling at how he could work a full day in the garden, at a rate that belied his years, without the half-smoked Gitanes falling from his lower lip. After several months of working for her, he now treated her partly as a revered guest and partly as a slightly daft daughter. It was an unsettling combination.

"There's always the possibility that I am prejudiced against my own countrymen when they are abroad," admitted Penelope. "They can be so . . . embarrassing. You don't want people here to think we are all like that."

"Like what?"

"Arrogant. Convinced that everyone will like them."

"Are you sure you are still speaking of this Don—or have you someone else in mind?" he asked slyly. "You say that you went with Laurent Millais . . ."

Penelope bridled. Had she been thinking of Laurent? Probably. "M. Charpet, I think the time has come for you to cut those plum trees down to size."

Then she felt so guilty about thinking badly of a sick compatriot that she went inside and called Clémence.

"I just wondered if you'd heard how Don Doncaster's doing," she asked.

"By all accounts, he's in a bad way—hardly conscious and in intensive care."

"Was it actually a choking, then, or something more serious like a heart attack?"

"Are you actually calling about Laurent?" asked Clémence.

"What? No!" Why did everyone keep presuming she was thinking about Laurent Millais? "What makes you say that?"

A pause. "Actually, I have just been speaking to Claudine Versanne," said the estate agent. "She was sorry that your conversation came to such an abrupt end last night, and she wondered if you would like to join us for coffee at the museum in Roussillon later this week?"

"I would love to," said Penelope.

Feeling more cheerful, she rejoined her venerable gardener outside where he was sawing with a vigour that would have put many younger men to shame. The simple country life with good food and plenty of wine obviously had much to recommend it, though she was fully aware that Charpet was a man among men. No one in St Merlot had forgotten his bravery and determination as a messenger boy between Resistance cells during the Second World War. It was the first thing she had been told about him, not that he ever mentioned it himself.

Penelope set to work by his side, thoroughly enjoying herself as she held some of the larger branches steady for him and snipped at plum suckers with secateurs. She collected the cut wood and took some much-needed exercise trundling the wheelbarrow up and down the garden to the newly designated wood store in a dry outhouse. The logs would be perfect for her brand-new woodburning stove.

The swimming pool in the walled garden was now covered over with a substantial tarpaulin. The wild flowers in the grass had died away, yet the sun still shone warmly most days. This was why she had come, she thought. She couldn't help but compare the cheerful light and space to the cold, wet, misty autumns in southern England and the impending gloom of afternoons that darkened at teatime.

Although she had to admit that when the wind blew here, there was an icy edge to it. She had noticed the breeze building as they worked and the gusts brought a distinct chill.

M. Charpet straightened up and looked down the valley. Clouds were racing across the blue sky. "*Le mistral*," he announced. "Tomorrow it is coming."

"Will it be a bad one?"

"Two or three days."

Penelope was not sure whether that was a harsh prospect or not. She had not yet experienced the famous Provençal wind that whipped down the Rhône Valley gathering strength and speed.

"It comes from the west, from the gap in the hills at Avignon," he went on. "It can be so violent that it brings madness. But then, suddenly, it will stop and the sky will be so clear that it looks new." His eyes were bright, almost mischievous, as he watched for her reaction.

"I'm looking forward to the experience," replied Penelope stoutly.

❧

WHEN M. Charpet returned to his house in the village for a three- or four-course lunch, cooked by his sister Valentine, Penelope heated up some soup and sat quietly at the kitchen table. It was only when the cold winds started that she noticed how ill-fitting most of the doors were. Drafts whistled hither and thither, lowering temperatures in seconds. Every so often a door would slam loudly in the interior of the house. She would have to see to them before winter proper.

Penelope could see how easy it would be to take her eye off the ball when it came to the house. You started off with all kinds of grand plans, and then got used to living in a quirky, imperfect building. There was a kind of ease in imperfection, she was finding. It was the newly replastered walls that gave cause for concern, as each day she thought she spotted old cracks returning. Charpet had been sanguine.

"These houses," he had said, "they move. The whole time. No foundations, you see? When the earth moves, so do the old stones."

It wasn't entirely comforting.

Lost in thought, Penelope finished her meal and pushed the soup bowl away. After all the years of marriage and motherhood, it still felt self-indulgent simply to eat what she wanted, when she wanted, with no one else to please, or cajole, or disappoint. Her children, Lena and Justin—her stepchildren, in actual fact, though she never thought of them as such—had been such fussy eaters when they were young. But in time, her life had opened up again. She had gone back to work, and it had felt like a holiday to have a pub lunch now and then with a colleague. Then came her years working in London as personal assistant to Professor Camrose Fletcher, the eminent yet maverick forensic pathologist. She smiled as she pictured him in his book-lined study, taking off his glasses after an intense morning's work collating evidence for a case, then giving her an irrepressible grin as he suggested they had earned lunch at their favourite Italian restaurant.

That brought her back to Don Doncaster. She was both irked and intrigued by the man. If she was honest, she had reacted against an odd frisson of recognition. He had reminded her a little too uncomfortably of her ex-husband, David Kite. Not in looks but in manner. After making partner in his City law firm, David had developed a layer of bombast in company that Penelope disliked intensely. That wasn't why they divorced, but looking back, that was when they started to grow apart.

Who was Don Doncaster, underneath all the bluster? Where did he come from, and what had brought him to France? Judging from the exhibition, it seemed highly unlikely that he was a professional artist, or even one who had studied at art school. So what had he done before? Weren't artists supposed to want to say something about the world as they saw it? It didn't seem as if Don's daubings actually said anything beyond the awful truth that he possessed no talent. So were they simply an entertainment, a grand joke at the expense of the gullible, the emperor's new clothes?

Penelope opened her laptop, went onto Google, and typed in "Roland Galbraith Doncaster." There were tens of thousands of hits, many from the French press: magazine and newspaper articles and art blogs. She trawled through them with bemused fascination. The accompanying photographs showed him mainly at play, a glass of wine close to hand. The backdrops were expensive Luberon interiors and far-reaching views. Pictures of the art itself were largely absent.

It was only when she filtered the sites by English language that she sat back in her seat, slightly thrown. The polished brogues made sense now, along with the confident stance and the strident voice. Don Doncaster had once been a barrister in London. Was that why she'd felt that vague sense of recognition? Court cases had formed a large part of her work with Camrose Fletcher.

She read a decade-old account in the *Telegraph* of a planning battle in Buckinghamshire, in which he had been the leading light of a successful campaign against a four-thousand-home development in an Area of Outstanding Natural Beauty, or AONB, next to a historic village. He was prominent in the accompanying picture, spraying a bottle of Moet & Chandon like a victorious racing car driver. Another article reported a large donation he had made to a children's hospital after a sponsored cycle ride from Land's End to Gravesend. At first she wondered if she had the right man, but the man in the photographs was definitely the same Roland Doncaster she had met, albeit rather younger and slimmer. He was also mentioned in a brief summary of a court case and conviction for public disorder of Fenella Doncaster during a student demonstration ten years ago. A daughter, niece, sister? That must have been embarrassing for a barrister, thought Penelope. There was no mention of any artistic endeavour whatsoever. Nor was there any clue as to which chambers he had worked for.

❧

ALL IN all, he was rather more impressive than she had expected. She sent silent good wishes for his swift recovery in hospital.

That afternoon the wind gathered force. Trees caught the gusts like sails. Windows and shutters rattled loudly. Dry leaves scraped along the stone terrace, and the garden danced ever more wildly. Even in the kitchen, which had always been such a warm, cosy room despite its good size, the temperature had dropped. Penelope went upstairs and put on a thick jumper.

4

THE WIND WAS STILL HOWLING ferociously as Penelope set off for the ochre museum in Roussillon a few mornings later. All along the road down the hill from St Merlot to Apt, the trees pitched and rolled as if they were a churning green sea.

The main valley road towards Roussillon headed due west into the mistral, and at times she felt the Range Rover, substantial as it was, struggle to make headway. Soon enough, though, the rusty red cliff on which the village sat rose majestically from the valley floor.

As the road climbed, the curves and wind-sculpted stacks of red soil emerged from the green pines like a fifties actress letting a fur slip from her bare shoulders. Soon the village came into sight. Unsure exactly where the museum was, Penelope drove slowly through the main street, looking out for a sign. The last time she had come, in high summer, it had been thronged with tourists. Now it was deserted, and the scent of wood smoke hung in the air.

On the far side of the village, a sign directed visitors downhill. She found the museum and an entrance to the car park on a bend in the road. Soon she was walking along a path through pine trees to the entrance of a long, low building painted in different shades of red. The wind whipped Penelope's carefully brushed hair first one way and then the other. It had started to rain, in a gentle but insistent manner.

"Ah, Penny, how nice to see you again! We hardly had a chance to speak the other night." In the reception area, Claudine Versanne gave her a warm smile. Today she was wearing black jeans, high-heeled boots, and a sloppy sweater that felt like cashmere when they leaned in to exchange kisses. It was a casual look that had probably taken considerable effort to perfect, from the impeccable fit of the jeans to the maintenance of the lean, narrow thighs.

"Clémence has called to say she is running late, but if you like, I could show you a little of the museum," she said. "Our latest project is outside, unfortunately—a large waterwheel that has just been restored. We are very nearly ready to start it again."

"This rain might help, then."

"It will take a lot more than this to fill the water channels. They descend from the lake at the top of the site. Now that the wheel is as good as new and has been connected with the old machinery, we will be able to show visitors how the ochre is crushed and ground into powder. It will be an exciting addition to the museum."

It was funny, thought Penelope, in these days of space stations and the Internet and mobile phones, how many people were thrilled at the thought of bygone engineering. Just like those back home in England who travelled the country to ride in steam trains.

They walked past walls of glass display cases where rocks, antique tinctures, and bottles of coloured dust told the story of paint production. According to an information panel, the modern ochre industry in Roussillon was founded in 1785, when a system of separating ochre from sand was discovered. By the time the railway came to the Luberon Valley nearly a hundred years later, ochre and paint washes were as vital to the local economy as the pottery and candied fruit that put the town of Apt on the map.

Penelope was genuinely interested in the exhibits, some of which would not have looked out of place on the shelves of a Victorian pharmacy: old bottles of violet-black ink, their ornate labels torn and foxed; different shades of alcohol varnish; stoppered glass jars of cadmium and manganese and potassium. A yellow-grey rock like a curled fist was labelled "*Réalgar (sulfure d'arsenic)*." A pile of broken shells labelled "*Murex*" was paired with wools dyed different tones and shades of purple. Claudine led her past a wall hung with strips of fine cotton, each dyed a subtle variation of each colour, so that a rainbow of soft vegetable dyes unfolded before them.

Even the names of the paint shades were evocative: "*Oxide de fer naturel violet*"—iron oxide with a dusty purple hue—and "*Terre ombre chypre naturel*"—earth shaded by a cypress tree. She had never seen such romantic names. Perhaps she should reconsider playing it safe with white and be more adventurous with the walls of Le Chant d'Eau.

"This is quite wonderful!" said Penelope. "I could spend hours here."

"I am glad. It has been much work, but it is worth the pain." Claudine was speaking in English—she had insisted—and she had the cosmopolitan's command of it, but now and then she slipped into transliterations. Penelope's French was rapidly improving and she enjoyed being able to recognise the linguistic subtleties. "*Ça vaut la peine*" would be more idiomatically rendered as "It's worth the trouble."

"This is what sparked Nicolas's passion for the ancient techniques," Claudine went on.

Exotic jars with Latin names stood on shelves. Plants steeped in alcohol, the colour leaching from their leaves—sometimes of a completely different hue to the underlying vegetation. In one glass cabinet under lock and key stood a number of old prewar tins and bottles.

"We have to keep these locked up. Some of them are very dangerous!"

"Dangerous?"

Claudine pointed at a small jar of a crystalline salt. "This is vermilion. It is made from an ore—cinnabar. It is a beautiful red, but one that comes at a cost."

"Very expensive?"

"No. The cost of your mind! Cinnabar is mercuric sulphide. It is poisonous, and when it splits, as it does when heated, to metallic mercury, that is even worse! The fumes can affect the brain."

"Yes, I remember hearing about mercury poisoning when I worked at the Department," said Penelope.

"Department?"

"The forensic pathology department of the Home Office in London. I once had to go on a conference with Cam . . . with Professor Fletcher, my boss. He was giving a talk about poisons."

"In that case, you may know about this as well." Claudine pointed out a yellow powder in a small glass-stoppered bottle, marked "*Giallo di Napoli*." "Naples Yellow—this contains lead and antimony. A very old paint. Apparently they found some on the tiles of Babylon. Then we have Indian Yellow, made from the dried urine of cows fed only on mango leaves. And we have a brown pigment in the next cabinet that was created from the ground flesh of ancient Egyptian mummies."

"Seriously?"

"Yes, absolutely. The trade in exhumed remains from Egypt began in Roman times, first for medicinal purposes and then as a base for paint."

"Wonderfully macabre," said Penelope. There was definitely something fascinating about all these luxuriously beautiful colours with their hidden malevolence. As Penelope studied the shelf, one particular item caught her eye. A very strong green pigment in another bottle almost glowed. Claudine followed her gaze.

"You have a good eye for danger, Penny! That is Scheele's Green."

Penelope looked again at the yellowish pea-green colour. "Containing arsenic."

"You know of it?"

"In the early nineteenth century, women wore dresses made of fabric dyed a beautiful green using this compound. Often with fatal results. And the houses of the wealthy were often decorated with sumptuous green-patterned wallpaper that also contained it. No one knew that the high mortality rate among the bourgeoisie and upper classes was attributable to this colour, which was so fashionable at the time."

"Exactly." Claudine looked impressed.

Penelope smiled. Sometimes her formidable memory could even take her by surprise. Distracted by thoughts about green arsenic, she followed as Claudine moved on. Something niggled at her, but she couldn't pin it down.

❧

CLAUDINE LED her out of the paint section into a café hung with naïve ochre and black pictures. A long window looked out on the valley where the hills were wreathed in low white lines of cloud. There were few other visitors.

They had just sat down with coffees when the familiar tap of high heels on stone announced Clémence's arrival.

Greetings over, the estate agent launched straight in. "Laurent called the hospital this morning. Don Doncaster's condition is stable, though he is still weak. On the positive side, his heart seems strong enough at present, so time will tell."

"Thank goodness for that," said Claudine.

"Do you know him well?" asked Penelope.

"Well? Not really. I know a lot about him and what he does because he is represented by Gilles."

"But?"

"I have never expected that we could be friends. He . . . is not an artist in the way that we would understand it. Though obviously I would not wish him any harm."

Penelope nodded. "Is he really taken seriously, or is it all a big joke?"

"I would like to say that his work is a joke, but I think he is a bit cleverer than that. I think he has decided to cater to popular taste. Nicolas thinks it is selling out—but at least it is selling!" said Claudine, with a short, grim laugh.

"How on earth does he get away with it?" asked Penelope. "I guess it must be charm—he certainly possesses that in spades. All those silly women were falling over themselves to get close to him. You should have seen the way they looked at me when he came over!"

Clémence nodded. "They cling to him like, like . . ."

"Limpets." Penelope finished her sentence.

Claudine and Clémence exchanged uncomprehending glances.

"*Coquilles.*" She knew this was not quite the right translation, but it sounded weirdly appropriate.

Claudine continued. "Gilles de Bourdan likes him. It's not actually about the art, you see. Gilles is a very clever dealer, and he knows all about the power of publicity. It is better that people have an opinion on art than no opinion at all."

"And Don Doncaster is a master of self-publicity," added Clémence.

"I'm sure he comes over well, however ridiculous his art is," admitted Penelope.

"Is it ridiculous to make a lot of money?" asked Claudine.

"From truly terrible art?"

"From truly terrible art," the museum director confirmed. "Both he and Gilles de Bourdan profit extremely well from it." She gave a small sigh that could have been disapproval but might have been tinged with envy.

Penelope shook her head. "I find that very hard to believe. I should think most of his money comes from his former career back in London."

"It's not just the art, you see," continued Claudine, sticking to her theme. "It is the life of the artist that Don has created. A serious artist like Nicolas, he works hard and believes in his work. But someone like Don . . . it is the playing of the artist character that becomes the art." Claudine's deep brown eyes searched for signs that Penelope understood.

"Too much wine, too many women, a little controversy." Clémence had picked up the baton. "A willingness to speak to journalists—to allow them to visit the artist's beautiful if eccentric house in picturesque Provence; magazine articles showing him living the good life in the sun—it all plays very well in the rest of the country. Doncaster bought into it all, and the public buys into him."

"What you must not forget is that Gilles is a brilliant agent," interjected Claudine. "He has done very well for Nicolas."

"And artists like Don are the sensational, showbusiness side of it all," added Penelope.

"Yes, that is a good way of seeing it. Gilles has a very good understanding of who will buy certain pieces. It's like the serious antiques dealers: they sell the most prestigious pieces very expensively to private clients. Nicolas's buyers are a very different market from the one Don Doncaster sells into."

"Do you think the collapse could have been a publicity stunt, then?"

"Who knows?" said Clémence. "He is always trying to—"

The café door swung open with a crash. Nicolas, dishevelled in paint-splattered jeans and T-shirt, dispensed with polite greetings.

"I have just spoken to Gilles. Don Doncaster died thirty minutes ago and the police are treating his death as suspicious!"

5

$\maltese$

"YOU'RE NEVER GOING TO BELIEVE this!"

Back at Le Chant d'Eau, Penelope had found it impossible to settle. It wasn't walking weather. She tried and failed to play her cello. Neither could she concentrate on a book. All she could think about was the prostrate form, belly up on the gallery floor, of the artist sporting those incongruous shiny British brogues. There was only one immediate solution: a chat with an old confidante who wouldn't judge her for being fascinated by it all.

"Never going to believe what? That you finally had dinner with Laurent?" quipped Frankie, her oldest, dearest, and—occasionally—most irritating friend.

"Er, well . . . no, I didn't actually."

Penelope explained why.

Frankie listened intently, interspersing sympathetic murmurs with loud shrieks of "Get off that sofa, you stupid animal!" and "If you touch that plate, you're out!," indicating that Perky, the large and demonic hound loved only by his mistress, was, as usual, laying waste to his immediate surroundings. At one stage she disappeared from the line, then returned breathing heavily and swearing a little. At the end of Penelope's story, she whistled.

"You can't seem to go anywhere without someone pegging out nearby in suspicious circumstances, can you?"

Penelope caught her breath. "Please don't say things like that."

"Of course, it's just a horrible coincidence. Though I do hope you haven't started as you mean to go on in France."

"Not helping, Frankie."

"Sorry. So what was the actual cause of death?"

"No one seems to know. The police have taken charge and they aren't saying."

"But you of all people know that things are very often not quite as they first appear, and you want to know the truth."

"Exactly."

"This time, though, it's nothing to do with you, is it? Though I know you can't help yourself. Presumably 'suspicious' doesn't always mean skulduggery—just that the cause of death hasn't been established and the authorities are looking into the possibility that it was not simply an unfortunate event, a public death due to natural causes?"

Penelope stared out of the kitchen window. The fig tree in the courtyard was swaying, the last of the autumn's sweet purple fruit being shaken from the topmost boughs by the wind. The mistral, though still lively, seemed at last to be dropping. "Of course." A pause. "All I did was go along to an exhibition to support a friend of Laurent's before going out to dinner. I was so looking forward to it, too!"

"Now we're getting to what this is really about . . ."

"You're right, it has nothing to do with me—but it does have to do with Laurent's friends Claudine and Nicolas. You remember, you met them at the dinner at his house. Nicolas is very upset, though it doesn't seem that he and Claudine have—had—much time for Don. They knew his appalling art was a moneymaking joke, and that made him a very different kind of artist from Nicolas. But they were represented by the same art dealer and agent, and it happened at a joint exhibition for the gallery's biggest names, so I suppose it all seems a bit close to home."

Frankie was silent for a while. Though she was usually noisy and larger than life in person, she had always known when to let Penelope unravel her thoughts in a conversation. During their school years in Bromley, South London, Frankie had lived in the neighbouring suburban street. They caught the bus to Bromley High together each morning in term time, and were co-conspirators in the absorbing pursuit of boys during the holidays. They had been appallingly giggly teenagers together, and there was a part of their relationship that would forever be so.

"When I think back on that evening," Penelope mused, "there was quite a bit of tension between the artists. They are—were— all very different, and perhaps there were some unresolved issues around the way the dealer promoted each of them. But this is all supposition on my part, reading between the lines of what Clémence and Claudine have told me."

Frankie gave a piercing scream. The dog was apparently now lunching on the curtains. "It sounds like I may have to pay you another visit soon, Pen."

Penelope pulled herself together, remembering the gluttony and rosé carnage of her friend's last descent on Provence. It had taken weeks to recover.

"That would be fantastic, but let's wait until the bathrooms are in. I'd love to get your views about making one of the outhouses into a *gîte*."

Frankie and her husband, Johnny, ran a very successful construction company. There was nothing more likely to deflect Frankie than the subject of building and renovation. "Aaah, you have decided to rent out a bit. Well, I'm not going to say I told you so, but . . ."

"But you just have, Frankie!"

⚜

THE NEXT morning Penelope awoke after an unpleasantly vivid dream in which she was trapped in the gallery in Avignon. There was no way out, and every wall was hung with ancient, rusting Deux Chevaux cars and sad puppies.

She got out of bed and put up a kettle of water to make a mug of tea, looked balefully at the fruit and yoghurt she had bought for breakfast, and then slammed the fridge door and switched off the kettle. Coat and boots on, she set off down the track and took the path up the hill through the woods to the village. There was only one thing for it when her thoughts were stuck in a cycle of speculation surrounding a suspicious death.

The bakery in the square at St Merlot was superlative. Which was a mixed blessing for a woman who found it hard to resist the lure of a traditional continental breakfast. The local master baker, Jacques Correa, produced the finest croissants Penelope had ever tasted: crispy, flaky, buttery delights with just the right amount of chewiness in the centre. She had made a deal with herself several weeks ago. If she wanted one—and one only, mind—she had to walk up and down the hill for it. Calories out before calories in.

The boulangerie occupied a narrow yellow building with a few chairs and tables outside under a vine canopy. During the summer, it was a popular morning spot for the villagers, with good coffee and a superlative view of the Luberon Valley. Now, though the outside tables remained, they were empty in the bright, chilly air left in the mistral's wake.

Penelope opened the door and entered a warm, steamy world of fragrance and temptation. A queue had formed and doubled back on itself. A hubbub of chat and laughter between the customers rose and fell, and was ably parried by Mme Correa behind the counter. Several people smiled at Penelope, and she nodded back. It was nice to feel that some of them knew who she was and were making her feel welcome. Jacques brought through a tray of croissants, newly baked, to a collective sigh of contentment from the clientele.

Penelope emerged with a bag containing her breakfast and, because she was a slave to her baser instincts where French pâtisserie was concerned, one individual hazelnut and praline tart for later.

"Caught you," said Clémence.

Penelope jumped. Laurent appeared, too, grinning over the Parisienne's narrow shoulder as she pulled an expression of amused disapproval.

"Just one croissant," admitted Penelope feebly.

"We thought we might find you here," said Laurent.

"Bit unfair," said Penelope, not knowing quite how to take that. "I've managed to resist for ages."

They already knew her far too well. More to the point, she felt, was that the bakery in St Merlot was surely not on Clémence's daily round. Had she and Laurent arrived together, and if so, what did that imply this early in the morning?

"Were you looking for me, then?" she asked.

Laurent gave her an ambiguous smile. "I have worked up quite an appetite this morning and am about to have a splendid breakfast at the mairie. Would you like to join us?"

Did he exchange a meaningful look with Clémence, or was Penelope imagining that? She reached into her basket and held up the paper containing the offending croissant. "I'll bring my own."

Only a short walk away, the mairie was a low modern building that also housed the village post office. The national trico-
lour flag rippled from a flagpole. Lantana shrubs and olive trees
in big galvanised metal planters waved in the breezy sunshine
with a jaunty Mediterranean air.

The three of them negotiated a passage to the mayor's office
through morning greetings from Nicole and Marie-Lou, who
ran the post office with their ears pinned back for intriguing
titbits of information, and a gaggle of customers, who were all
more interested in any village gossip than sending packages or
buying stamps.

Laurent closed his door, switched on an elegant modern coffee machine, and soon they were sitting around his desk with
pungent cups of espresso eagerly discussing the suspicious death
of Don Doncaster.

Clémence, predictably, ate nothing. Penelope ate her sublime
croissant with as much delicacy as humanly possible. Laurent
rapidly disposed of a croissant, a *pain au chocolat*, and an almond
twirl. Surely it was not possible to look as fit as he did and eat like
that every morning! Or were French metabolisms different from
British ones, in some mysterious and manifestly unfair way?

"It is all most unfortunate," said Laurent.

Penelope snapped out of a momentary daydream. She assumed he was speaking about Don Doncaster's demise, not over-
active fat cells in the middle-aged Englishwoman.

"His body had suffered a trauma, for sure, but no one thought
he would die. He seemed to be recovering yesterday morning."

"What happened after he left in the ambulance—what state
was he in when you got to the hospital?" asked Penelope.

"He was groaning, coughing, then he relapsed. To be honest,
I thought he had gone to sleep, that perhaps he had choked in
the first place because he was very drunk."

"Was he very drunk?"

"He often was," said Clémence. She wrinkled her pretty nose in distaste. "That was one of the reasons his wife left him. And of course his drinking got worse after she had gone."

Penelope shook her head.

"A classic expatriate story, I am afraid," continued Clémence. "The long-married couple. Perhaps the move is meant to fix their problems. But it makes them worse. The excitement fades. Too much wine, too much time, too many distractions. The dream becomes a nightmare."

"Cheers. I'll remember that."

Laurent laughed.

"How long did it take for the Doncaster marriage to unravel here?"

"A few years, four or five, maybe."

"And how do you know all this?"

"I sold them their house when they arrived here. And I'm hoping to sell it again soon."

"Ideal clients, then!"

Clémence allowed herself a slightly smug smile.

"So did she go back to the UK, then?" Penelope hadn't reckoned on a wife. Given her own recent experience, she found herself more interested than she should have been in the anatomy of a middle-aged divorce.

"No, she is still here."

Laurent rolled his eyes. Either he did not think much of the behaviour of English ex-wives in Provence in general, or he knew Mrs Doncaster. Penelope was aware that the French in general looked askance at the antics and eccentricities of northern incomers, and there was every reason for the British to be considered prime offenders. With a jolt of shame, she realised that she hadn't actually brushed her hair before coming out. She tried to smooth her mop and give it some body by raking her fingers through it.

"And?"

"Fenella Doncaster is also an artist. Most people would say she is a much better artist than her ex-husband. But like most painters, she is not successful commercially, at least not compared to him," said Laurent.

"Fenella?" Penelope thought back to the court report she found online. Not a daughter or niece, but his wife who was convicted of affray, then. "Did the Doncasters part on friendly terms?"

"Absolutely not. They detested each other by the end," said Clémence.

"What does she do now that she's on her own, then?"

"She still lives in Goult. She still paints. But she earns her bread and butter by teaching art classes at various picturesque venues, like the Manoir at Gordes and the Château Carmin at Roussillon. She is a very good teacher, apparently."

"Pity Don didn't take some of her classes! Presumably she also lives on his alimony. So she wouldn't want to see him dead. Out of sight and mind, maybe—but not dead."

"I don't think anyone is saying that Fenella Doncaster is a killer," said Laurent.

"No, of course not."

"Though if it is a suspicious death," fished Penelope, "then doesn't that imply that someone is? What exactly are the police saying?"

Although she knew she shouldn't, Penelope felt a tingle of excitement. She was thoroughly enjoying sitting here playing at detective again, as well as the feeling that both Laurent and Clémence valued her opinion.

"They are still saying nothing beyond the fact that it *is* a suspicious death," admitted Laurent.

"They won't give you any more information at all?" asked Penelope.

"Nothing."

No one said anything for few moments.

Clémence looked deadly serious before she broke the silence. "By the way, Penny, you have croissant flakes in your hair."

6

WHEN DRIVING IN FRANCE, PENELOPE'S favourite radio station had always been Nostalgie, which churned out a cheerful selection of pop hits from the 1960s to the 1980s in all their cringeworthy splendour. Who could take classical music all the time?

Sometimes she even caught some peculiarly awful French pop ditty she remembered hearing during a family holiday to France when she was twelve or thirteen, driving south on the *routes nationales* through tunnels of plane trees. There was something about the French language, she thought, that just didn't work with rock and roll. Nevertheless, those songs never failed to tug at the heart, inviting fond memories of her parents: her mother in the front passenger seat of the Ford Granada, swathed and crackling under a large Michelin route map; her father sucking at a pipe that he did not light in the car out of consideration for his family.

Penelope's father, a GP and police surgeon, hid his own thoughts under a bluff, no-nonsense exterior. He had often seemed too busy for family life and his only child when she was growing up, but on holidays in France, he was all theirs, relaxed and carefree, focused on seeking out castles and beaches and good restaurants. Happy times. It was thanks to one of his old colleagues, a pathologist who became a friend of the family, that she had found her first secretarial job at the Home Office pathology department when she decided to reassert her independence while she was still married.

She allowed herself a moment of sadness that her parents were no longer alive. They had both loved Provence. How they would have adored Le Chant d'Eau. Along with her divorce settlement, it was thanks to the sale of the substantial family home in South London that she had been able to buy the farmhouse outright and live a very comfortable life.

Now that the tourists had retreated north, she still felt a thrill at the thought that she was staying rather than reluctantly counting down the days until she had to pack her suitcase and head home. This *was* home. How lucky she was.

She would have gone to the V comme Vin wine boutique in Apt, recommended by Clémence, to buy the supplies for a lunch party she had planned for Sunday, but the conversation over breakfast at the mairie had set her thinking. The Château Carmin winery in Roussillon had an excellent reputation for local rosé, and Penelope reckoned it also offered an ideal opportunity to find out a bit more about Fenella Doncaster and her art classes there. There was even a possibility that she might run into the ex-wife at the end of the Thursday-morning class that was advertised on the winery website.

Had she allowed herself careful examination of her motives, Penelope might have concluded, uncomfortably, that they encompassed not only a certain curiosity about the intriguing Don Doncaster, but a need to impress Laurent Millais and Clémence Valencourt with her investigating skills. As it was, she justified her actions with the prospect of the lunch to which she had invited M. Charpet and his sister Valentine, along with her farmer neighbour Pierre Louchard and his new partner Mariette. They would drink plenty of wine, and it made perfect sense to buy it somewhere interesting.

❧

THIS TIME she did not need to go into the village. The Château Carmin lay to the east of Roussillon, set on a hillock above impressive vineyards. It had the most elegant drive of any winery Penelope could recall. Cypresses and olives alternated on the bumpy road, interspersed with oleanders. An old tractor was posed scenically by a stone hut on the brow of the hill. The *vinicole*, less a château than a collection of imposing farm buildings, was painted a luscious dusty rose.

She entered a cavernous room with a large, rustic bar on which bottles cooled in metal ice buckets. Battalions of glasses waited for potential customers to request a tasting. Several up-ended barrels were serving as tables. To the right was the shop counter, behind which was displayed all the glory of the estate in white, rosé, and red.

"*Je peux vous aider, madame?*"

A young woman with a high ponytail and skintight jeans tucked into boots took up her position expectantly behind the counter.

"*Je voudrais goûter du vin, s'il vous plaît,*" said Penelope.

Before the wine tasting was permitted, full disclosure was required of every course she intended to serve her guests for Sunday lunch, the herbs to be used in the cooking, and the cheeses Penelope intended to offer. The young woman listened intently and then made her judgement. Penelope took tiny sips of the recommendations, and it was clear that the products here were excellent. Buying the wine was going to be the easy part. Staying upright, less so.

Getting ready to settle up for six bottles of full-bodied red, six of a deliciously fruity rosé, and three of a thoroughly decent white, Penelope's thoughts moved to how best to raise the subject of Fenella Doncaster when she spotted a pile of advertising flyers for an "Introduction to Painting" course. Her luck was in. The artist-teacher was indeed Fenella Doncaster and there was even an email address and a phone number for her.

Penelope scanned the flyer casually. "I've heard these classes are very good."

"They are quite popular, it is true, madame."

"I've been thinking of taking lessons myself. Oh, Thursday morning! Is there one taking place now? It might be a good idea to get a sense of what this course is like before I signed up. Would that be possible, do you think?"

"*Ah, non.* Unhappily, not."

"Oh?"

"Mme Doncaster's class has been cancelled this week. I understand there has been a bereavement in the family."

"Oh, I'm sorry to hear that. Doncaster? Now you say the name, I believe I have may have met . . . Mme Doncaster, she's the wife of Don Doncaster, the British artist who lives in—?"

"She is, madame . . . sorry, that is, she was. She called this morning, in a terrible state, to tell us that her husband has died and that she would be suspending the art classes for the next week."

"How dreadful for her. What a shock."

The sales assistant extended the card machine for Penelope to pay. "Yes, it will be hard for her."

"I'm sure it will," said Penelope. It was odd, she thought, that the girl was speaking as if the Doncasters were married, not divorced. She took the card machine, but then set it down on the counter and examined the label of a slim bottle of rosé from a display of special offers. So pale was the wine that it offered the merest pink blush in the bottle.

"So the police are involved, then?"

"Oh, yes."

"Do they think someone wished to harm him?" She stopped short of using a more violent word.

"Possibly, yes."

"Was he a man who gave others reason to dislike him?" She entered her card code in the machine slowly, and handed it back.

"I cannot say, madame."

It was a diplomatic answer, and Penelope thought better of seeming too keen to pursue the subject. She accepted the proof of purchase and the directions to the *cave* where she should collect her order.

The assistant was not quite done yet. One had to do justice to gossip of this quality. "But Fenella said that the police have even been searching her house, and a number of others."

"And what are they looking for?"

"Poison, madame! M. Doncaster was poisoned."

❧

PENELOPE WAS still processing this news as she approached the *cave*. Cardboard boxes of wine were stacked floor to ceiling and on wooden pallets on the floor. A couple of men in blue boilersuits were chatting loudly in the far corner.

As she went in, she caught the words "*mort*" and "*artiste*." It had been a good idea to come here. The demise of Don Doncaster was clearly the topic *du jour*. Penelope strained to keep up with the torrent of words in the broad Provençal accent in which "*vin*" was pronounced "veng" and "*maison*" was "maiseng." She edged closer and pretended to be absorbed in examining her receipt.

Disappointingly, there was not much to overhear that she didn't already know. In fact, she probably knew more than they did. The rumour mill had already converted the gallery opening in Avignon into a studio in Ménerbes, and Don's collapse into a discovery of him slumped and blue in the face at the easel. The men made no mention of his wife, or ex-wife.

They were so busy swapping theories that neither registered her arrival. She listened as one man suggested that the Russian mafia had come up from Nice and Cannes to execute him, though for what crime other than that against Art itself, Penelope could not imagine. The other countered by invoking his public persona as a well-known British drunk and would-be Lothario.

"He had 'parties' at his house, if you know what I mean. It was well known locally," said the Ménerbes studio theorist. "It's always the way with these rich foreigners. They wouldn't behave like that in their own country," replied the other.

Blimey, thought Penelope, that's a bit of a sweeping generalisation. Out of respect for the dead, she coughed and waved her proof of purchase.

One of the men came over and dealt with her order, finding the right wines and carrying the boxes to her car. He could not have been more helpful, even though he must have noticed the British plates on the Range Rover.

❧

AS SHE retraced her route down the hill from the château, Penelope tried to order her thoughts and the insights she had garnered. She was concentrating hard on recalling the exact words used in the conversations. Was it true about the poison?

A wrong turning found her on the road back up to the centre of Roussillon. The village was a honeycomb of narrow streets and smart restaurants, art shops and galleries, each building rendered in terra-cotta colours. Murals on courtyard doors and the sides of houses gave it a bohemian artists' colony atmosphere.

She drove slowly through the village before realising that she had unwittingly rejoined the road that would take her past the ochre museum and on towards the main valley road. Round the next bend she caught a glimpse of it through the pines.

Two police cars were parked in front of the old factory buildings. On impulse, she braked sharply and turned into the car park. Cautiously, she took one of the spaces furthest from the museum, then sat quietly assessing her options. She wondered whether Nicolas and Claudine would thank her for suddenly appearing, or whether she was grossly overstepping the mark.

"Rats!" said Penelope, cursing her own impetuosity.

A few minutes later, she got out of the car and walked onto a wooded path that led directly to the water channels once used to power the watermill. The roots of evergreen firs and pines clawed at the surface of the sandy red ground, seeking out every crack and rock for purchase. She emerged at a vantage point where she could see how the hill behind the old factory was criss-crossed with narrow water channels. A lake at the top supplied the water to turn several large mill wheels. A couple of these ponderous artefacts were crusted with rust and moss, but the one closest to the buildings was pristine. Presumably, this was the wheel Claudine was so proud of having restored.

Penelope walked over to it, trying to look nonchalant, as if she had simply decided to come and have a closer look. There was no sign of life at the back of the museum. Close up, the wheel was impressive, almost twice her height. The axles disappeared inside the building to power the crushers and grinders. It was a brutal piece of equipment and it was a fair bet, she thought, that it had seen some accidents over the years.

A movement in the glass exterior wall of the museum sent her ducking behind the wheel, aware she was acting suspiciously. This had not been a good idea.

Penelope squinted through the slats in the wheel. A man was standing and looking out through the large glass window of the exhibition area—a policeman or a member of the museum staff? Had he seen her? She held her breath. Another man with dark clothes and a confident strut approached him, followed by a woman. With the light on the glass, it wasn't possible to be sure, but she thought she saw Claudine further inside the room, talking with a man whose back was turned, but whose cockerel stance and diminutive stature reminded Penelope of someone she most emphatically did not want to encounter.

She remained stock-still, hoping they would move away from the glass wall. It would be embarrassing, to say the least, to be caught spying. What excuse could she possibly give?

After five increasingly clammy minutes, the visitors left the exhibition room. As they disappeared behind the solid wall of the corridor back to the main entrance, she ran for cover back in the direction of the wooded path and the car park.

"Holy guacamole, that was close!" She spoke out loud, in between gasps for breath.

Back in the Range Rover, she closed her eyes. She had a nasty feeling she had made herself look ridiculous. Come what may, she was going to have to brazen it out. She couldn't just leave now. That would look worse.

She climbed out and walked towards the museum's main entrance, but hung back by a thick tree by the edge of the car park when she saw the short, stocky figure strutting over to the

larger blue police car. Penelope swallowed hard. The tall policeman emerged, followed by a non-uniformed man carrying what
looked like several evidence bags. She stayed where she was until
the police cars had departed.

Penelope tried to strike a neutral expression as she approached
the museum. She was a few paces from the entrance when Claudine emerged, her face quite white. She started when she saw
Penelope, then tried, and failed, to compose herself.

"Something awful has happened!"

Penelope reached out to Claudine.

"What is it?"

"It's about Don," said the museum director.

She was in a mild state of shock, thought Penelope. "Tell me,"
she said.

"The police think he was poisoned!"

In her office, Claudine made a conspicuous effort to put up a
calmer front. She poured two glasses of Badoit, and they sat in a
pair of Scandinavian leather chairs by a high, arched window.
The impressive pictures on the white walls were surely painted
by Nicolas: raw ochre colours overlaid with a mysterious veil of
purple-black in his characteristic style.

Penelope was almost certain she knew what the police had just
taken away, but she waited patiently to hear it from the museum
director herself.

"I am so angry. They didn't actually accuse me, but the implication was there." Claudine took another sip of water.

Penelope nodded, not wanting to interrupt.

"It was so sudden and unexpected. The police . . . it was as
though they wanted to see . . . my reaction."

Another nod.

"All morning they have been here."

Silence.

"Did they find what they were looking for?" asked Penelope at last.

Claudine looked her in the eye. "As a matter of fact, yes. That room I showed you where the old paints and dyes are displayed—they have sealed it off and then removed some of the exhibits."

Penelope was fairly certain of the answer to her next question. "Do you know precisely what they took away?"

"No. I was not allowed to see. This is ridiculous! I mean, why would the police suspect me of poisoning him? What would it gain me?"

"Well, it may not be you that they suspect. More likely, it's the old paint. The toxins that may or may not remain in them. They haven't arrested you, have they?"

A shake of the head.

"I'm sure they are simply covering all possibilities. Ruling out anyone with a connection to the deceased, and those who were at the gallery in Avignon on the night he collapsed." As she said it, Penelope felt a worm of unease. She, too, had been there that night. A confrontation sooner or later with the diminutive yet cocksure official she had seen leaving was inevitable. It was not a happy prospect.

"I'm sure you have nothing to worry about," she said. "It's very standard procedure for the police to rule out all the obvious lines of inquiry and coincidences at the start before the real detective work begins. They couldn't ignore the presence of poisons here, but that doesn't mean they believe they were used."

Claudine nodded, visibly pulling herself together. "You're right. Thank you. I needed to hear that."

"A visit from the police can be very intimidating. But they are only doing their job properly." She declined to ask whether one policeman in particular had been rude and intimidating.

This was not the time. "I saw the restored waterwheel," she said carefully, wanting to find out if she had been spotted. "It's very impressive, I must say."

"Did you?" said Claudine vaguely.

"I had a little walk in the grounds just now. I saw the water channels, too." Best to be straightforward.

"Did you? It's going to be wonderful when the project is complete. It will give a real sense of how the factory once worked."

It didn't sound as if she'd been spotted. "Yes, it will. I'd love to see it when it's started."

"There's going to be a special opening that we are hoping will help to attract some more visitors in the quiet winter months. Even the local TV company is coming to film it. You must come along."

"I'd like that," said Penelope. With any luck, by then normality would be restored, too.

7

ON SATURDAY MORNING, A THICK mist clung to St Merlot. The visibility was terrible as Penelope navigated her way carefully down the hill. Not that this stopped several cars from overtaking her, once by a large woman shaking a crutch out of the window. On market day, Apt was still busy, though Penelope managed to squeeze into a parking space just beyond the main square, a feat quite inconceivable in summer months.

Stalls filled most of the centre of the town with kaleidoscopic arrays of fruit and vegetables, all kinds of squashes and pumpkins, large truckles of cheese and legs of smoked ham, salamis, olives, sun-dried tomatoes, and olive oils.

Penelope had a long list for her lunch party. She set a course through the narrow streets towards the best butcher. She considered shoes in one of the boutiques. She peered through the window of the chocolate shop like a child of ten. She succumbed to some delicious-looking macaroons, laid out in a rainbow of colours from a stall dedicated only to biscuits. The market was more than just a stocking-up exercise. It was an affirmation of life in Provence.

When Penelope unpacked her shopping back at Le Chant d'Eau, she couldn't quite believe how much she had bought. Preemptive action was needed. Preferably before lunch.

❧

PENELOPE PRESSED Start, struck a pose more or less Latin, and began to swivel her hips. The pulsating samba music made her feel young and free again. Unfortunately, the message hadn't reached her feet as the Zumba class leader on YouTube cruelly increased the speed and complexity of the moves. Penelope toppled over mid-merengue march and hit the living room floor in a tangle.

It was not the best time for a visitor to put his head round the door, nor an elegant bottom that greeted him. It was Laurent Millais. Of course it would be.

He was obviously hugely amused. "Outside, it's a quiet village in the Luberon. Inside, it's carnival time! You didn't hear me knock, and the back door was open."

"Oof," said Penelope breathlessly as she staggered to her feet and stood with her legs pressed tightly together to minimise the size of her Lycra-clad thighs.

"I admire your . . ."

Penelope waited, a hot flush rapidly spreading up from her knees, curious to know what, if anything, there was to be admired in being caught red-faced in bad exercise gear, defeated by a step-swivel-step-turn.

"Spirit," said the mayor, still grinning infuriatingly.

Penelope hit Pause on her computer.

"Was there something I can do for you?" she asked, mustering as much dignity as she could. She felt herself blushing deeper as the double entendre insinuated itself in her consciousness. Why did this man always reduce her to an awkward teenager? It really was not seemly in a woman of her age and experience. She moved to the other side of the sofa, effectively shielding her legs from view, and motioned him to sit.

"There are many things you could do for me, Penny," he replied, not helping matters at all. He gave her a lingering blue
stare, and flopped down into a chair. "But I wanted to ask you
something about Don Doncaster. What did you think of him
when you met him at the gallery?"

"Why?" she blustered.

Laurent smiled. "Well, I like the way you think. It is a different way of thinking, and sometimes that is a good thing."

Clearly not always, but Penelope let that go.

"Well . . . Don struck me as a certain type of expat, a bit
pleased with himself . . . though not unpleasant . . . Sorry, forgot my manners, would you like a coffee? I'll go and make one,
won't be a moment."

She was fully intending to go and find a long cardigan to hide
in, but to her mortification, he followed her into the kitchen. Unfortunately she forgot, until it was too late and she was standing
by the kettle with her back to him, that her backside in leggings
must be the width of a rhino. She pulled her stomach in as tightly
as it would go and turned sideways.

"Are you OK?"

"Yes, why?"

"You gasped and suddenly went stiff."

"Did I? I'm fine. It's just . . . well, it's what happens to English
people when they haven't had a . . . a good, strong cup of tea for
a while. At least two hours. Just one of those things. You get used
to it."

Sitting across from him at the table, she felt more relaxed.

"I saw Claudine yesterday," she said. "More or less by accident. I happened to be passing and saw police cars outside the
museum." Better to be straight with him, rather than let him
hear it from anyone else.

"I know."

Too late.

"Best not to spread it around that the police have been speaking to the Versannes."

"Of course." Penelope saw exactly where his concerns lay. Laurent was ever loyal to his friends. "I'm sure the police are just covering all the obvious bases. If they think it was a death by poisoning, that is."

"Quite so. Claudine and Nicolas have enough to worry about."

"They're good friends of yours, aren't they?"

"They are."

"How do you know them?"

"I was at university in Paris with Nicolas. When we both married, Claudine and my ex-wife Eloïse became good friends, too."

"Close ties, then."

"Yes. There is something about the relationships one makes at university. After the intensity of those years, you may not always agree with your friends, but you can forgive them anything."

Penelope knew what he meant. Her student days at Durham University had given her several close and valued friends. No matter what, knowing each other in the heady years of early adulthood made for an unbreakable bond, even when you hadn't met up for a while.

It was lovely to sit mulling over the events of the past weeks with him. When she made him laugh, it was like winning a prize.

"That's a lot of shopping, Penny."

The evidence was all over the worktop near the oven and on the end of the table: vegetables and fresh herbs, fruit, flour, and other items that didn't need to go in the fridge; three half cases of wine and litres of mineral water; a stack of new roasting pans, generously sized; and flowers from the market.

"For one?" Only the raised eyebrow indicated amusement, or it might have been bemusement.

Penelope felt a blush flame. "For five."

She didn't elaborate. It could do no harm for him to think she had made lots of friends beyond the enclosed world of St Merlot.

"Speaking of sharing food, when shall we try again to have dinner together? One evening next week?"

"Sounds good to me."

When he had gone, Penelope punched the air in delight. Result! She cranked up the YouTube Zumba class again and salsa-partied with renewed purpose.

8

PENELOPE WAS TAKING A BIG risk. She had decided to serve
a traditional English Sunday lunch: beef and Yorkshire pudding, followed by steamed syrup sponge and custard. She was
well aware that a "pudding" with the meat would be a strange
concept to her French guests, but Penelope was confident in her
ability to produce a batter that would bake to a consistency that
was light as air, with a satisfying crispiness on the outside. She
had hunted high and low for parsnips and finally found some.
There was nothing as delicious as parsnips roasted until they
were naturally caramelised! Peas and haricot beans, and baked
onions and a rich unctuous gravy would give them all a taste of
her home country. The idea for dessert had presented itself when
she had unexpectedly found some Tate & Lyle's golden syrup at
the hypermarket.

For some lunatic reason she had also decided to make her own
horseradish sauce. Her eyes streamed as she grated the white
root, releasing its pungent sharpness. The kitchen was beginning to resemble a battlefield, as various surfaces became covered with pots and pans, and a thin white film of flour. Still she
soldiered on, and just about in time to allow for some beautifica-
tion, all preparation was completed and the room restored to a
semblance of order. She shut the kitchen door quickly before she
noticed anything else that needed doing, and went upstairs to get
herself ready.

Soon the whole house was infused with the aroma of roasting beef. She had a sudden qualm that she ought to be offering a starter, that the French would expect one. It was the first time she had cooked for her new friends and neighbours, and she wanted to hit the right note.

She decided to explain that this was exactly what she would cook for her family back in England, and hope they entered into the spirit. A final polish of the glasses, a smoothing of the white linen cloth, and the big table along the length of the kitchen windows looked splendid. The large, stone-flagged room was cosy despite its spaciousness.

Beyond the windows, the previous day's mist had lifted, and the garden unfurled to meet a view of the rippled blue mountains. Birds wheeled in the clear sky.

Penelope had only just opened some red wine to let it breathe, when M. Charpet and his sister Valentine knocked on the back door.

"*Bonjour, bonjour!*" she cried.

Kisses and flowers and wine were heaped upon her, everyone talking at once.

M. Charpet was wearing his dark grey Sunday suit, as she had expected. Valentine wore a floral dress. They admired the settings at the table, and Penelope could see them surreptitiously eyeing the kitchen worktops for clues as to what gastronomic treats awaited. Stomachs rumbled. They assured her they had brought their appetites. On the occasion that Penelope had gone to the Charpet house for lunch, Valentine had prepared a gourmet experience on a magnificent scale. The pressure was on. Penelope hoped she had prepared enough.

"I intend to show you a typical British Sunday lunch," she announced, more confidently than she felt. What her menu lacked in the number of courses, it more than made up for in stodge. "I am not going to claim it has finesse, but M. Charpet, Valentine, I want to see you struggle to even crawl out of here!"

"It takes a great deal to defeat us where food is concerned!" Valentine waggled an index finger.

Penelope laughed nervously. The crispy roast potatoes and caramelised parsnips could go into the oven again now for a final blast. The sponge and a second tin of golden syrup were consigned to the steamer at the back of the hob, which rattled and shook alarmingly, every so often disgorging a large puff of steam, like Robert Stephenson's prototype Rocket engine.

As the clock's hour hand reached one, there was another knock at the kitchen door. Penelope opened it to a smiling M. Louchard and his fiancée Mariette. How things had changed in the past three months. Her farmer neighbour, a former Foreign Legionnaire, had been a lovesick recluse when she arrived. But now the loneliness and shyness had disappeared from his demeanour. Penelope noted with approval the large bottle of his homemade plum brandy in his hand. It had magical properties, of that she was convinced.

She showed her guests through into the sitting room. They were all keen to see the changes she had already made and offered helpful advice. "It is your blank canvas, madame," said M. Louchard, "waiting for you to make your mark on it."

He was obviously in one of his philosophical moods. Now that Penelope had come to know him better, she appreciated Pierre Louchard's idiosyncracies and the way he found simple pleasures and solace in nature. Whilst tending to his field of lavender and his herd of *brébis*, a goat-like breed of sheep, he would speculate on the world's ineffable questions, and then expound his revelations to all and sundry. It had earned him the nickname "The Thinker," after Rodin, in a not entirely respectful fashion. For unfortunately his delivery of the Great Truths while out in the fields never quite attained the heights of his internal musings. Put bluntly, many of his fellow farmers never had any idea what he was talking about.

"A blank canvas," said Penelope. "Mmm, it is rather white, isn't it! I may have to tone that down. Even with my woodburning stove, it might look too chilly in winter. I'll have to see."

"A curtain, still waiting to be pulled," said Mariette. She grinned widely, as if she was only joking. Whether or not she was poking gentle fun at her fiancé, Penelope judged it wiser not to laugh out loud.

While the four of them sat down facing each other across a coffee table on huge comfortable sofas, Penelope brought in pastis and well-chilled champagne. As usual, the men chose pastis.

Mariette was looking prettier every day, thought Penelope, as she handed her a flute of champagne. A bad marriage to a ne'er-do-well had put paid to the light in her eyes and any effort to retain her youth, but now she was happy and free after the death of her husband in a brutal murder that had rocked St Merlot and drawn Penelope into the tight-knit community. In the aftershock, Mariette and Pierre Louchard had rekindled their teenage romance and it had not taken long for their love for one another to become serious. Her dark hair was now cut in a gleaming short bob, and she wore a waisted trouser suit that skimmed her curves and took years off her. Not for the first time, Penelope felt that she and Mariette had much in common and might in time become good friends as well as neighbours.

"I had some good news this week," said Mariette, raising her glass. "We are getting a new Bibliobus!" She was one of the drivers of the mobile library that trundled around the Luberon villages. But the ancient lavender-painted coach had become ever more prone to breaking down, much to everyone's chagrin. Like other village monuments, the old Bibliobus was both a talking point and a perfect venue for catching up on all the current gossip. There had been some concern that the service might be axed. A few people were even worried about their supplies of reading matter.

"*Santé!*" they chorused.

"That is very good news," said Penelope.

They all agreed that it would have been a crying shame to lose the vital service provided by the Bibliobus. Indeed, only this week, Mariette had picked up some excellent new titbits along its route.

"You have heard about the English artist who was murdered? Well, apparently he had three women in his life and one of them was seriously deranged." Mariette made a circular motion with a finger at the side of her head. "She could not cope with not being his only lover, so it was she who strangled him."

Interesting, thought Penelope, but mainly because it showed how rumours spread like bushfire, even when they were wrong. "Which stop on the route did this bulletin come from?"

"Let me see . . . it was either Goult or Ménerbes, on Friday. I had quite a crowd, all longing to hear the latest. Ménerbes, it must have been. There was a woman there who occasionally used to clean for the artist. He had a studio there, apparently. She was in demand, as was the owner of the bar who had heard all kinds of speculation. Apparently Don Doncaster might even have had a fourth woman."

"Was that where he lived?" asked Penelope, trying not to sound too interested.

Valentine helped herself to a goats' cheese, sundried tomato, and basil leaf canapé. "It said in *La Provence* that the dead man lived in Goult. Why would he have a studio in Ménerbes?"

"If he was to satisfy four women . . ." M. Charpet pulled a cheeky face.

"Most people seemed to agree it was only three," said Mariette.

"It's always difficult to separate fact from fiction with people like this," said M. Louchard, handing around a bowl of gleaming black olives flecked with thyme.

"These olives are delicious," said Valentine, rather pointedly, as if she were keen to move on from the subject of a private life of dubious morality. "But, you know, for the very best, you must go to Goult. There is an *épicerie* there, well known for its special recipe—olives stuffed with almonds and marinated in a special brine. It is a renowned speciality of the region, but I don't think they make it anywhere else."

Penelope shifted forward in her chair. "Stuffed with almonds you say? Is that unusual?"

"Not that unusual, but the herbs they use are a unique blend, and a closely guarded secret. You should try some next time you go to Goult."

I fully intend to, thought Penelope.

Penelope attempted casually to re-introduce the subject of Don Doncaster and his amorous entanglements.

"So, Mariette, what else did you hear about Don's women—who were they?"

"Did you know him, Penny?" asked M. Louchard.

"Not really." She glanced at her gardener, remembering she had already told him about the fateful night at the gallery. She didn't want to make it seem as if she took a constant ghoulish pleasure in local deaths. "I only met him once . . . I was at the exhibition when he collapsed."

The others exchanged glances.

Mariette rescued her. "He had a wife and two mistresses. That was what I understood."

"Ex-wife, I think," said Penelope.

"I distinctly remember the *femme de ménage* saying that M. Doncaster was married. Maybe it was a mistake."

"Maybe," said Penelope. "Who were the two mistresses?"

"Maybe he had two wives and one mistress," suggested M. Charpet, not helping.

So intent was Penelope on trying to square this with what Clémence had told her, that she took longer than she should have to react to a trail of smoke that had started to creep through from the kitchen door. Followed by a distinct smell of burning. She shook herself violently.

"Oh, my God—the Yorkshires!"

Leaving behind four French guests utterly bewildered by this strange outburst in English, she plunged into the kitchen. The tray filled with beef fat that she had put in the oven was smoking heavily and she pulled it out just in time. Upon being flung in the sink, it sizzled fiercely and released a cloud of smoke. Luckily for her pride, she had managed to flap away the worst of it before M. Charpet plunged into the room, hand over his mouth, and flung open a window with a French oath.

"Thank you, monsieur, thank you," murmured Penelope weakly. This was not going according to plan, she thought. But as the air cleared, so did her mind. Nothing had been ruined . . . yet. She ushered Charpet out of the kitchen with the bottle of pastis, and opened the other window and the back door to clear the air.

Twenty minutes later, they sat down to eat.

∞

THERE WAS silence as Penelope brought the meat to the table, and a certain frozen quality to the smiles on the faces that looked up at her. Gastronomy was a powerful weapon in the entente cordiale between the two proud nations, but she detected some signs of Gallic scepticism.

"Roast beef . . . with . . ." Lacking the French for "all the trimmings," Penelope hesitated.

"*Ahah! Le rosbif! Avec une rosbiffe!*" M. Charpet doubled up in mirth at his joke before being poked by his sister. Mariette and Louchard looked into the wineglasses, trying not to laugh.

"*Rosbiffe avec le rosbif!*" Charpet was almost overcome with the elegance of his wit.

"Yes, got it—very good." Penelope soldiered on. *Les Rosbifs* was the affectionate, or maybe not so affectionate, French slang for the Brits—based on what they liked to eat. Exactly the same as the British referring to the French as "frogs."

"Roast beef," she repeated, in English, enunciating each syllable like a 1950s BBC newsreader, "and Yorkshire pudding."

This was too much for Pierre Louchard, who snorted into his glass. "*Rosbif* . . . and pudding? Together? Penny, you are so funny!"

There was a little whispered conversation between him and Mariette, who smiled broadly at the notion of what they were calling "poo-ding." "You're joking, aren't you, just to test us!"

Penelope was getting a tad irritated. "I am not joking!" She fixed Louchard with a beady glare that rapidly wiped the smile from his face. "Yorkshire pudding is the pride of Britain, and it is not a dessert. Now, would you like to pour the wine, Pierre?"

She turned and returned to the business end of the kitchen. At the table, amusement was now mingled with some apprehension. Ladling roast potatoes and peas into tureens with one hand, and stirring the gravy with the other, Penelope inched slowly towards readiness. The Yorkshire puddings were in the oven and looked like they were rising, to her great relief. With such a critical audience, she could not afford to put a foot wrong.

Five minutes later, the various dishes were laid on the table, along with hot plates, mustard, horseradish sauce, and the gravy. Finally, she carved the glistening joint of beef at the head of the table, the slices satisfyingly rare, as she knew the French would demand. Then, taking the lids off the china dishes, she announced with a flourish, "*Rosbif,* Yorkshire pudding, parsnips, roast potatoes, vegetables—*servez-vous!*"

The reaction was a little more muted than she would have liked. There was definite approval of the meat, even the odd appreciative nod. But the group's main focus was on the dish of Yorkshire puddings. Like a team of botanists discovering an entirely new species of plant, they leaned forward on their chairs and peered over the rim of the bowl, incomprehension writ large on their faces. Penelope took the lead and deposited some of the round (and beautifully risen, she noticed) national delicacies on her plate. The others followed suit, except for M. Charpet, who put one on his side plate and attempted to butter it.

M. Louchard looked thoroughly alarmed at the two alien puddings on his plate. It was true that, on second glance, some of them had not risen quite as she'd hoped. There was some solid consistency in the middle. Was it the flour? She tried to explain that this was not what she had anticipated. They all insisted on trying them but she could tell they were being polite. Neither did the gravy have the silky sheen she usually achieved.

They commenced eating. Penelope was itching for someone to begin a conversation, but her attempts were for the moment ignored, as the serious business of tasting progressed.

Finally, M. Charpet came up for air. "Mme Penny, the roast beef is delicious. And the poo-ding, he is . . . very interesting."

There was a concerted nodding of heads at the table, and they continued to tuck in. Penelope counted that as a win.

As the wine flowed, so did the conversation. There were some

intriguing snippets about Laurent Millais and his business deal-
ings and political ambitions beyond the office of mayor. Penelope
was very careful indeed not to seem too interested. Luckily, the
subject of Pierre and Mariette's impending wedding was a fruit-
ful subject, covering everything from love, to food, and the best
venue for the party.

⚭

IT WAS time for the second offering to Franco-British gastronomic relations, the syrup sponge. A saucepan of custard was
warming on the hob. Eschewing all offers of help, Penelope
heaved out the frankly oversized pudding from the steamer, and
with some difficulty upended it on a large dish. There was a loud
and embarrassing fart as the sponge pudding parted from its
glass bowl onto the dish. She paused to let it recover its dignity,
while she ladled custard into a jug.

"*Mesdames, messieurs! Le golden syrup pudding, avec custard.*"

"And this is also a poo-ding, Penny?" asked Pierre Louchard,
clearly trying to be open-minded.

"Yes, it is." It came out more severely than she meant it to.
"And custard is only *crème anglaise.*"

Delighted that they were aware of the provenance of at least
half of the dish, there were renewed smiles all round. Penelope
carved out slabs of the sponge and poured over the custard. It
looked good and smelled ambrosial. The extra syrup oozed like
golden lava down the sides. How could they possibly not like
this? She crossed her fingers.

Bravely, they put their spoons to the syrup pudding. In its plain,
domed splendour—half a cannonball on the serving plate—not
only did it look unlike anything a French cook would have dished
up, it clearly tasted foreign to them. "Save room for the cheese!"

said Penelope, brightly, giving them all a chance to save face by releasing them from their obligations. But all was well. A contented silence fell, and when the bowls were clean, expectant faces all round encouraged her to ask if anyone wanted more.

"*Absolument!*" exclaimed Valentine Charpet. This was praise indeed. M. Louchard nodded towards his plum liqueur on the kitchen island and suggested it might go well with it. "As a digestif?"

They fell on that suggestion with wholehearted enthusiasm. The party had definitely warmed up since its early hiccoughs. "I bet it's lovely with cheese," sighed Penelope, as greed and relief made her reckless.

"But we should have had the cheese before the dessert, no?" Valentine furrowed her brow.

"But not in England," explained Penelope. "Always afterwards."

This was another very odd practice, the others agreed.

"My house, my rules!" Penelope laughed. And they toasted her, joining in.

By the time the cheese had been sampled, and coffees served, the sun was sinking behind the hills in a blaze of light as warm as the bonhomie around the table.

❧

AT SIX o'clock, her guests departed, making a show of groaning and holding their stomachs. She fervently hoped it was a show, anyway. Penelope sank into her sofa and allowed herself to relax completely. Lunch had gone pretty well. She would do the washing up later—she had yet to purchase a dishwasher, and if she was going to enjoy entertaining in the months and years to come, it was surely a necessity. She was tired but happy, and still floating pleasantly on the Château Carmin's very quaffable wines.

She put her head back on the cushions and gazed at the vaulted ceiling, feeling the heaviness in her limbs, letting her thoughts run free. Snatches of the conversation replayed in her head, especially the words of appreciation for her cooking or choice of ingredient. She smiled at the reactions to the Yorkshires and doubted she would ever convert them. The French took such delight in the simple pleasures of food, with such knowledge and precision. The perfect cut of beef for the recipe. The ideal potato for the dish. The best olives. Penelope sighed contentedly.

An image swelled of Don Doncaster tackling a bowl of olives stuffed with almonds, swearing they were the finest in the region. His insistence that she take one and join him.

Penelope got up rather more quickly than she should have, and immediately regretted it. Groggily, she dragged herself upstairs to her bedroom and found the handbag she had taken to the gallery in Avignon. She delved down to the bottom, fished around, and pulled out a livid green olive.

9

❧

THE SKY WAS A DEEP hyacinth blue the next morning and intense light sharpened every scar and outline of the hills. Penelope popped on her sunglasses. It felt so glamorous to wear them in November.

She parked the Range Rover close to St Merlot's main square and waited. A few minutes later, Laurent bounded down from the mairie and jumped into the passenger seat.

"Thank you so much for doing this with me," said Penelope.

Finding the olive had put her in a quandary. She knew that the tiniest possibility always had to be considered in an investigation. Could this olive be connected to the poisoning of the person who had been eating all the others? Statistically, the answer was probably no. But there was always a faint chance that it might. Was it worth taking it to the police?

In the end, she had called Laurent. As mayor of St Merlot, he could make the decision. Now they were on their way to the police headquarters in Avignon.

A large white van rounded the corner in front of them, and flew past well over into the middle of the road without any attempt to slow down. Penelope's knuckles tightened on the wheel and she clenched every muscle as the Range Rover rocked from side to side, caught in the slipstream.

"Ah, Gérard—always the racer. He thinks he's Sebastian Vettel, that one. Rumour has it that he once overtook a bus by

driving through a petrol station. Did you see the excitement on
his face?"

"Laurent, just for that moment my eyes were closed so tightly
I saw nothing at all."

"You might like to keep them open round this bend. I saw
another car I recognise coming up."

Seconds later, an ancient rust bucket scorched towards them,
apparently from nowhere. For a moment it appeared that no one
was driving it at all. Then, under the rim of the steering wheel,
she noticed the steely eyes of an equally antique old woman. Penelope had to take evasive action, almost going off the road.

"Hell's bells."

"Mme Etienne. She is over ninety and she still makes wonderful goats' cheese. At the far side of the village in the hamlet of
Les Beaux Jours."

"Amazing," she muttered. It *was* amazing that the woman
had made it to old bones if she had always driven like a speed
freak on these roads full of blind bends.

They crawled the remainder of the winding road down to
Apt. Penelope relaxed only when they reached the main road.

"Is this straight enough for you?" asked Laurent. "It was the
old Roman way known as the Via Domitia."

They bowled west towards Avignon. No matter how many
times she travelled along it, Penelope knew she could never grow
tired of the route, with its ever-changing views of hilltop villages: Bonnieux topped with a church spire; the austere castle of
Lacoste; the vertical chasms of the mountain ridges facing each
other across the broad, fertile valley.

"During the time of the Roman Empire, this was the main
route between Turin and Avignon," said Laurent. "Imagine all
the legions marching down, Roman eagles pointed skywards,

swords glittering, bent on conquest and destruction as they expanded their new province."

"Which is why it's still called Provence?"

"Exactly."

"And now the invaders are marauding Dutch caravans and mad Belgian drivers bent on destruction," said Penelope.

"Er, the British can be just as bad. They are notorious for setting off on the wrong side of the road after lunch with a little too much wine."

"*Touché.*"

Laurent directed her through the gorgeous little town of L'Isle-sur-la-Sorgue. It sat on a maze of waterways, the streets lined with antiques dealers and *brocante* shops. Penelope struggled to keep her eyes on the road as they passed fantastical objects: ornate stone urns, lanterns, Victorian pergolas, and stuffed birds in cages that made her think of Mme Bovary, statuary, fabulous chairs, and bedheads. Penelope vowed to come back and explore.

Far too soon they were approaching Avignon. She felt nervous again, knowing she could be on a fool's errand. But she knew she could not have ignored the livid green souvenir from the gallery.

֍

THE PLACE de l'Horloge would have been a lovely place to relax at a street café. Crisp leaves were falling from the plane trees that gave shade in the summer. An elegant theatre stood across the road. The life-sized figures inside the Gothic arches of the clock tower atop the Hôtel de Ville, the city hall, began to strike the hour with their hammers. Penelope counted eleven chimes as they walked towards it.

A vintage carousel, ornate and gilded, stood at the foot of the Hôtel de Ville. At that moment a wedding party came down the steps of the municipal building, led by the bride and groom. They headed straight for the merry-go-round and got on prancing white horses, friends and family riding the rest of the herd and taking seats in red-lined carriages. The carousel began to move, with the remaining wedding guests cheering them as they went by, waving.

Penelope waved back.

"OK?" he asked as they looked up at the imposing Hôtel de Ville and considered less pleasant matters. It was a building that implied the might of the French Republic in the stone pediments, Corinthian columns, and carvings of its frontage. "Liberté, Fraternité, Egalité" was engraved prominently on either side of the entrance. The police must have a presence there, as they did in Apt's equivalent.

She nodded.

A residual worry coalesced in the form of the small, cocksure figure glimpsed at the ochre museum, but she reassured herself that he worked out of Apt, not Avignon.

"Let's sit here," said Laurent, rather surprisingly indicating a table at the nearest café. "We can have a coffee."

Penelope wasn't going to argue.

Smells of autumnal dishes wafted from the interior. The menu chalked on a blackboard offered a three-course menu to the locals for the price of a starter in August. She salivated, feeling piqued that this was no occasion for a long lunch. If only she were here with Laurent Millais under different circumstances.

The waiter had barely turned away after serving them, when Laurent straightened his shoulders and stood up. Penelope followed his gaze.

At first she thought she was mistaken, that she was imagining the worst-case scenario. But no. He was real enough. A most unwelcome addition to the party was making his way over to join them.

"Mme Keet. We meet again," said Georges Reyssens, chief of police at Apt. It was not a warm greeting. He puffed up his chest as she stood from the table. The suspiciously dark hair that fell across his forehead, giving him a Napoleonic air, seemed to have slipped its moorings so that it slanted at an improbable angle. Penelope was convinced it was a wig.

They shook hands formally. Reyssens narrowed his eyes, confirmation that her appearance on the scene was as irritating to him as it was unwelcome. Their relationship had been tense from the beginning, when Penelope had become unavoidably involved with the murder of Mariette's husband. Although her detective work had led to the solution, there had been little thanks from him.

Laurent turned to her. "I thought it would be best if we did not make this matter . . . bureaucratic. It is, after all, only a very small piece of evidence that may or may not be of consequence. And it is only because M. le Chef de Police has already seen you in action, so to speak, that he has agreed to consider it."

"Very gracious of him," yammered Penelope.

"You may not know this, Penny, but our chief of police was promoted after the successful conclusion of the St Merlot murders. He is now responsible for a much larger municipal area, and is based here in Avignon."

Crikey, he might have warned her! This policeman had made her first few weeks in the Luberon extremely uncomfortable, and she did not expect this encounter to go much more smoothly.

"I understand you may have some potential evidence in the

Doncaster case, Mme Keet," opened Reyssens with a gritted smile and frosty eyes. "Why, madame, am I not the slightest bit surprised by your involvement?"

Penelope decided to ignore the scarcely veiled disdain. "I am concerned that I may be in possession of something that could be potential evidence."

"And exactly what do you have for me, madame?"

She presented him with the ziplocked plastic bag. Reyssens's expression was priceless.

He looked at the exhibit with disgust. "An olive?"

"Yes," said Penelope. "An olive offered to me by M. Doncaster, out of a bowl he was eating from at the exhibition. I understand that he may have been poisoned."

"But why do you still have this olive? Do you make a habit of hoarding canapés?"

"Of course not. I was trying to avoid eating it after it was offered to me. I don't much like green olives, and I thought the colour was particularly offputting."

Reyssens eyed the olive. "It is certainly green."

Quite a specific green, thought Penelope. It looked very like the arsenic-laced Scheele's Green. But she knew better than to say so before forensics had tested the evidence. If the police had taken the sample at the ochre museum, they would soon know for certain.

Inspector Reyssens stood up, pinching the ziplocked bag between forefinger and thumb with unconcealed distaste. "May I make a request?"

"Of course."

"Kindly make it your business, Mme Keet, not to investigate this case any further, nor to talk to anyone about it, nor to bring me food remains again."

Laurent laughed until he had to dry his eyes on a paper napkin after Reyssens had bobbed off across the square. "Come on, let's go somewhere nice and have lunch."

Penelope was quite cross with him. "You might have told me! Honestly, that man. You see how he always treats me like an idiot. That wasn't fair, Laurent."

She had an awful feeling that he had been having some fun at her expense, too. The thought was crushing.

But the mayor was unrepentant. "It was for the best that we did it this way. Look, Penny, did you really want to make it official? With an olive? And before you say it, I know that your experience in the field of forensics means that you could not ignore what you found. You did the right thing by contacting me rather than the police first. Can you imagine the capital that ridiculous man would have made of it, had you presented it officially at police headquarters?"

She had forgotten that Laurent Millais had little respect for Apt's former chief of police. Penelope softened.

"You know it makes sense," he said.

"I suppose the investigators would have made the connection in other ways," she conceded. "They would have asked questions about what he ate at the party. But he was eating all the olives, so they may not have found any to test for poison. I had to be sure they had all the evidence possible."

"And Reyssens will be delighted to present his detectives with a new and potentially vital piece of evidence that he alone has discovered so brilliantly. You did the right thing. And I think I did, too."

"But—"

"If you had known you were heading for an encounter with Georges Reyssens, would you have enjoyed the drive to Avignon?"

He was right.

"What were you saying about lunch?" asked Penelope, deciding to make the best of it.

⚘

THE MASSIVE, bulky shape of the Palais des Papes reared up into the heavens across the great cobbled square. As Laurent escorted Penelope to a restaurant he knew, she felt a tingle of excitement, the medieval Gothic grandeur adding to the sense of occasion. He pointed upwards at the frieze on the Hôtel des Monnaies where festoons of ripe fruit and vegetables decorated coats of arms. It was once the house of the infamous Borgia family, he explained.

In the stones of the most ostentatious buildings were carved celebrations of the simple joy of living in the sunshine with the richness of nature: grapes and pears and even courgettes and pumpkins.

At the restaurant in the far corner of the square, a few tables were still set under the trees, the first customers already seated. With the patio heaters on, it was still warm enough to sit outside.

"What do you think?" asked Laurent.

"Perfect."

It never failed to amaze Penelope how the customers in France took the bustle of service, the superb food, and picture-perfect setting for granted, hardly seeming to acknowledge the baskets of fresh bread, the aromatic herbs judiciously sprinkled on garlic prawns and sizzling cuts of beef, the divine crispness of the *frites*, the unctuousness of the speciality cheeses and the tempting elegance of the dessert confections. They simply accepted it all as their due. For her, lunch out in Provence would never stop being a delicious, almost guilty, pleasure.

She gazed around, quietly enraptured. The figures on the battlement paths above the square were specks on the horizon. A group of late-season tourists was following a guide with a sign. From this vantage point, in the wide expanse at the feet of the palace, the famous broken bridge on the Rhône was out of sight, but not far away.

Across the table, Laurent was perusing the menu. His white shirt and sunglasses accentuated the suntan that had scarcely faded since the summer. The finely sculpted face showed few signs of age, though he was only a few years younger than she was. He was smiling, pleased perhaps to have spotted a favourite dish. There was something very attractive about his generous mouth and the way it lifted at the corner.

He looked up. "Have you seen anything you like?"

Was that a hint of amusement?

"Er, yes—well, not quite decided yet." Penelope buried her head in her menu, praying her face wasn't red. Fortunately, many of the dishes on offer were so enticing that she soon forgot about any potential for embarrassment, and they ordered.

Penelope felt curiously at ease as they chatted about how Laurent had come to leave Paris after his divorce and make a new life in St Merlot, close to his boyhood home in Saignon. He opened up about the pleasures of having old friends on the doorstep, and how he admired Nicolas's talent and determination. Dessert was looking like a distinct possibility, as was finding a discreet way to raise the question of Clémence and whether the two of them had resumed their long-standing on-again, off-again affair.

As she perused the menu, though, a shadow fell across the table. She looked up to see, outlined against the sun, a tall, dark figure standing behind the mayor. Laurent turned around. "M. de Bourdan. What a surprise."

"Gilles, please, M. le Maire. And this is—?"

"Mme Penelope Kite," said Laurent.

The gallery owner gave her a dazzling smile. He looked considerably more relaxed in jeans and a blazer than he had at the gallery on the night of the fateful exhibition. He must have been around fifty-five, and clearly kept himself in shape. Penelope, already exhilarated in the company of one attractive man, stretched out her hand to another. *"Bonjour, monsieur."*

"Call me Gilles. The pleasure is all mine. I have been looking forward to making your acquaintance properly. Nicolas and Claudine have told me all about you, and I am intrigued!" He turned to Laurent. "I hope you do not mind if I join you for a coffee?"

Laurent indicated the chair next to Penelope.

Gilles turned to Penelope. "So, madame, what brings you to Avignon?"

Penelope caught a raised eyebrow from Laurent and decided to remain discreet about their intentions. "A lovely lunch! And the chance to see the sights without the summer crowds," she added quickly. "We were just talking about poor Don."

Gilles's demeanour changed abruptly. In the softest of voices he sighed, *"Aah, mon ami, le pauvre Don.* So misunderstood, you know."

"Did you see him before he died?" asked Laurent.

"Alas, no. Not after the night he was admitted to hospital. I was reassured by the staff the next morning that he was stable, then I had to go to my gallery in Nice for a meeting with an important client. That was what I wanted to speak to you about, though. Did you return to the hospital before Don died?"

"No. But I checked on his condition with a doctor I know there."

"Do you know whether he had any visitors?" asked Gilles.

"He was in intensive care. I'm not sure anyone was allowed to see him. Why do you ask?"

"It's probably nothing. A feeling, that's all."

They stared at Gilles expectantly.

"As I said, it's probably nothing. I don't want to incriminate anyone. But if you do hear anything through your semi-official channels, Laurent, I would be most grateful if you could let me know. Such a tragedy."

Laurent nodded. "You know he was probably poisoned?"

"The police interviewed me, as you would expect. But I read that in the newspapers."

Penelope felt aggrieved on his behalf, especially if Reyssens had been involved.

"Yes. It is always sad to see a person cut down in his golden years." Gilles's brown eyes became moist. He shook his head.

"I'm sure justice will be done," said Penelope, more confidently than she felt.

"Mind you," continued Gilles, "there will certainly be plenty of suspects. Most of the artistic fraternity for a start, who resented his success. Apart from the clique of adoring women, he wasn't very popular."

"Among your other artists?" asked Penelope.

"Well, it's complicated. It always is, isn't it? Rivalries, jealousies . . . Scarpio disliked him intensely."

"The artist who only paints black pictures?"

His dealer raised his palms as if to object, then conceded the point.

Laurent interjected. "We all know Scarpio can be trouble. My friend Benoît keeps an eye on him over in Reillane. He is not quite . . . normal, is he?"

Gilles did not deny it. But he leaned forward confidentially. "I got the impression Don and Nina were avoiding each other. Then, there is Nicolas."

"You cannot possibly think that Nicolas has anything to do with this! That is quite ridiculous." Laurent tossed back the last of his wine.

Gilles shrugged. "It would not seem possible, I agree. Of all the artists I work with, Nicolas is the most gifted. But there, I have said it. Don was envious of his talent. He was forever criticising Nicolas's work, sometimes to his face. He was so condescending. I had trouble keeping my own temper under control at some of his awful English arrogance. No offence, madame, but the French often struggle with the patronising tones of the British."

"Funnily enough, we think exactly the same about the French," said Penelope cheerfully.

"And of course, if it is poisoning we are talking about, then Nicolas has all the requisite raw materials in that museum his wife runs."

Laurent attempted to interrupt, but there was no stopping Gilles.

"As an art historian of some repute, Nicolas specialises in the history of ancient pigments. He has even written a book about the more bizarre and dangerous ones. There is little about the colour of poison that he does not know!"

Laurent sat back in his chair, folded his arms, and muttered a few words in French that Penelope did not recognise. For a moment the two men stared coldly at each other.

"What about Fenella, Don's wife or ex-wife, whatever she is?" asked Penelope.

"Crazy woman," said Gilles. "Though I cannot understand why she would want to kill off the source of her wealth."

"I thought she taught painting?" said Penelope.

"Yes, she taught a few classes, but that would never have kept her in the style to which she had become accustomed. She needed Don's money for that."

From what he was saying, there was a veritable tribe of potential suspects. As the three finished their conversation and their coffee, Penelope was longing to get back home for some serious pondering without the offputting glamour of these two so uncomfortably close.

Gilles stood up and gave a cursory nod to Laurent. After which he took Penelope's hand and planted a warm kiss on it. The warmth that she felt had nothing to do with the ambient temperature, and she desperately tried to stop herself smiling too widely.

"I must return to my gallery. I look forward to seeing you again. *Au revoir.*"

He turned tail and strode purposefully to the corner of the square.

10

M. LOUCHARD'S LAVENDER FIELD GLISTENED with November dew. Midway through the morning the sun was bright,
but not warm enough to burn it off. The air had a sharp, clear
quality that took Penelope's breath away as she walked.

The trip to Avignon the previous day was still circling in her
head. She had a sinking feeling that she might, yet again, have
made herself look foolish. That dratted olive! She really ought
to concentrate on more pressing matters, such as chasing up
the bathroom fitters who had failed to call when they said they
would. So much had happened unexpectedly that she had taken
her eye off the ball where the house renovations were concerned.

Over a cup of strong tea back at Le Chant d'Eau, she rang
the firm whose quote she'd accepted and was put through to a
messaging service. She made a list of improvements in order of
priority and went online to look at kelim rugs. While she was
there she thought she'd see what the consensus was on black
leather trousers for the over-fifties. "Sticky" was the most common verdict.

A search for "Scheele's Green" brought up little new. Next
she typed in "Realgar" and sat back to read the results.

"The natural colour of realgar in crystal form is orange-red,
and as such it was once known as ruby sulphur or ruby of arsenic. Its use as a red painting pigment can be seen in ancient
works of art from China, India, Central Asia, and Egypt. In

Europe, it was used in fine-art painting during the Renaissance. It was also widely used as a cloth dye."

Over time, the red crystals changed colour to yellow. That would explain why the lump in the cabinet at the museum was lemony-grey, thought Penelope. It was clearly a very old piece. She read on, wondering whether it might still be toxic.

Penelope sat back in her seat. What about the other minerals and pigments—how many of them were also poisonous?

⚜

HE PICKED up on the second ring, a sure sign that she had timed her call perfectly and he was sitting at the desk in his book-lined study in Manchester Square.

"Hello, Cam."

"Penny! How are you, my dear?"

Penelope was touched by the instant recognition. She pictured his full head of white hair, the mischievous cornflower-blue eyes behind his black-rimmed glasses, and the classically handsome, weathered face. "I'm well—and you?"

"Very. To what do I owe this pleasure?"

It was so good to hear this lovely, well-modulated voice with a warm hint of North Country in the vowels.

"Curiosity," said Penelope, smiling.

"Don't tell me you've got yourself involved in the dark side again?"

"We-ell . . . no, not really. I was just there the night it happened, and not involved at all—but puzzling, if you know what I mean."

"You'd better tell me."

Penelope did.

"Heavy mineral pigments do not generally lose saturation

over time, so it is possible to speculate that it is still poisonous," said Professor Camrose Fletcher. "There are some most fascinating cases, in which a vermilion-red dye made from cinnabar, a mercury-based sulphide, spontaneously produced swelling and blistering in elderly men who had been tattooed in their youth. Although it is impossible to know for certain without physical testing, it does seem as if, even in minute quantities, such as those contained in red tattoo ink, it can cause problems many decades later. And bear in mind that red is rarely used as more than an accent colour, or for a small heart, perhaps, especially when tattoos were the preserve of sailors and hard men, not the fashion they are today."

"Still active, then."

"Unstable but still potent."

Another man might have made a clumsy joke about that phrase equally referring to him. But that was not Camrose Fletcher's style. He was supremely—but quietly—confident, never falsely modest but rock-solid in his own expertise and achievements. Over the years Penelope had worked for him, increasingly closely, he had been the man in her life, though she hoped he never knew that. She cherished the memory of a conference in Stockholm when, for one weekend only, they had been lovers. On their return to London, without a word being said, they reverted to trusted friends and colleagues. No awkwardness had ever ensued.

"There's something very odd about this case," said Penelope. "First they think the victim will survive, that it was a heart attack, then he dies suddenly in hospital. Next we know, the police are saying he was poisoned and they raid a museum and take away a load of nineteenth-century paints and rock crystals kept under lock and key in display cabinets."

"But when you visited the museum, you were intrigued by the presence of arsenic. The same would be true of others, surely."

"I suppose so."

"It's common knowledge that arsenic is an extremely effective and unpleasant poison. Once known as 'inheritor's powder' because it was popular with impatient heirs who couldn't wait for nature to take its course before they could get their hands on their family fortune. 'White arsenic,' the compound arsenic trioxide, looks to all intents and purposes like flour or icing sugar. It has no taste and so is virtually undetectable to the victim in small doses in food and drink. The fashion for arsenic poisoning—"

"That's a chilling phrase . . ."

"Indeed. The *fashion* for arsenic poisoning in the mid-nineteenth century left the over-imaginative souls of Victorian Britain terrified that the slightest tingle in the hands or episode of vomiting could possibly have been caused by malevolent persons known and unknown . . . though the clinical signs of arsenic—vomiting and diarrhea—were easily mistaken for those of common diseases such as dysentery and cholera if the poison was administered in small doses over a period of time. This also increased the risk of cardiovascular disease."

Penelope shivered.

"Myocardial infarction can be induced by low to moderate arsenic concentrations."

She sat back in her seat. "Don's heart attack."

"It's possible."

"So how long before . . . that might be the outcome?"

"The nature and length of the victim's suffering depends partly on their genetic makeup and general state of health. Victims of very low-dose poisoning can survive for months, aware only that they are suffering low-level bad health, with symptoms ranging from nausea to stomach problems."

"So someone might have been poisoning him for months . . ."

"Again, it's possible."

"And does it stack up to you that his condition could seem to be stabilising in hospital, and then all of a sudden, he's gone?"

A pause. Penelope could see him in her mind's eye, his gaze wandering in the direction of his bookshelves while his focus directed inwards to his own inner reserves of knowledge.

"And again, possible."

"But not a conclusion you would want to draw without specific pathology—I understand that," said Penelope. "I'm just thinking out loud, really. There are many other sources of arsenic besides old minerals and paints, though, aren't there? I mean, everyone knows about weedkiller."

"Of course. Worldwide, drinking water is actually the largest source of arsenic poisoning—usually ingested foods from crops grown in arsenic-contaminated soil or irrigated with arsenic-contaminated water. Tobacco can contain arsenic."

"Don was a cigar smoker," said Penelope. "I smelled it on him."

"It's also found in industrial products such as those used in tanning. It's rather more prevalent that people might imagine."

Penelope made some notes. It was comforting to be reminded of the days they worked so happily together.

"Just one more thing," she said. "You never came across a barrister called Doncaster, did you, in all your expert witness years?"

A pause.

"You mean, this is him? Good grief. Now you mention it, I do vaguely remember the name. A prosecution silk—or was he a silk? I'll ask around at CPS. I do have a spot of work coming up with them."

Penelope smiled. The Crown Prosecution Service were clearly as loath to respect Camrose's retirement as he was himself.

"So how's the house renovation going?" asked Camrose.

"Not too bad. Waiting for the new bathrooms, but the place is perfectly habitable."

"And the music? You said you had started playing again."

"Well, quite good actually. Though I am still some way off my best, there's a group I might be able to play with here. In fact I'm meeting them tomorrow, so fingers crossed."

"Good luck, Penny, though I know you won't need anything of the sort. That is good news. I might find myself in the South of France quite soon."

"In which case, it would be lovely to see you, Cam." Penelope had the feeling he was floating an idea to gauge her reaction. "Just let me know when, and I can come and meet you somewhere, or you're always welcome to stay here."

Hard to make it plainer without coming across as a little desperate, she thought.

"I'll keep you posted, then, if I may," said Camrose.

"Do."

She put the phone down and did a few spontaneous Zumba steps.

11

⊙⧚⊚

THE SUN WAS SETTING OVER the valley as Penelope parked in Viens. She walked up steep winding streets until she reached an arch embellished with a stone crest. The Valencourt residence was a *grande bâtisse*. Behind a wrought-iron gate, the bright red Mini Cooper was parked at the foot of the stone staircase leading up to the house. She pressed the buzzer on a modern intercom and gave her name. The connection went silent. For a minute, she shifted from foot to foot waiting. After a long pause, the gate opened.

At the magnificent entrance door, she was met by a diminutive elderly woman in a black dress without a flicker of recognition, and invited into the cavernous hall. A stylish console table and ornate mirror were the only items of furniture. From there she was shown to an open double door.

"Come in, come in!" said Clémence airily. Of M. Valencourt there was, as usual, no sign. The housekeeper poured a glass of white wine from the silver tray on the table and handed it to Penelope.

"How lovely, thank you. I've been looking forward to this evening."

"We have an hour before the concert starts, so we might as well relax."

"You'll never guess who I met yesterday."

"Gilles de Bourdan?"

Penelope felt a quick, sharp moment of irritation. Why was it that this woman seemed to know everything that was going on, sometimes it seemed before it had even happened? She was about to say so when Clémence got in first.

"I saw Laurent this morning. He told me of your trip to Avignon. I don't think he appreciated Gilles interrupting your cosy lunch." Clémence's eyes glinted with an emotion Penelope couldn't quite read, and once again, she found herself blushing.

"Yes, I noticed a slight atmosphere between them. Is there some history there I should know about, Clémence?"

"I don't think so, though they do know each other. I believe that Laurent feels that Gilles is not treating his friend Nicolas very well."

"Yes, I got that impression, too."

"I would guess that it is to do with money—it usually is."

"Perhaps. But yesterday, Gilles implied that as Nicolas had access to the old poisonous paints and dyes at the ochre museum, he could not be considered beyond suspicion."

"But that's outrageous!"

"Laurent certainly thought so."

"He didn't tell me that," murmured Clémence.

"Probably didn't want to upset you. And Gilles did talk about other people who hated Don. Though in my experience, it's not always hate that kills. Sometimes it can be love."

"Jealousy?"

"Certainly," said Penelope.

"A crime of passion!"

"Or, what about those who kill their loved ones to end their suffering? Though with Don and his art, it was the rest of us suffering. Sorry."

Clémence laughed. "Don wasn't mortally ill, as far as we know."

"Poison is often thought of as a woman's weapon," said Penelope. "It makes the victim suffer, but does not necessarily have to be witnessed by the murderer. We also have to consider where the poison might have come from. It could be something crude, like weedkiller. Anyone can buy that from M. Bricolage. It could be pharmaceutical or a natural substance. Something that would only kill certain people."

"How does that work?"

"If the victim suffered from a certain allergy, it would induce a reaction, potentially fatal, which simply doesn't affect the person next to them in any way."

"Nuts!"

"Precisely. Nut allergies can be very nasty indeed, and yet most people pop them in their mouths and crunch away without a second thought. The question is, did Don have any allergies that a very few people knew about, but unfortunately those few included his killer?"

"His wife—ex-wife—would know," said Clémence.

"Indeed."

They stared at each other.

"What's she like?" asked Penelope. A vision of the kind of middle-class Englishwoman she knew very well came to mind, and then she remembered the assault conviction at a demonstration.

"Not what you would imagine. Dresses like a student. Angry—very angry. But she paints well and is an excellent gardener. A woman of contradictions, I would say."

"But they were divorcing. She didn't need to poison him. All she needed to do was sell the house, do her packing, and adios!"

"Perhaps it was her parting present. She wanted to punish him."

They exchanged looks that may or may not have contained suppressed amusement. It was interesting how the subject of wives besting ignoble husbands quite often seemed to bring Clémence to the brink of confiding some experience of her own, but then she backed away.

"What exactly was Fenella's status—wife or ex-wife?"

"As far as I know, they were in the process of divorce. Just as they were in the process of selling the house in Goult. They'd argued about the best way to market it. And if they are not yet divorced, then Fenella would presumably inherit her husband's share of the estate after his death." The estate agent raised her glass in an ironic gesture.

Penelope raised her eyebrows. "I think I should go and see Fenella. As a fellow Brit, I might be able to pick up anything that's out of kilter."

Clémence shook her head. "That may not be a good idea. She wouldn't thank you. Fenella Doncaster is a . . . has become . . . very radical. A very modern feminist." She pulled a face. "Last time I saw her, she informed me that I am sexist against women myself! She is very vocal about it. Crazy!" A finger whirled at the side of her head.

"Ah. I'd better go in some dungarees and clompy shoes, then."

Penelope relished the visible shudder this vision induced. She hastened to assure the Frenchwoman that she currently pos-sessed no such items. "I might still have a go, though."

A deep exhalation and shrug from Clémence wished her luck with that.

"What about Don's other women? Maybe we should talk to them. See where we get."

Penelope was hoping for another glass of wine and a jolly good gossip. Clémence had proved an excellent co-detective during those first grisly weeks at Le Chant d'Eau, and she was showing potential in this matter, too. But they had a concert to attend.

They surged off in the Mini Cooper, out of the village and down the hill towards Oppedette, Clémence changing gear aggressively and putting her foot down to take the bends at fearsome speeds. Penelope gripped her seat belt and braced herself.

❦

THE CHAPELLE St Ferréol was a small stone building beautifully situated in the valley beside a lavender field. It had gradually fallen into disrepair until rescued from ruin by a rich local patron of the arts. Now it was a venue for cultural events, Clémence informed her as they pulled up sharply. Concertgoers were converging on the flat-fronted chapel topped by a bell in its arch and a homely roof of terra-cotta tiles. A stately tree grew by the wall close to the entrance. Penelope made a mental note to return in high summer, when the lavender in flower would scent the evening and lend another sensuous layer to the music.

Inside the chapel, the stone walls were so painstakingly restored that they were almost white. But it was the vaulted ceiling that made her heart soar: a dense flock of birds in black outline wheeled across a blue yet cloudy, stormy, sunset-hued sky in a modern mural. Were they birds? When Penelope looked closer, she saw they were human figures swimming.

"It's absolutely stunning!" whispered Penelope to Clémence. This was what the French did so well. It was modern, but somehow completely appropriate. "Who painted it? It's not a Chagall, is it? I mean, it can't be . . . but all the same."

"Local artist, I think. Nicolas knows him."

Clémence stopped to speak to a distinguished-looking couple. The mayor of Viens and his wife were glad-handing one and all as if their lives depended on it.

Penelope stood happily by herself under the swimmers in the sky, allowing her thoughts to swirl alongside them until they took their seats.

Beyond the open door, the musicians gathered. In front of the stone altar, their chairs and music stands awaited. The hubbub of chatter faded to an expectant hush as five players, all women, filed in with two violins, two violas, and a cello.

The concert was delightful. It consisted of a trip through French chamber music from the early arrangements of sixteenth-century chansons, to some ravishing songs by Fauré. The concert finished with Debussy's String Quartet, a piece Penelope remembered playing at university. As the final chords drifted up to the rafters, she stood and started clapping loudly along with the rest of the audience, who had clearly enjoyed it as much as she had. She was very much looking forward to meeting the musicians.

The applause died away to be replaced with the general hubbub of friends taking their leave and a rush for the bar. Clémence grabbed her arm and shepherded her in the other direction, towards a small side room. She found herself ushered into the centre of the musical group.

"*Mes amies*, can I introduce Mme Kite? Penelope is the Englishwoman who has retired to St Merlot."

Less of the retired please, thought Penelope. Her smile stiffened slightly as she shook hands with a number of the group whilst Clémence beckoned the waitress over and took two glasses of white wine from a silver tray.

"Mme Kite studied with the Royal Academy of Music in London when she was younger." Clémence, as befitted her job, was comfortable with a certain level of exaggeration. The others nodded and looked at Penelope with a degree of deference.

"You are a professional musician?" asked one of the violinists. She was an older woman with grey hair and wide-set eyes behind steel-framed glasses.

"Sadly not," said Penelope. "I . . . I changed paths. I didn't think I would be good enough." Clémence had misremembered, far too flatteringly, what she had once told her of auditioning for the Royal Academy.

Clémence was undeterred. "I know you are always looking for new members, and I have to say, having heard Penelope, you should snap her up quickly before another group hears of her talent."

How easily the sales patter comes to her, mused Penelope, knowing she had to find her way carefully. She did not want to step on any artistic toes.

"You have a beautiful instrument," she said to the cellist, a woman of around her own age with long salt-and-pepper hair caught on the crown of her head with a clip. "And you played it marvellously, too. The middle passage of the Debussy was exquisite."

The woman beamed. "Thank you, that's kind. Orla," she said, extending her hand.

"*Enchantée.*" Penelope shook it, and decided to cut to the chase. "How would you feel about having another cellist in the group?"

"Couldn't be better! I don't always want to, or have time to, rehearse for concerts. I just like playing. If we had another cellist, then that would suit everyone. If we both wanted to play, even better."

"Sounds good!" Penelope found herself pulled towards one of the violinists, who shook her hand by pumping her arm up and down. She was in her early fifties, with very short brown hair, no makeup, and sensible shoes. Laughter lines fanned from the outer corners of her dark eyes. She had the clear-eyed look of a model in a health-and-exercise magazine from the 1930s. "I am Monique, the longest-serving member of the group, always hoping to welcome new players. Madame, Clémence has been telling me she heard you playing Rachmaninov. You must be very good indeed!"

Penelope gave her a big grin. "Well, I can usually muddle my way through."

"No one can 'muddle through' Rachmaninov, madame!" said a smiling younger man as he joined them. "Sylvain. I am the conductor for larger events, and not even I can 'muddle through' Rachmaninov. I will however be 'muddling through' some Mozart shortly for our next concert, and I hope you might enjoy participating."

⚘

PENELOPE RETURNED home around eleven o'clock and slumped down into her sofa with a satisfied sigh. She had thoroughly enjoyed the concert, and the musicians had been friendly and welcoming. Rehearsals had already been scheduled before the next concert, which was to be in Roussillon in a month's time.

She was rousing herself to prepare for bed when the phone went. It was late, which always worried her. She picked up.

"Mum—at last! Where have you been? I've been calling all evening."

"Hello, Lena, darling, how lovely to hear from you. I was at a concert in a nearby village. It was—"

"I have a wonderful surprise, Mum. I'm coming out to see you."

Penelope closed her eyes. She had known this would happen sooner or later. It was just a bit sooner than she had envisaged. "Well, you know I'd love to see you but it's a bit tricky right now, sweetheart. The house is barely habitable just for me. I've only just started painting the second bedroom."

"We don't need much. Just a bed. We won't be any trouble. You'll hardly know we are there."

That was highly unlikely. Penelope had a horrible feeling she was about to be taken for a mug, as usual where the family was concerned.

"I've found it very hard since you left," said Lena.

"You cope very well. You've always been able to manage more than you think." Perhaps she just needed an injection of confidence.

Privately, Penelope thought that Lena had made a rod for her own back with her lax attitude to basic discipline. Zack and Xerxes, four and three, respectively, were tiny tyrants. Lacking the boundaries set by Penelope on at least three days a week, had their appalling behaviour spiralled out of control?

"Zack got sent home from school. What kind of school sends a four-year-old home?" wailed Lena.

"Well . . ."

"They said he was biting as well as kicking."

Penelope herself had too often been on the receiving end of one of Zack's mule-like right-footers. She didn't want to say I told you so, but my goodness, it was tempting. Persistent as ever, Lena ploughed on. She always knew how to wear Penelope down.

"It's been hell with him fighting with Xerxes. Honestly, some days it's been like one of those drawings in *The Beano* with all the flying fists and feet. It's just so draining. And now James is going away for three weeks to Thailand!"

Her husband, James, was in the process of setting up an adventure holiday business. Even so, three weeks seemed a little excessive, maybe even a tad selfish. Penelope found herself feeling sorry for Lena with her two exhausting boys and another on the way. Though she needed to think fast. She absolutely could not allow Lena to park herself in Provence for three weeks.

Without any actual agreement on Penelope's part, it was apparently settled that Lena was arriving in ten days with Zack and Xerxes. Whittling the allotted time down to a week felt like a triumph.

12

THE NEXT MORNING PENELOPE WOKE with a sense of irritation. Not only had she been railroaded by her daughter, she worried about having the children to stay before the house was comfortable and safe. Almost grounds for a walk to the bakery, she thought, but decided to exercise some self-restraint. No sooner had she finished her yoghurt and fruit breakfast and started on her daily music practice than the phone rang again.

"Hello, Mum."

"Justin! How are you?"

Justin had heard about Lena's proposed trip.

"Hannah and I have been longing to come out and see you," he said, a slight edge in his voice.

"Really?" said Penelope disingenuously. They didn't want to miss out, more like.

"It's been a terrible worry, you know. Not knowing exactly where you are, not being able to support you through all that dreadful business when you first moved in."

As Penelope couldn't remember Justin doing much to support her while she was living in Surrey after the divorce, she wondered what exactly this might have entailed. She waited while he exchanged a few terse words with someone in his office in the City.

"You do realise that I am very far from being visitor-ready, don't you?"

"But we could come and . . . I don't know, see if we can help out somehow. We won't be any trouble. You'll hardly know we're there, apart from in the evening. We can all have dinner together."

"Oh, have you learned to tile bathrooms and cook since I left, Justin?"

"No, but if we have to, we can always eat out. Besides, Hannah's very run-down. She could do with a break."

"All I can offer is glorified indoor camping. There's not even a bed in the third bedroom. It'll be blow-up beds for the children. The guest bathroom is nothing more than bare walls at the moment."

He was not to be dissuaded.

Penelope went back to her cello practice. But it was impossible to focus on playing the ethereal music of Bach while thoughts of one practicality after another popped into her head. In the end she gave up. She picked up the phone again to call the company whose quote she'd accepted for the new bathrooms. Then thought better of it.

Ten minutes later she was in the car heading for Saignon, the neighbouring village. This was one advantage of her plan to use local businesses for the renovations. The pressure she needed to apply would be best done in person.

❧

FORTRESS-LIKE ON its rocky outcrop overlooking Apt, the village of Saignon was an enchanting blend of shuttered houses, bistrot restaurants, quirky bed-and-breakfasts, and arty-crafty shops, but none of it too overdone. A prominent auberge covered with bright red Virginia creeper and a fountain topped with a statue of Ceres stood at the end of the main street.

Penelope stopped at the foot of the lichen-encrusted statue, which dripped water into a mossy basin, to consult the map on her phone for the precise location of the plumbing company.

"*Bonjour*, Penny!"

Penelope recognised the voice. She wheeled round.

"Oh, *bonjour!*" Penelope didn't really know what to say. "Gilles! How nice to see you again."

The gallery owner was dressed casually in jeans and a brown suede jacket, and a dark blue shirt patterned with tiny white birds. "What an excellent coincidence!" He stuck out a hand, then seemed to think better of it and went in for the familiar three kisses. "I wanted to call you but haven't yet managed to get your number from Laurent Millais. Is he trying to keep you all to himself?"

"I doubt it. Why did you want to get in touch? Sorry, that sounded rude. I didn't mean—"

"There was a matter I wanted to discuss with you . . . after the conversation we had in Avignon."

"I see," said Penelope, though she didn't.

"May I buy you a coffee?"

"I'd love to, but I'm just on my way to sort out an urgent bathroom crisis. In my house, I mean, I don't mean personally, nothing wrong there," she blithered. "I urgently need to talk to the plumbing firm in the Rue de Jas before I have a house full of visitors."

He looked disappointed.

"What did you want to talk about?" she asked.

"I will go to the café, over there on the corner, and I will wait for you to join me for a coffee," said Gilles. It was hardly unreasonable.

"I'll be as quick as I can."

She was true to her word, and within twenty minutes, she had returned to the café to find Gilles sitting at a table outside next to a heater. He immediately stood to attention.

"I must say, you look most alluring this morning."

Penelope tried to keep a level head in the face of such a charm offensive, and just about succeeded.

She sat down, and Gilles clicked his fingers at a glum-faced waiter who stood in the doorway.

"*Deux kirs royales, s'il vous plaît!*" barked Gilles. The waiter nodded without moving the rest of his forlorn countenance.

"I presume you like kir?"

"Well, I do . . . but . . ." What was it about France that every time she went out, she ended up drinking? She decided to stand firm. "I'll have a coffee, thanks."

"Of course, Penny, and you must call me Gilles." He smiled widely. "And the kir?"

"Oh, go on, then. I can resist anything except temptation."

He laughed. "That is very good! I like that."

"It's not original."

A pause.

"How did you get on with the plumber?"

Penelope rolled her eyes. "He wasn't there, but I spoke to the woman in charge of the office. Apparently a job is overrunning and the firm is booked solid for the four weeks after they finish. Realistically, the earliest they could fix my bathrooms would be December, and that's too late. I'm not sure what I'm going to do."

"I could help."

"Don't tell me plumbing's your hobby?"

"Because you would not believe it?"

He smiled in a way that assured her he was a man of many talents. Or was he taking the mickey out of himself? Without Laurent there, he was being quite flirtatious. His brown eyes didn't leave hers but seemed constantly amused, as if he didn't take life too seriously.

"No, I wouldn't."

"You are right. But I know plenty of people. Leave it with me, and I will ask. There are more firms to choose from in Avignon."

"That is extremely kind, thank you."

Her coffee and the kirs arrived. Penelope decided to drink the kir first. Why not? It was such heaven sitting outside in the sunshine with an attractive man. What would she have been doing back in Esher? The most exciting it got there was lunch with some women friends at Café Rouge. How her life had changed!

Gilles took a sip and leaned across the table. "I expect, Penny, that you are wondering what it is I have to ask you."

"Oh, yes." She'd completely forgotten about that, what with the annoyance over the bathrooms, the distraction of the drinks, and the glorious setting.

"I would like to propose to you."

Crikey, she hadn't seen that one coming. They barely knew one another. "Excuse me?"

"My proposal is that you do some work for me."

Penelope felt a hot flush coming on. It wasn't the first time that a misleading similarity between French and English words had caught her out.

"What kind of work?" she croaked.

"I have found out about you. How you solved the murders in St Merlot. I find this most impressive."

She wondered what was coming.

"Mme Kite—Penny, I would like to engage your services to examine the circumstances of the death of Don Doncaster."

Penelope snorted as her drink went down the wrong way.

"Sorry. You want me to do what? That's what the police are doing, surely?"

"But are they . . . ?"

"Well, Gilles, I mean . . . I find it most flattering that you could think that I would be of any use at all, but—no. You can't compare my efforts when it was a matter that happened on my doorstep and involved me, whether I liked it or not. I cannot be involved with a crime that is already being investigated by the correct authorities."

"Even so."

Silence as his implication percolated through.

"But Reyssens . . ."

Gilles cocked his head and raised his palms. "Exactly."

Another pause.

"Your involvement would be known to no one except ourselves. But you must let me be the judge of how useful your . . . opinion would be, Penny. Consider this from my point of view. I am one of the most successful art dealers and agents in the South of France. I look after many artists, not just the four you saw at Roussillon. I even organise overseas exhibitions for some of my artists. It is an expensive business."

Penelope nodded.

"What happened to Don was deeply distressing. He may have been talentless—oh, do not think I was blind to his faults, Penny—but he had many other attributes. It was Don who earned much of the money that kept some of the other, far better, artists in paint and rent. He attracted attention and may have been controversial, but he was effective in getting people to my galleries and putting our names in the media."

"Did the other artists appreciate that?"

"Some did. Others were not so . . . pragmatic."

"And you are nothing if not pragmatic?"

"Indeed."

Penelope found she had finished the delicious kir. A warm

surge of recklessness hummed in her blood. She felt light and airy, as if anything was possible.

She rapidly got a grip. "I'm not going to work for you, Gilles." He sat back and sighed.

"Which is not to say that I am not very curious already about who or what killed Don. As it happens, I have been asking my own questions . . . and I would be more than happy to discuss anything I find with you, if you share what you know with me."

A smile spread slowly to Gilles's eyes.

"That would be a most acceptable proposal."

❧

THEY ENDED up having lunch. Of course they did. This was France.

Over a fifteen-euro set menu of *oeufs en cocotte* with shavings of truffle, *daube de boeuf*, a palate-cleansing lemon mousse, and a glass of wine, they happily discussed the details of Don's final night at the gallery and last days in hospital, his bohemian life and his many women.

"Did you mean it the other day, when you said the other artists hated him?" asked Penelope.

Gilles exhaled theatrically. "There is always competition and jealousy. But Don was the one they all hated the most—well, apart from Nina Chiroubles, of course."

"Why, of course?"

"You don't know? Don and Nina were . . . how do you say it . . . ? An item. For a while, anyway."

"Really . . ."

"Yes. She was his mistress for several years—"

"While he was still married to Fenella?"

"Definitely. But then Nina caught him with someone else.

After that her love turned to loathing. I suspect she hated him even more than the others by the end."

"You don't seriously think Nicolas Versanne had anything to do with it, though, do you? Laurent was quite upset about that."

As soon as the words were out, she kicked herself for not being more discreet. But Gilles nodded sympathetically. "I would have expected nothing less. And I would have defended a friend just as he did."

"Why on earth would Nicolas hate Don? He might have been irritated by him, or tainted by association even, but he can't have been jealous of his non-existent talent."

Gilles wiped his mouth with his napkin. "Don never missed a chance to boast about how much money he was making. As if the buying public are any measure of the true artist! But it infuriated Nicolas."

"But Nicolas does well financially, too—doesn't he?"

"He does. But his wife is a genius at spending it. They argue a lot about money. That museum takes a lot to run, for a start. Sometimes it's more like a charity for struggling artists. She pays people like Nina far more than the going rate for the job."

"What?" Penelope sat up. "Nina works at the museum?"

"Now and then."

"Interesting. I thought her work was extremely expensive to buy."

"It is. But it almost never sells."

"So why—?" Penelope's head was spinning with all the implications.

"It would sell even less at lower prices," said Gilles. "It's a very strange market, installation art. It's more about money than anything else."

Penelope would have liked to know more about the financial

arguments between the Versannes. Perhaps that was what Laurent meant when he said they had enough to worry about.

The bill arrived. Gilles automatically reached for his wallet, insisting on paying. As he handed the unsmiling waiter his gold card, he fixed Penelope with another dazzling smile. "Come to Nice, see my gallery there! We can continue this conversation and have a delightful dinner together as we discuss all this further."

Penelope felt a little jolt of excitement, swiftly followed by disappointment. "I can't at the moment, the family is arriving, you see."

"You have a family?"

"Well, stepson and daughter, and their offspring."

"But no Mr Kite?"

"Long separated, now divorced."

The Frenchman gave her a distinctly twinkly look. His brown eyes softened and did not look away from hers. "Well, after they have left, then. It is such a lovely drive to Nice from here, through the Basses Alpes, and then down the Route Napoléon."

Penelope nodded. It was impossible to argue with this man, she thought. His charm was quite intense.

Not only was the prospect of a break in Nice with Gilles a pleasure in its own right, but it could prove interesting. After all, he controlled most of the Provençal art world from his galleries in Avignon and Nice.

❧

LATER, WHEN Penelope told Clémence that Gilles de Bourdan seemed to have taken a bit of a shine to her, a tiny expression of disbelief crossed her enviably smooth brow. Penelope recognised it immediately as the register of puzzlement that very attractive

women reserved for their less alluring sisters who had inexplicably managed to interest a man who could take his pick.

"I do quite like him," said Penelope, feeling her cheeks start
to burn.

"Well, you'll find out how much you like him as soon as you
get to his house, won't you."

"I'm not going to his house! I am going to his gallery. After
which, I am going to indulge myself with a night or two at the
Château Eza and meet him for dinner. And, God knows, after
the children, I'll have bloody well earned it!"

A pause.

"What's his . . . relationship status . . . by the way?" Penelope
had deliberately not asked Gilles himself.

Clémence opened her eyes wide. "Single, as far as I know. I
believe his wife died some years ago."

Penelope left it there.

It was hilarious in its way, the way her friends reacted when
she let slip that Gilles had invited her to his gallery in Nice for
a weekend, and that she had accepted readily.

Even Laurent seemed rather put out.

13

GILLES WAS AS GOOD AS his word. The next day, she received a call from a bathroom installation company in Avignon, promptly followed by an acceptable quote and the excellent news that they had had a cancellation and could start on Monday. Timing would be tight, but plumbing for all the family was just about achievable.

In the meanwhile, Penelope was going to make the most of her time alone.

FIRST ON the list, in defiance of Clémence's warnings, was Fenella, the ex-wife.

Penelope habitually drove past the turning to Goult on the main road to Avignon, but now she found that the village was a hidden gem. There were pretty tree-lined squares where cars could be parked in the old-fashioned way: simply drawn up and left, unlike in Britain, with no annoying fiddling around for change for ticket machines that might or might not work the first time.

The houses were solid, flat-fronted, and painted in pretty shades that didn't shy from bold blues and reds. Yet the most appealing beauties were those where the stucco had faded, even blackened in patches.

The artisan food shop was announced in beautiful cursive script on a hand-painted sign: *"La Ruche"*—the beehive.

Penelope experienced a delicious sensory rush as she opened the door. In the middle of the floor stood a large grinding stone. There were still traces of flour on it, presumably replaced every morning with admirable care and attention to detail. In fact, there was the air of an exhibit about the whole place, the very essence of Provençal epicureanism distilled into one outlet, where lavender vied with strings of garlic, mottled salamis butted against the cheese counter, and a myriad of candles and soaps fought a battle of the scents against spices in open hessian bags: yellow turmeric, deep red paprika, cinnamon, powdered ginger, cumin, and every type of dried herb. Tins of pâté and variations on the insides of local wildlife were piled on shelves behind, all clearly homemade. Large hams hung from hooks on the rafters, located so that one had almost to brush against them whilst moving round the shop.

At one counter towards the back of the shop, which seemed to extend for ever, there were a number of half barrels, full to the brim with olives of every size and colour. The green olives stuffed with almonds announced themselves as special in every way: their position in the centre of the delicatessen display, the lavish decoration around the display bowl, and the astronomic price. On the wall behind was a painting. Penelope moved closer to confirm her suspicions. It was indeed a particularly gruesome offering from the late Mr Doncaster: a simpering child set in a blood-purple lavender field.

"Bonjour, madame." A pleasant youngish woman caught her attention. "What can I do for you?"

"Bonjour. What a wonderful shop! I am looking for the special almond-stuffed olives, which I was told could only be purchased here."

"*Merci, madame.* Everything is organic of course, and most comes from within fifty kilometres of this village. I think these must be the olives you are searching for."

The assistant scooped up an olive with a long-handled teaspoon and offered it to Penelope. It seemed a touch less lividly green than the one she had taken from Don.

"I have tasted them at parties. They are superb," she said quickly, to avoid having to eat it. "I will take a hundred grams, please."

"Marinated for a year in herbal brine made from a secret recipe, there is a twist of lemon peel, and the sweet almonds are picked only from trees in a sloping south-facing orchard where particular wildflowers grow between their roots."

"You must have a lot of people asking for them."

The woman nodded serenely. "Our customers even come from neighbouring regions. They will make a special journey."

"I was introduced to them by an Englishman," said Penelope. That was nothing less than the truth. She let her eyes drift over to Don's hideous painting.

"We have an international reputation."

Penelope kept her gaze on the picture. "The artist told me he was a regular customer."

"He loved them," said the woman.

"Did he often come in to buy them?"

"Occasionally, though it was usually one of his women. He was very good to us—he would mention the shop by name in one of those Provence lifestyle interviews he gave to the press, and that brought in more customers. Naturally, he often went away with a free gift. He always had them on special occasions. He used to say they were like champagne to him—celebratory."

"Did Mrs Doncaster buy the olives for his last party?"

"I can't recall who it was."

Penelope settled up for the olives, along with some goats' cheese sprinkled with dried red currants and thyme and some fishy *brandade de morue* made of salt cod and potato.

"I'd like to pay my respects to Fenella," she said. "The house is . . . remind me?"

"Carry on down the hill, and turn left. The salmon-pink villa, you can't miss it."

⚭

"FENELLA IS out, teaching," the girl told Penelope. "I am her assistant, Anya."

She was a beautiful girl in her twenties, with long glossy hennaed hair that fell halfway down her back. Skinny jeans showed off her slim, shapely legs. Her black sweater was covered by a paint-smeared apron.

From the threshold of the house Penelope could see down the hall to a garden room with views over the valley. "Do you know how long she'll be out?"

The girl looked at her watch. "Maybe not so long now." The accent was Eastern European.

"In that case, I don't suppose I could come in and wait for her?"

Inside, the walls were hung with paintings, some of which Penelope quite liked, all signed "Fenella S." Of the Doncastrian oeuvre there was no sign. Various rugs, many depicting parts of the female anatomy, sat on looms in different stages of completion. Bookcases overflowed with an eclectic mix of paperback novels and leather-bound histories. A well-stocked drinks tray was crammed with specialist gins and vodkas.

Anya showed her through into the conservatory-like room overlooking the garden. A sturdy jasmine was still flowering, alongside lemon trees in pots and hothouse orchids. It was clearly the work of an accomplished gardener.

"I came to France from Prague three years ago," said the girl as Penelope gently asked her about herself. "I could not get a job in my country. For one year I was an au pair to a family here, and then I met Don and Fenella nearly two years ago."

"How did you meet them?"

"In the summer I was working as a waitress in Bonnieux, a restaurant they often went to. They were kind to me. Then I would work for them, maybe only a few hours a week at first, but then more. Now I clean the house and take bookings for lessons and prepare the easels and materials for the art classes. Sometimes I drive the car to classes, and I do the shopping."

"So they were still together when you started working for them?"

Anya tilted a hand up and down. "*Comme ci, comme ça.*"

"This was here, at this house?"

"Yes."

So this was the one that Clémence was selling. Penelope looked around the spacious room with its glorious light and length-way views of the Grand Luberon and thought it wouldn't be long before it was snapped up by an eager buyer. Though now Don was dead, perhaps Fenella wouldn't need to sell up.

"I only met Don once but I was very sorry to hear of his passing," she said.

Anya looked away.

"I loved him," she said. "Fenella did not mind at all. I think she was happy it was me and not some woman she did not know."

Penelope stared, still processing the girl's startling admission. A more unlikely conquest she could not have imagined.

"Oh, not so much recently. Don had cooled off. He was not so much fun, and he was always tired. He started to look older and he wasn't interested in sex. Before, we used to laugh so much and play around, he was a delightful lover."

She stopped. "You look at me like that, but obviously you did not know him. He was a gentleman and I was very excited that he chose me to be one of his lovers. At first, that is. But then he seemed to get tired of me."

"Just tired, maybe—with so many women eager to . . . spend quality time with him," suggested Penelope.

"I always knew I would not hold on to him," Anya said sadly.

Penelope gave her a sympathetic smile.

"I did not want to make a fuss, to be one of those women who cannot accept the end. He always hated that."

"Did it happen a lot?" asked Penelope, still slightly incredulous. Don clearly did have something about him.

"All the time. It is alluring to be close to such a talent. Some women cannot give it up."

Penelope didn't trust herself to comment on that. "So he always had many different women around him, and he had plenty of flings?"

"Flings?"

"Romantic liaisons. Affairs."

"Yes. That is true."

"And each of these women accepted that, sooner or later, he would move on to the next affair?"

Anya shrugged her thin shoulders. "Mostly. But some did not."

"Did you know of any who did not go quietly, who did not want to end it with him?"

"There was one."

"Really?"

"I used to hear the fights between Fenella and Don. Fenella did not much care about his lovers by then, as I said. But she did care about this woman who continued to telephone him and turn up here at the studio when he was supposed to be working."

"Who was it?"

"Why are you asking this?"

"I'm . . . just curious. Don was a very interesting man."

"Are you a journalist?" Anya's eyes had widened, presumably with fear that she had overstepped the mark and said too much to a friendly stranger who could too easily betray her in print. The compulsion to speak about a man she had admired had been too strong.

"No, I'm not," Penelope assured her. "I'm just . . . a fellow compatriot from England. I thought Fenella might appreciate having someone to talk to in her own language. I was at the gallery the night that Don . . . was taken ill."

She held her breath, but she had clearly said the right thing.

Anya nodded and dried her eyes with the back of her hand.

"It can't be easy, for either of you."

A shake of the head.

"He was not well in the weeks before he . . . went. He did not seem as energetic as normal. He complained about feeling tired and wanting to go to sleep. His stomach hurt, he said."

"Had he been drinking more than usual?" asked Penelope.

"Perhaps. As I say, he was worried. But he always drank a lot. When he was happy, when he was sad, when he was painting, and when he was not. It never seemed to affect him."

"Had he changed in appearance recently?"

She fished out a cleaning rag from the apron pocket and began to twist it in her hands. "I think so. He had lost a bit of weight, and his face was redder. I did not think he was *beau*, at first," Anya went on. "Not at all. Only when I got to know him. I had never liked older men before, but Don was different. So . . ."

confident, so assured. And he was so kind. He helped me to . . . understand so much." She looked away and blushed.

Only if you were too young to know better, thought Penelope. It was all too easy, in your twenties, to confuse infatuation with the real deal. She should know.

"How long did your romance with Don last?"

"A few months . . . four, maybe."

"The woman who kept coming round . . . was that before you started seeing Don romantically, or after?"

"It was before Don moved out of the house. But he went soon after."

"Fenella and Don separated over her?"

"I think maybe, yes."

"Why was that, what was different this time?"

Anya shook her head.

"Did you never ask Don?"

"No! He hated unpleasantness and being asked about his other relationships. He said it was all unnecessary and that we should all just live for the moment, not spoil it with petty emotions like jealousy and resentments."

Yes, thought Penelope, that would be typical of a certain kind of cake-having and cake-eating man. She let the silence run.

"It was because the other woman was her friend Nina."

Penelope tensed up. The longer they waited for Fenella to return, the more awkward it was going to be. "You know, Anya, I think I'll come back another day after all. Is there a better time to catch Fenella when she's not teaching?"

14

ON HER RETURN TO LE Chant d'Eau, Penelope fished in her bag for her keys and found a slip of folded paper. On it was written the name Monique and a number. It took a while before she remembered that Monique was the music group's long-serving violinist, who had given it to her after the concert in Viens. Penelope decided to call her. She had been intrigued by the chance of playing again, and the suggestions for the concert at Roussillon excited her. One particular piece was an old favourite of hers, and she was determined to be part of it.

"Come this afternoon, if you like," said Monique, five minutes later. "Don't be shy."

AT THE chapel by the lavender field, Monique and Orla, the other cellist, greeted her warmly, and introduced her to another viola player, a septagenarian called Philippe. He looked like a teacher. Which was exactly what he was, it transpired: a retired history teacher. Sylvain, the conductor, sat at a piano.

They attacked a Schubert quintet and then tried a Beethoven quintet with two violins, two cellos, and viola. It had been a long time since Penelope had played with other musicians, but she held her own and didn't make any mistakes.

When they took a break for some coffee—Monique had brought two large vacuum flasks—Penelope had another chance to admire the inside of the chapel, stark yet appealing with its blend of clean lines and medieval stonework, its striking mural on the vaulted ceiling.

"What was it like before the renovation?" she asked.

"Mostly in ruins," said Monique. "The woodwork was rotten—damp and full of wormholes. The wooden seats were so weak they could hold nothing heavier than a mouse."

"It smelled of mice, that's right! A terrible smell of mice!" said Annette, the other violinist.

"There were some parts that survived. Some pretty panelling. Not all the benches were beyond saving. But it was decided to take it all out. It all had to be restored, or none of it. It was too expensive to restore all the wood, so it was decided that we should have modern seats. Which is much better for concerts, anyway."

"And more comfortable," said Penelope. "But what a shame. What happened to the panelling and the benches that weren't in too bad a state?" She tried to keep the interest out of her voice. It had occurred to her that a couple of church pews might be perfect for either side of the long pine table in her kitchen, but didn't want to appear venal.

"They were stored in M. Bérenger's barn, weren't they?" Monique turned to Annette.

"Rows of them. Yes, rows of them!"

"Bérenger's the village carpenter. Some of the stuff was sold to benefit the works, but after a while, when everyone who was interested had had a look and bought what they wanted   which, frankly, was not much—anything that was left over was given to him. It is probably still there. Why, are you interested?"

Penelope wished her thoughts were not always written so clearly on her face.

"Well, I am in the process of renovating my house. And I love the idea of incorporating a piece of history. If there's a chance of having a look, at least to see what remains, then I am interested."

"I can ask him if you like," said Philippe.

"I'd appreciate that, thank you very much."

"Or, it's not far, you can drop by anytime," said Monique. "How are your renovations going?"

"All right. A few problems, but I'll get there. I hope."

Monique raised her palms. "There are always problems. But equally, there are always solutions."

"Very true," said Penelope positively.

Gentle and understanding, Monique clearly loved music. Her touch on the violin was sensitive and quite lovely. She dressed in the same homely way Penelope had done around the house in Surrey, before she encountered the chic Clémence and her critical eye.

"I'm so glad Clémence introduced me to you," she said. "If this works out, then it's just the boost I need to start playing more often."

"How do you know Clémence Valencourt?" asked Orla, another woman who had also let herself go, by French standards. Salt-and-pepper hair spilled over her shoulders.

"She sold me my house," said Penelope.

The women seemed surprised. "Mme Valencourt doesn't often stay friends with all the satisfied clients who buy property through the Agence Hublot. Especially not the foreign buyers," said Orla.

Penelope did not want to explain the precise circumstances

of their unlikely friendship, with its background of murder and mayhem. So she diverted to more property talk. "The Valencourt house in the village is very grand, isn't it?"

"It has been in the family for a long time," said Annette. "A very long time."

Penelope's curiosity got the better of her.

"What's her husband like?"

The women exchanged glances. Penelope fought to keep the ferocity of her interest under control. She examined her bow.

"He's . . . an old-fashioned kind of husband."

What did that mean? He didn't seem very old-fashioned with regard to his wife. He never seemed to be home, for a start.

But the other women were looking at her as if she had unearthed a ticking time bomb. A couple of them edged away.

"He's a remarkable man," said Monique, as if that settled the matter. Not that it was any more enlightening.

The others nodded, though Penelope sensed reservations.

By the time they took their seats and resumed playing, she had heard nothing that made M. Valencourt any less mysterious.

❧

NO TIME like the present, thought Penelope as she waved and pulled out of the chapel car park.

The carpenter's barn was on the edge of the village where the road branched down from Viens, exactly as Monique had described. It smelled of sawn pine and was packed to the roof with new and old wood, ancient doors, and battered old cupboards.

M. Bérenger was a tiny man with white hair. He shook his head sadly. "I regret, but there is nothing left now of the chapel's former fittings."

"Nothing?"

"Nothing. Not a plank."

"Are you sure?"

"Of course I'm sure." The carpenter was tiring of this. "Some old hippie came and bought the lot a few months ago."

"Oh, well, never mind," said Penelope. "It was only an idea."

Even so, it was a bit of a letdown. Her mind's eye had sanded, polished, and placed the satiny pews either side of her kitchen table, and even sewn plump cushions in Provençal fabric for the comfort of her guests.

❦

BACK HOME, there was a message light winking next to the landline.

She called Camrose back before she'd taken off her coat.

"Doncaster," he said. "Crumhorn Chambers. Competent when not distracted, bit of a ladies' man, is the consensus."

"That could well be him!"

"Known as Bonker Doncaster. Or 'Bonkaster,' apparently. Good-looking. Pretty bumptious. In fact, I shared a case with him many moons ago. The Earnshaw case. The cat and the milk that was off."

"Of course!" It was a lightbulb moment for Penelope. "The elderly woman left to die by the burglar."

She hadn't been working for Camrose very long, and it was one of the first times she'd seen the full drama of a court hearing at the Old Bailey. So she had actually recognised Don, or at least partially. As a barrister, he would have worn his wig in court.

"Don Doncaster shredded the defence," recalled Camrose. "It was touch and go whether the pathology was strong enough for a conviction, but his prosecution won the day. Must have been, what—ten years ago?"

"A bit longer."

"Poor old Doncaster."

"Well, I'm going to do my best for him now," said Penelope, much more confidently than she felt.

15

"FENELLA DONCASTER IS A HOWLING hyena!" said Clémence. "She has just announced that she is no longer selling the house. This, after all her unreasonable demands. Targeted marketing to women's collectives. No use of gender-specific pronouns in the advertisements. Intrusive assumptions about my private life."

The estate agent's annoyance was clearly audible on the phone.

"What are you doing today? I don't suppose we could meet?" asked Penelope. "There's lots more to talk about."

"I have a meeting in Lacoste this morning, and then one in Céreste to view a property. But I could meet you after that, if you like."

"That would be perfect. I've got plenty to do here, then I'll see you in Céreste."

They made arrangements and rang off.

Penelope looked up at the ceiling. An electric drill was competing with various thumps and shouts. The challenge of getting the bathrooms fitted before the family arrived was on. Penelope had always been rather sniffy about all those reality property makeover programmes on TV, with the inevitable race against the clock to get everything finished before the first paying guests arrived or a wedding party was scheduled. It was all so much unnecessary drama that only ensured that corners were cut and the outcome so much less polished than it should have been. Unfortunately, now she was living it.

Upstairs, Le Chant d'Eau was a building site. Penelope had painted the walls of the spare bedrooms herself, and new beds had been delivered. She had an obstacle course to clear before she could clean her teeth or have a wash. But on the plus side, the bathroom fitters were a cheery couple of young men who arrived at eight on the dot and didn't take too long over lunch. On the minus side, the tiles she'd ordered were suddenly out of stock and delivery was delayed, and a carpenter was having to replace some rotten joists in the floor that had to support the second bathroom.

Gilles tried to reassure her that these fitters were renowned for their sprint finish, and she had to trust in that. With five days left before Lena and her little boys were due, it was going to be a close call.

✣

JUST AFTER midday, Penelope joined Clémence in the market square at Céreste. Even in summer, Céreste had the feel of being just outside the main tourist area. Now, as winter encroached it had become even quieter.

It was quite a relief to be with someone who didn't want to devote the middle of the day to a big lunch. Over a couple of mint teas at a café-bar, Penelope brought Clémence up to speed with what she had discovered about Don, and they picked over Fenella Doncaster and the financial advantages Don's death had bequeathed her.

"So it could have been Fenella, for a purely financial motive. You said she hated him by the end of the marriage," said Penelope.

"Even so, I am not convinced. I have known her for years, and I cannot see it. It can't have been jealousy of his other women because that was no different to how it had always been."

"With the exception of Nina Chiroubles, it seems," said Penelope, recalling what Anya had told her. "Did you know they used to be good friends?"

"Nina?"

"Yes. I think Nina's affair with Don really hurt her. Fenella expected loyalty there."

"Maybe there is a special bond between artists," suggested Clémence.

Penelope was sceptical.

"Between Gilles's artists, then."

"The guy in black, Scarpio, was very rude about Don at the exhibition," said Penelope. "Didn't seem much love lost there."

Clémence drummed her red-varnished fingernails on the table, as if she was making up her mind. "Perhaps we should go and see him. I know where he lives—not far from here. Benoît keeps an eye on him. Makes sure he doesn't get into too much trouble."

Benoît was Laurent's friend, the priest—ordained by Internet, in order to run a renowned arts centre in the former monastery in Reillane. He was better known as the former French film star Benoît Berger who had embraced a simpler life in Provence.

"I heard that. But not what kind of trouble," said Penelope.

"Sex and drugs and rock and roll," said Clémence, confirming Penelope's prejudices. "And too much fighting."

"I have to say I don't see him as a fighter."

"He can't fight—that's why Benoît keeps an eye on him. Last time he almost got killed, apparently. A very bad idea to do deals with thugs, and an even worse one to go on the attack when you don't like what they supply."

Penelope shook her head. It was at times like this that she felt she had lived a very sheltered life in Surrey.

"He lives out beyond Reillane. It's not far."

Why not? It was better than sitting around speculating, thought Penelope.

⁂

THEY WENT in the Range Rover, as it would deal better than the Mini Cooper with the rugged track to the old mill house Clémence described. They took the swooping road to Forcalquier, through avenues of plane trees that would cast deep shade in summer, ever further away from the glitzy end of the Luberon. The land was more agricultural, the villages less well tended. It was like travelling decades back to a time before the valley became a chic destination.

They climbed towards Reillane, passing through a square where bunting from the summer fête still hung in tatters from trees and lampposts, stopping only to toot at a dog that lay in the road blissfully unaware that it had escaped death only because Penelope rather than Clémence was driving.

Behind the village there was a plateau, empty save for the astronomical observatories where the clear air, unpolluted by city light, attracted scientists and stargazers. Though it looked flat and uninhabited, the plateau concealed a number of deep rifts where the water had eaten away the limestone, scarring the landscape with steep gorges. Several of these held old houses, built into the sides of the ravine to shelter the inhabitants from the worst of the mistral and the snow that often covered this area in winter.

The road suddenly fell away at an alarming gradient, plunging down the slope towards a stone building with a large wheel attached to one side. Penelope could see that half of the house had been hollowed into the rock face. The bright cold of the day was instantly replaced by an unappealing damp gloom. The leaves on the trees hung lifeless, with the morning's dew still dripping from each bough. The forest seemed to swallow all sound, as they made their way down, with the bare rocky cliff faces towering ever further above them.

"This is it," said Clémence, indicating a stone mill by a stream.

The two women crossed a small stone bridge to the house. It looked dark and mouldy. The upper storeys were in a state of disrepair, with no glass in some of the small windows.

"It has tranquility, but little in the way of charm. A project," said Clémence, slipping into agent-speak.

Penelope shuddered. Not for most normal people, it wouldn't be, she thought. The sky was a long way above the ravine. Apart from the water dripping from the trees and a faint gurgle from the stream, all was silent.

Clémence's knock on the front door elicited some muffled thumps inside. Eventually, the door opened. The spindly Scarpio scowled at them. "*Oui?*"

Clémence took charge, introducing Penelope as an art collector. Scarpio looked distinctly under the weather. But he was clearly unwilling to turn down a potential sale.

They found themselves in a large hall crowded with easels, palettes, small paper drawings, and, everywhere, half-finished tubes of black acrylic paint.

Penelope was immediately knocked back by the intense aroma of cannabis. She felt quite light-headed. "What are you working on at the moment?" she asked feebly.

Scarpio gestured at a large square canvas on which had been drawn a black comma on a background of darkest grey. Six identical wooden panels were smeared with black daubs.

"Black is certainly your signature colour," said Penelope. "Which is, of course, fascinating in itself . . ."

Scarpio collapsed on a chair. "It is black to you, *mesdames*, but to me, it is all the colours of the rainbow!" Possibly the effects of the dope, thought Penelope. His dark eyes glistened like black olives in oil, and his hair hung lankly.

"Where do you get your inspiration from, monsieur? I am always interested in the artist's motivations."

His Spanish accent was all but impenetrable. "Madame, my motivation comes all from here," he stood up and beat his heart theatrically, "and from here!" He brandished a joint at her. "My mind is flying, as . . . as . . . as—"

"A bird?" proffered Penelope.

"Yes, madame, a bird, a little black bird."

Of course.

"Are you working on anything else?"

This seemed to excite him. He rose from his chair and went over to a table. The effort took its toll and he doubled up for an instant, as if in pain.

"I am getting bigger!"

She looked at his emaciated frame with some puzzlement.

"*Voilà!*" He handed her two large photographs. The first was of Mont Ventoux. The second was of Mont Ventoux photoshopped to look shrouded in black plastic.

"The world looks at the stony summit of Mont Ventoux and imagines snow, white snow. Not anymore!"

"Very . . . interesting."

Scarpio became animated, though still slightly disoriented. "All the black plastic in Provence I need for this."

Penelope didn't dare look at Clémence. "To cover the real thing?"

"What a statement it will be!" crowed Scarpio.

Completely bonkers, thought Penelope.

"What do your gallery colleagues think of it?" asked Clémence, clearly trying not to laugh.

"They do not understand me! No one does! That is how I know I am destined for immortality."

"Do you understand their works of art, though?"

This brought on a frenzy of gesticulations. "Works of art? That is not art! That idiot woman with her strings of bottles and big words—art? And Nicolas with his old colours. And worst of all . . . worst of all, that Don with his nauseating lavender fields and little children with the big eyes. Rubbish! God knows why Gilles bought so much of his work."

"Can't disagree with you about Don's work," said Penelope. "Yet it was very popular at the exhibition."

"Popular! Maybe to the public who know nothing. He is no artist. We had a fight once."

"A fight? Why?"

"I don't want to talk about it. But he was stronger than I had realised, and next I knew I was on my back with a broken nose. A monster he was!" Scarpio paused to light a roll-up from the ashtray that sat on the table, stuffed to the brim with old nicotine-stained fag ends. "I cannot imagine why Gilles de Bourdan would take him on."

"So you didn't like Don very much?" asked Clémence.

"I could endure him not, that English voice—sorry, Mme Keet—that voice, the arrogance . . . The man deserved to be whipped. Mind you, being upper-class English, he might have liked that!"

A withering look from Penelope stopped him from elaborating further. He took another drag on his roll-up.

"You know he was having relations with Nina?"

Penelope nodded.

He coughed violently. "She was so upset when he went off her. I was almost sorry for the bitch."

Clearly the milk of human kindness ran in short supply around here, thought Penelope. "So you didn't like her either?"

"Pah! She's all words and no art. What is twenty bottles in line with tomato ketchup dripping from them? It is not an artistic statement! It is . . . it is . . . McDonald's!"

He was working himself into a fury.

"So why are you asking about them? You are not from the police?" Scarpio's face darkened like one of his paintings as he succumbed to a further bout of coughing.

Penelope was no medical expert, but she didn't like the sound of that racking cough. "No, no, just interested in your work. Do you think the darkness of the mill has contributed to your use of monochrome?"

He explained that he was a qualified carpenter and he was renovating the mill very slowly and had plans for more windows.

"At present I am treating the beams for insects." He held up a can of evil-looking black liquid. "This is not nice, but it works! Soon there will be no living thing within these walls, except for me."

"Well, I hope it will soon look as elegant as your art, monsieur," simpered Clémence, "and I look forward to seeing it in its finished state."

Scarpio smiled wanly at the pair.

"I also look forward to that, señoras. And now I must get back to my work. Adios."

He turned away, but swayed, knocking into the can of insecticide balanced on the edge of the table, then doubled over again as the tin sailed off and hit his foot.

"Fah-kin' 'ell!" he yelled in unmistakably harsh London vowels.

Clémence stepped back neatly, with a startled sideways look at Penelope.

Penelope had to steady him as he rubbed his toes. That must have hurt. He was only wearing thin canvas espadrilles. "Are you sure you're all right?" she asked in English. "You really don't look well."

Another bout of coughing prevented him from replying. He doubled up, and dropped to the floor. Penelope managed to keep him out of the pool of black gunk while Clémence righted the pot.

"It's all right, take it easy. We can help you," she said.

The artist blinked at her with bloodshot eyes.

"I want to help you," said Penelope. "Here, give me your hand. We'll get you sitting up."

He allowed himself to be helped onto a dirty sofa streaked with so much black paint it was like turning him over to the care of an enormous zebra. His breathing was laboured. Clémence pulled a small bottle of Evian water from her bag and offered it to him. He took it gratefully.

"Which part of London are you from?"

He coughed again, this time nervously.

Several seconds went by before he answered. "'Ackney."

Penelope gave him a stern assessment. "I'm guessing Scarpio isn't your real name?"

But the artist's only response was to start retching. He rolled over on the sofa, face to the floor, twitching uncontrollably in some sort of seizure.

"I will phone for the ambulance," said Clémence. "Do you know first aid, Penny?"

"Well, I did once go on a course at the Home Office . . ."

"Good. Then you must help him."

"What!" Penelope did not like the way this was developing.

"You know, Penny, make sure he is breathing, give him the Kiss of Life." Without waiting to hear the answer, Clémence ran outside to get a signal on her phone.

Penelope looked at the recumbent figure and shuddered. At that moment a little ball of spittle dribbled from his mouth and ran slowly down his chin. Let us hope it does not come to that, she prayed. Having pulled him over into the recovery position, she breathed a sigh of relief when, ear to his chest, she heard the weak beating of a heart and the rhythmic expansion of his lungs.

Clémence re-entered.

"The ambulance is on its way. Is he breathing?"

Penelope stood and brushed the dirt off, each stroke leaving little puffs of dust that hung in the air, glittering in the shaft of light from the open door.

"I am massively relieved to say yes, Clémence."

"I have also phoned Benoît. He did not sound entirely surprised. He told me that Scarpio has had various 'episodes' in the past. Some of the psychotic drugs he dabbled with in the nineties had effects that remain with him."

It seemed like an age before the sound of a siren announced the arrival of the ambulance. A few minutes later two red-faced paramedics carrying a stretcher rushed into the room.

"What's your real name?" she asked the patient urgently.

Silence.

"The hospital will need it," persisted Penelope. "They will need to cross-reference your records."

His eyes were closed. He mumbled something.

"What?"

"Barry Finch."

Minutes later, an old Jeep rattled to a stop outside. It was Benoît de Reillane, a handsome silver fox, for once without his trademark red Ferrari.

He was just in time to reassure the artist that he was in good hands, and that he would look after the mill and the paintings.

The ambulance set off as fast as the track would allow, and the two women took turns telling Benoît exactly what had happened. Clémence described the convulsions that overtook the sickly artist.

"I wonder whether that was just one of his episodes, or something else," said Penelope. "How long has he been ill?"

"He hasn't been truly well for a while," admitted Benoît. "But I put that down to his not eating properly and his terrible lack of hygiene."

"I noticed the plates and cups he had lying around," she said. "Some of those plates could have doubled as a nature reserve! But loss of appetite, seizures, coughing, that horrible breath . . . these are nasty symptoms. How much do you know about arsenic, Benoît?"

He fixed her with steely Clint Eastwood eyes. His chiselled movie cowboy's face did not seem as shocked as it might have done by the question. He grinned in amusement, in fact.

"Mme Penny, on the detective trail again, I see. Like with the poisoned olive!"

"You know all about that?"

"Laurent told me."

Of course he had.

Benoît pulled up a chair and sat down, legs akimbo. "You think Scarpio has been poisoned?"

"It's a possibility. Too much of a coincidence to ignore."

Benoît sighed.

"Alas, there is so much evil in the world. At least if he is in hospital, this can be checked."

A fat lot of good that did Don, thought Penelope. "By the way, did you know he was British, not Spanish?"

"Does it matter?"

"It might."

The "priest" smiled dismissively. "So many people come here to start a new life, Penny."

She decided not to mention what else she had seen amid Scarpio's clutter.

16

BACK HOME, PENELOPE OPENED HER pocket diary. In the back pages she scribbled a list of names, starting with Scarpio (aka Barry Finch). Next came Fenella Doncaster. She drew an arrow from his to hers and closed her eyes as she tried to visualise the card she had seen on Scarpio's chest of drawers. It was for another of Fenella's art classes, on Friday mornings in Fontaine de Vaucluse. A note had been scribbled on it. "Anya" with a mobile number. And "Don" followed by something unreadable. "Fungus" or "Fungal"? She wrote this down.

Then she added Nina Chiroubles, the final artist in Gilles's circle. For a moment, Penelope let her thoughts settle, then made her decision.

She was going to have to work fast before the family arrived. But she could combine this line of investigation with a trip to the furniture and homeware stores on the outskirts of Avignon.

According to the Bourdan Gallery catalogue, Nina Chiroubles was born of a French father and an American mother: "She lives for the earth and the wind," gushed the biography. According to Gilles himself, when Penelope called him for a chat and an update on Scarpio—he was doing well, under observation in hospital in Forcalquier—Nina lived a pretty hand-to-mouth existence, often having to keep herself afloat with various odd jobs.

"Like in the ochre museum," said Penelope.

"Exactly. Though she does have family money that comes her way now and again, but she spends it very rapidly."

"Family money?"

"I believe so. She comes from a wealthy family," said Gilles.

So Nina's turquoise cockatoo hair, the dress from the wackier end of the layered garments habitually sold by Provençal market clothes stalls, the long grubby fingers painted with black nail polish—all these nods to penniless bohemia were an affectation, it seemed.

"By the way, I'm assuming you did know that Scarpio was from East London and that his name is Barry Finch?" said Penelope.

"Of course. But people deserve second, even third chances, no?"

"I don't think it's actually a crime to come from Hackney. What do you mean?"

"He had some troubles in the past. He might have spent some time in prison. I don't know the details. Drugs, probably. I didn't pry too much. He has been a great help with his handiwork skills. Framing, carpentry, you know."

Penelope stayed quiet, hoping he would spill more.

"Nina's currently living in a painted gypsy caravan in a feminist commune between Avignon and Le Thor," said Gilles.

❧

THE NEXT day Penelope did a lightning swoop on the homeware hypermarket in Montfavet, spending a fortune on a king-sized goose down duvet, good-quality white cotton sheets, duvet covers and pillowcases, curtains, towels, and pillows. More haste, less speed, she admonished herself as she drove away without soap dishes, loo brushes, and toothbrush holders. It would take a while for her to live up to her ideal of being the perfect hostess, able to welcome guests apparently effortlessly into her charming and elegant home.

Too bad. For now, her priority was finding Nina. She followed the directions she had noted down from Gilles, keeping the piece of paper visible on the passenger seat. The turning from the main road became increasingly stony and unmade. She concentrated on trying to avoid the worst of the potholes on the track, swinging the Range Rover from one side to the other.

The first intimation that she had arrived at the edge of the feminist encampment was a series of artistic representations of intimate female organs on the walls that surrounded it. In the compound, a dozen tents and mobile homes had been drawn in a circle as if the occupants were expecting an attack from nineteenth-century Native Americans. It was a depressing piece of scrubland, in Penelope's view. Surely they could have found somewhere more scenic?

Penelope parked considerably out of the way by the inner wall, and walked over dust and weeds. Nina—instantly recognisable by her turquoise hair—was boiling a kettle on a wood fire outside a gaily-painted gypsy caravan. She looked up at Penelope with some curiosity and a little disdain.

"Hello," said Penelope.

"Who are you?"

Penelope gave her name in what she hoped was a friendly tone that also implied that she was not to be trifled with. "I saw your work at the Bourdan Gallery and I was interested in knowing more." She was getting rather good at being economical with the truth, she thought. Though whether that meant she was becoming an unpleasantly sneaky kind of person was another matter. She hoped not. It was all in a good cause.

"Are you that English woman?" asked Nina, hitching up a leather belt like a gunslinger. She wore a small ruby piercing in her nose.

"Which English woman?" retorted Penelope, not to be outdone.

Nina returned to stoking her campfire. "The one who came to my exhibition and immediately hit on Don."

"I beg your pardon?" Penelope did a double take, then moderated her reaction for the sake of politeness. "I can promise you that wasn't the case."

"That's not what it looked like to me."

They glared at each other.

"You say *your* exhibition, but it was for four artists, wasn't it?"

"You can't imagine people wanted to see the other charlatans, can you? That beanpole in black, Scarpio. I've seen traffic signs more interesting than his symphonies in darkness! And Nicolas, with all his heritage this, and ancient that . . ."

Penelope bridled slightly. "I rather like Nicolas's work."

"Well, you would."

This was not going well, thought Penelope, as she felt her temper start to fray slightly at the edges. With the exception of sweet young Anya, Don's women were awfully spiky.

Nina sniffed, wrinkling narrow nostrils. The skin around the ruby piercing looked slightly inflamed. "His paintings . . . were . . ."

What was Nina going to say? This was crunch time for any claim the woman had to artistic judgement, thought Penelope.

". . . such shit. But he was a good man. And now he's gone! None of us can have him. Not you, not me, not Fenella, no one!"

Penelope took a bottle of water out of her bag and offered it. Nina grabbed it and took a swig.

"How did the two of you get together?" asked Penelope sympathetically.

Silence.

"It's good to share," said Penelope, grimacing inside.

Nina's face was pinched. Her skin was bad. She might have been pretty if her complexion hadn't been so dry and blotchy.

"I was a friend of Fenella's," she said, the fight leaving her. "We shared a big studio in Ménerbes for a while. One day he came in and it was like electricity between us. The next time I saw him at a party, and the same thing happened. We managed to keep it a secret for quite some time, but as always these things get out eventually. Fenella went crazy. I arrived at the studio one day and found all my stuff outside with the garbage. Fenella never spoke to me again. I think that was the final straw for her. She chucked Don out of the house in Goult a few weeks later. Not that it was all roses and wine for Don and me either. We were on, we were off. We had fights, we made up. But the electricity was still there."

It was hard to imagine them together. Penelope had to put some disturbing images out of her mind. "You were living together?"

"Not really. He took over the studio in Ménerbes when he left Goult, and I would stay over. But we always needed our space. We're so different."

You can say that again, thought Penelope.

"I needed to find the powerful woman in myself again. I came here for a labia painting afternoon."

Penelope decided not to ask her to clarify the ambiguity. "So how long have you been living here?"

"About two months now. I needed a big change to my dynamic."

Penelope looked around. Two women had emerged from their tents and were pretending to secure guy ropes and shake rugs out. Another very slim young woman in Turkish harem pants, with a ring through her nose and violently dyed purple hair, slouched watchfully nearby.

"So where do you put together your art? It can't be here."

"I use a studio in Avignon near Gilles and the gallery. Close to the university, too. I am taking an evening course in post-feminist Marxism. We all need to learn how to live beyond the male totality."

"Ri-i-ight," said Penelope, none the wiser.

"You need to confront the political rationality of gender."

"I'll certainly give it a go," said Penelope.

A tear slipped down Nina's cheek. "Why did he die like that? He was getting better. All the nurses and doctors said he was improving."

"Were you there the day he died?" Penelope asked.

She nodded. "He was still unconscious, and hooked up to various drips, but breathing normally. He seemed quite comfortable. I left, then he . . ." The tears took over and she could not finish.

Penelope offered solidarity in the form of another Kleenex.

Nina snuffled into it and blinked. "We had only just got married."

"Married?" Penelope felt the bounds of reality loosen. "But I thought he and Fenella were separated, not divorced!"

"Divorced. The decree came through in July and we were married two weeks later. Such a lovely little service, just us two on a deserted beach in Phuket. Nina put her hands over her face. "We would have worked it out. We were both making big changes."

They sat in silence. In the valley a police siren could just be heard on the main road.

Penelope looked around at the array of females pretending not to watch the pair from their tents.

"The bonds were strong. We had started to see each other again, but within different parameters."

"Sorry?"

"We were both making *big* changes. And now it's too late. Oh, Don! Who could have done this?"

The sound of sirens in the distance grew louder.

Nina wiped her eyes. The thick eye makeup she wore had run in black rivulets down her cheeks.

"I'm sure the sisterhood will be kind to you," said Penelope against the wailing of the sirens. They seemed very close and getting nearer.

She was still consoling Nina when two police cars with flashing lights drove at speed into the camp. Doors opened, and with a sinking feeling Penelope saw a familiar short stout figure step out. Worse still, he appeared to be heading towards the caravan where she and Nina were sitting.

Inspector Reyssens stopped in front of them and pulled a thin smile.

"Mme Keet. It seems that we cannot stop meeting."

"Monsieur, the pleasure is all mine." Penelope knew it irritated him when she pretended not to understand his sarcasm.

"However, it is not you that we wish to speak to, enjoyable as that would undoubtedly be. It is Mlle Chiroubles."

He turned to face the panda-eyed artist.

There was a stunned silence as a policeman put handcuffs around her wrists.

"I say, that's a bit unnecessary, isn't it?" said Penelope.

"Mme Keet," snarled Reyssens, "do not interfere in police business!"

He did not see the approach of a large woman dressed in a voluminous kaftan. She was extremely light on her Birkenstock sandals. She pulled him round, forcing him to look up at her moon face haloed by an orange afro hairstyle.

"Typical male oppressor! It's always the woman's fault!"

Penelope held her breath. This woman could probably kill Reyssens just by sitting on him.

"Why are you inserting yourself into our space?" called another woman, before ducking back behind the flap of her tent.

Reyssens ignored her. "Nina Chiroubles, I am arresting you in connection with the murder of Roland Doncaster."

17

FOR ONCE, PENELOPE HAD THE upper hand when she phoned Clémence the next morning.

"Nina Chiroubles! Who would have guessed? Did Reyssens say anything else? Arrested on what grounds?"

Penelope filled her in as best she could. "Clémence, I would love to talk more, but I'm up to my eyes in cleaning and organising here."

"If you wish, I could send Gabrielle over from Viens to help."

"Thanks for the offer, but I am nearly done," replied Penelope as brightly as she could. She felt embarrassed just thinking about the Valencourts' housekeeper seeing the state of the house.

"While you are entertaining your family, I will do some more investigation myself, and report back. *À tout à l'heure.*"

As she tackled the builders' dust, getting the house ready for two grown-up children, one partner, and three young boys, Penelope reflected on this new twist, and wondered how she could find out more. By late afternoon, the new bathrooms were gleaming—if still drying out—and the bedrooms were clean and pretty. It would be a squeeze to have them all at once, but they would manage. As for other matters, there was no immediate chance of finding a solution.

❧

THE FIRST arrivals at Marseille Airport were Lena, Zack, and Xerxes.

Lena looked exhausted. Her long chestnut-brown hair was pulled back in a ponytail and she was wearing glasses rather than her contact lenses. Her baby bump was now prominent over her jeans.

She dropped a large bag and almost fell into Penelope's open arms. The two little boys, Zack blond like his father, Xerxes with Lena's darker colouring, grabbed hold of her skirt and legs with cries of recognition.

"We made it!" exhaled Lena. "I've missed you so much."

"I've missed you, too. It's lovely to have you here," said Penelope.

She grabbed the handle of an enormous suitcase on wheels and took Zack's hand as they set off to the car park.

Two expensively hired child seats with heavy-duty restraints passed without comment and they set off up the autoroute. The shouting and screaming and fighting from the back was even louder than she remembered. Lena said nothing to her sons to get them to turn the volume down. Penelope started to think it was going to be a very long week.

Le Chant d'Eau did its best to charm. The stone of the farm-house caught the last of the sun. The outbuildings glowed and hid their decrepitude. The pines waved a gentle welcome. The boys were released into the garden to burn off some energy, while Lena flopped into a sofa in the sitting room and surveyed the house from there.

For the rest of the afternoon and evening, Penelope provided a full hotel service, cooked and served supper, put the boys to bed, and offered a sympathetic ear to Lena. With every new indignity and complication—the schools, the neighbours digging out their base-ment for a home cinema and gym, the unreliability of the trains, the parking difficulties, the overpriced supermarkets—Penelope increasingly felt she had done the right thing in moving from the crowded southeast of England and its London-centric stresses.

Lena stood dreamily at the window, her slight figure almost overwhelmed by pregnancy. She looked washed out. "It's completely dark and silent outside here. The stars are so bright."

"You can see the Milky Way arching right across the night sky."

"It's fantastic. I might just sleep for a week."

Much as she wanted her daughter to be able to rest and relax, Penelope fervently hoped that she wouldn't.

∿

ZACK AND Xerxes started shouting and running around at half past six. Penelope got to up to give them breakfast at quarter to seven, to give Lena a chance to lie-in.

"It's very cold," said Lena in an accusatory tone when she came down at nine.

"Well, I'm sorry about that. Next time I will make sure the weather knows you're coming. What's your ideal temperature, so satisfaction can be guaranteed?"

"There's no need to be sharp. I was just saying. We brought our swimming gear. You said you were still swimming."

"That was last month. And it was pretty cool *then*, but the exercise was very invigorating."

"I thought it was always hot in the South of France, that's all." Lena had always been dogged. She pushed her thick-rimmed glasses back up her nose, clearly not about to let it go. "When you said you were still swimming and you sent photos of sunny blue skies, it was reasonable to assume that we would be able to swim when we got here. The children are very disappointed. I said there would be swimming. I packed swimming stuff."

A howl of outrage from three-year-old Xerxes went right through her. "Want to swim, want to swiiiiim!" he added, giving her a challenging look.

Penelope sighed. It was all heart-sinkingly familiar, the way things were always her fault. One of the other very good reasons she had moved to Provence in the first place. "How about going on an expedition?" she asked, confronting Zack and Xerxes with a steely enthusiasm. "Who is brave enough for that?"

"Me! Yeah!" They jumped up and down.

"Shall we go on a bear hunt?" Penelope punched the air.

"Yay!"

"You go on, then," said Lena. "I think I'll just stay here and have a little rest."

Ah, right, thought Penelope. She had been going to suggest they head to the Colorado adventure walking trail in the same ochre landscape as Roussillon, where the boys could run off their excess energy, pretend they were stalking in the desert and get satisfyingly red with dust. But if she was going to be solely responsible, she thought better of it. They could climb up through the woods to the village and hunt down some treats at the bakery.

She got the boys ready in their coats and glared at them. Penelope had never had any truck with drippy parenting methods. "I love you very much, boys, and I want us to have a brilliant time. But. I. Am. Not. Taking. Any. Nonsense. Do you understand? Otherwise we will come *straight* back home."

Two sets of grave eyes. Two heads nodding.

"Good. Now let's go. Let the expedition commence!"

Zack smiled back at her, looking angelic. "Let expedition commence! Gan-ma! Let expedition commence!" he yelled.

Penelope smiled. Then he calmly leaned forward, turned to his younger brother, and jabbed him in the eye.

Xerxes let out a horrified scream and began to whine uncontrollably. As Penelope's hackles rose, she reverted to a more obvious approach.

"Be quiet, you two! *Right. Now.*"

They both did.

Five minutes later they were happily finding walking sticks and tracking bears through woodland, around dog-rose bushes, and along a rocky path up to the village.

※

THE SCENT of freshly baked bread, vanilla, and caramelised sugar wafted out across St Merlot's square. Inside the bakery, the different styles of loaf were displayed behind the counter: the trusty baguette; the *pain tradition*; the *matelas*; the *rustique*; the *ficelle*; the *fougasse*. Penelope tried and failed to avert her eyes from the pâtisseries in the display behind glass. Jacques Correa's peerless hazelnut praline tartelettes had proved a particular downfall of late.

In baskets on the counter were several varieties of mouthwatering pastries, from plain and almond croissants, to the chocolate-filled *pains au chocolat* and *pattes d'ours*. "You'll like those," Penelope told the boys. "*Pattes d'ours* means bear's paws. Can you see how they look like a big paw?"

They stared, nodding vigorously, eyes like saucers.

"I want that," said Zack.

"No," said Penelope. "You *would like* that, *please*."

The baker's wife smiled approvingly. She always rather sweetly attempted to explain the intricacies of their pâtisseries to Penelope by slowing her phrases down and speaking in chunks of French rather than whole sentences. "Baguette crust . . . best in the region . . . crust with the softness inside . . . see . . . smell it . . . the scent of the spirit of the yeast . . . continue the old tradition . . . these sacristans . . . see . . . the dusting of fine sugar like light snow . . ."

Penelope nodded eagerly and stored away the phrases. She was getting quite fluent, especially in conversations about house renovation or boulangeries. Well, there were worse specialist subjects, she thought.

Jacques emerged from behind the curtain of plastic strips, face patched with flour. He opened his mighty forearms at the sight of a loyal customer. *"Mme Keet, toujours un plaisir!"*

Penelope made a show of formally introducing her grandsons. They shook hands so solemnly that she felt quite overcome for a few proud moments. Then they spoiled it by grabbing at the croissant basket and tipping it up so that several fell out onto the floor and they were honour-bound to buy them.

It was not warm enough to sit outside, so the boys bore large paper bags full of goodies back to the house where they were consumed almost immediately. Lena was somewhere "resting." Penelope felt not one jot of guilt about polishing off her croissant.

The rest of the day passed pleasantly enough, with an afternoon trip down the road to Saignon. They sauntered along, picking up some food for supper in the little shop, stopping for coffee, and letting the boys have a run around the fountain and the old washing pool—splashing up the water in both, of course.

⚬⚬

THE FOLLOWING day, she drove to the Avignon train station to collect Justin, Hannah, and their son Rory. The valley looked brown under a bleak grey sky. There were few cars, even on the main road, and she spent the now-familiar journey thinking about her recent meetings with the artists. Of all of them,

Nina seemed the least likely suspect. What did the police have on her?

Penelope was lost in thought as she reached the city walls. She turned into an avenue of venerable cedars, whose mighty roots had hefted up the road surface. The Range Rover tipped and bumped over them, with no room to manoeuvre into the other lane.

Forcing herself to concentrate, she found the right slip road. The steel and glass structure of the station crouched over the car parks like a watchful armadillo. Inside, passengers dragging luggage scurried from the coffee shop to the escalators up to the platforms on the skyline. The train from Paris came in. A thoroughly English family emerged from the crowd, hauling two large suitcases.

Having not seen him for months, Penelope found it disconcerting how much Justin looked like her ex-husband when he was younger. He had his father's height, thick dark hair, and handsome bone structure. And a very similar expression of displeasure at any minor inconvenience. His girlfriend—partner, fiancée, whatever they called it these days—Hannah was a slim, pretty English rose with shoulder-length light brown hair. She was transforming year by year into the archtypal banker's wife, with her discreetly expensive clothes and well-groomed air. She never looked particularly thrilled about it.

Rory was a sweet boy, very similar in looks to his cousin Xerxes, but without quite so much of the attitude. He ran ahead to Penelope and she swept him up in a hug.

"Good to see you, Mum," said Justin, kissing her on either cheek.

"And you."

Hannah greeted her warmly as well. The journey had been hassle-free and Rory had even slept on the train.

Outside, Penelope was non-plussed to find Justin striding off in the direction of the hire cars. "I thought I was collecting you," she said.

"I thought you'd come to show us the way," said Justin.

"Oh! Well, you don't need to get a hire car now. Your chauffeur is here."

But he insisted it was a good idea for them to be independent, if necessary, and Penelope realised he was right. Though it could be done, there wouldn't really have been room for all seven of them and Lena's bump in the Range Rover. They drove back in tandem.

❧

JUSTIN AND Hannah were impressed by the house and extensive garden, no doubt about it. Penelope felt a profound happiness when they were immediately seduced by the far-reaching view. It was important that her children grasped the lure this place had had for her, and why she had decided to uproot herself in pursuit of a new life.

That evening, she cooked a special dinner, full of ingredients she knew they loved: spicy butternut squash soup, turkey and chestnuts and cream sauce, with a tangy lemon tart to follow and Justin's favourite, chocolate ice cream, on the side. "For the children," she said, winking at him.

As they ate by candlelight at the table in the spacious, rustic kitchen she felt that this was the way it was always supposed to be. Lena looked less tired. For once, Zack and Xerxes were on their best behaviour. Rory was glued to a game on an iPad, but Penelope decided not to interfere.

Justin and Hannah threw back the Château Carmin red at a frenetic pace. Penelope noted the speed at which the levels dropped in their glasses and supposed it was only in the time-honoured way of stressed city workers suddenly released into a holiday. After spending so much time with Clémence, she had learned to sip like a Parisienne.

Conversation was easy and uncomplicated. She caught up properly with their news, the battles at work and issues with other mums, the plans for house extensions and dreams of travel. In return, Penelope entertained them with tales of the mystery she had solved, the people she had encountered and places she had been, while glossing over most of the worst moments.

Justin fixed her with a sad and serious expression. "So, how long are you going to go on hiding out here, Mum?"

Penelope did a pantomime double take. "Sorry?"

"I mean, playing at being someone you're not. This," he swept a hand around the room, "this fantasy life of turning detective, drifting around in hats and a cloud of perfume. Pretending that you live here when you have a perfectly nice house and friends in Esher."

His face was quite red. Again she was reminded of a young David, and found that inexplicably painful.

"I am not pretending anything," she said calmly, determined to avoid being drawn into an argument that might sour the evening. "I just love it here."

"I mean," he repeated, "it's a great holiday home and all. I'm sure it'll be fantastic for us all in the summer, especially while the boys are young and we need an extra pair of hands to keep an eye on them . . ."

Penelope frowned.

"All right, mixed metaphor. You know what I mean."

"Not the figures of speech that worry me," murmured Penelope. She stood up to start clearing the table.

Justin reached forward to drain the last of the bottle into his glass, then leaned back in his chair. It creaked ominously. "But it's just not practical for you being here, is it?"

"Isn't it?"

"Well, no. Of course it isn't."

"Why's that, then?"

"Well, what do you do with yourself all day long? You don't work. You'll be bored in no time."

"And then what? Take to drink?"

The edge in her voice was clearly lost on him. She noticed Hannah shoot him a look as if to tell him to shut up.

But he was too far gone. "A woman of your age, making a fool of herself going around with all these different men you've been telling us about. You don't know them. They're just after your money, you know. *Our*—"

"I think that's enough, Justin," snapped Penelope. She had a good idea where this was going, and she did not like it one bit.

An awkward pause settled.

"We need you, Mum," whispered Lena, and burst into tears. "We miss you!"

⚜

JUSTIN APOLOGISED and helped her with clearing up while Hannah and Lena went to put the boys to bed. He clearly felt ashamed of his outburst. Penelope blamed the pressures of work, much as she used to excuse his father's short temper. She hoped he would be able to relax over the coming days.

Bloody cheek, implying she ought to while away the rest of her life in boring old Esher so as not to endanger their inheritance! They seemed to think that turning fifty meant playing it safe— they had no idea yet how young it still felt!

And she had a mystery to solve. Not that she was going to tell them that.

18

❧

PENELOPE MADE GREAT EFFORTS TO counteract the still-rumbling disappointment over the lack of swimming weather by laying on a full programme of events. They visited the Abbaye de Sénanque near Gordes, the windmill at Goult, and the ruined castle at Lacoste. No *brocantes*, though. Hannah was keen, but the potential for damage with the boys around too great.

There were lunches out, perhaps a few too many. Penelope could feel her waist beginning to thicken. At her age, it didn't take much to slide right back to the full Michelin Man look when it came to spare tyres. But the visits kept the children active, which meant they were tired by evening. Zack and Xerxes were clearly a bad influence on Rory, whose behaviour markedly declined.

On the Friday morning, she suggested a trip to Fontaine de Vaucluse. The boys could enjoy themselves running along the river path to the ancient pool where the River Sorgue sprang from beneath a rock face. And Penelope could look out for the workshop at the fifteenth-century paper mill where, according to the card she'd seen at Scarpio's mill, Fenella Doncaster would be holding a class.

Fontaine de Vaucluse was as picturesque as all the travel sites promised. In bright sunlight, the emerald-green river was sprinkled with diamonds. The family wandered happily past the restaurants and shops selling a Provençal dream, which consisted mainly of tablecloths and pottery garlic graters. The

paper mill was a long, old industrial building on the river promenade. It now served as a living museum, with a huge wheel
festooned with wet green weeds turning ponderously at one
end, driving huge wooden mallets that crushed raw timber and
cloth into pulp.

Penelope was just wondering where the entrance to the work-
shops was when they heard a commotion on the path in front.

A group of women stood by easels that held paintings in vary-
ing stages of completion. None of these looked remotely like the
surrounding views. It didn't seem too much of a stretch to assume that this might well be Fenella Doncaster's female-only art
class. An argument with a man who kept pointing to a shop
behind them was in full swing.

Penelope adjusted her sunglasses. Logic dictated the teacher
was the one shaking a finger and shouting at the man as he
stood his ground, demanding that she take the class elsewhere.
The woman's cyclamen-pink hair was shaved on the sides of her
head, with the rest pinned up with green plastic combs. Brave
choice, thought Penelope. Other women were joining the remon-
strations, several of them of a decidedly masculine cast.

"Look, Mummy, that lady has a hairy moustache and legs just
like my teacher!" shouted Zack.

"Just as well they can't understand us," said Lena out of the
corner of her mouth.

"I think you'll find that some of them can!" snarled the woman
with cyclamen hair.

Penelope stuttered out some inane reply and tried to walk on.
This was not the sort of introduction she would have chosen.

The angry woman was having none of it. Green eyes blazed
from a deeply suntanned face. She had a demolished beauty that
the pink hair and loose utilitarian overalls could not diminish.
"Very rude little boy! Come back and apologise!"

Penelope tried diplomacy. "Sorry about that. He's only four. Young children do come out with silly things like that."

"A young male learning early to look down at us! That's what leads to this kind of situation."

The shopkeeper objecting to the class setting up on the pavement space by his tablecloths and kitchenware made a rash comment concerning obscene subject matter on one of the easels, unleashing more indignant remonstration.

"I'm sure my grandson doesn't see it that way." Penelope needed to douse the fires of indignation rapidly if she was to get anywhere. "Zack, come here and say sorry."

He did so, relatively politely.

"Well, let's hope you *are* sorry," said the woman. "Words do so much damage."

Whatever happened to sticks and stones, and words could never hurt me, wondered Penelope. Lost to the sisters of perpetual umbrage. "You're not Fenella Doncaster, are you?" she asked.

"I don't use the surname anymore." The woman's tone was icy. "But yes."

"I saw your advertisement when I was last at the Château Carmin, and I've been hoping to meet you."

"You're interested in painting?"

"I am, indeed."

Fenella narrowed her eyes, as if assessing Penelope's likely comfort in the class. "We are painting our cycles."

Penelope shuddered internally. Now was probably not the time to mention Don. She was going to have to play a longer game. "Do you have any places on any of your courses at the moment?"

"I may be stopping my classes. I haven't decided."

"How can I get in contact with you?"

"Speak to my assistant Anya," said Fenella. "She deals with all my admin."

"All right, thanks. Time to go," Penelope urged Zack and Lena.

Justin and Hannah and the other boys had sidled away. They caught up with them by the Museum of the Resistance.

※

"YOU'RE MILES away, Mum," said Lena.

After walking up the river path to the source and exploring the mill—the boys especially liked the hammers that pounded the paper pulp—they were sitting on the terrace of a pizzeria next to the river's swirling green waters.

Penelope had been thinking about Fenella and Anya. Had Anya mentioned that an Englishwoman had already called at the house and asked all kinds of questions about Don? Why exactly had Scarpio made a note of this class of Fenella's? Was it possible Scarpio's illness was not self-inflicted? Could it be linked to Don's death? What if Scarpio had been poisoned, but had survived thanks to a more robust constitution? Was this particular group of artists a target—and if so, why? Don Doncaster was a former barrister. Scarpio had been to prison. What if they had met before? Was it beyond the bounds of possibility?

"You *are* very quiet," said Justin. "What are you thinking about?"

"Oh, nothing, really," she replied brightly.

Several pizzas and ice creams later, they wandered back to the car along the narrow street. It was too cold to indulge in the other sport that Fontaine had to offer, the canoe trip down the river to L'Isle-sur-la-Sorgue. But Lena was keen to stop at the lavender museum on the way back, much to the annoyance of the male members of the party. They piled into the car amid some harrumphing from Justin.

Hoping to lighten the atmosphere, Penelope switched on Radio Nostalgie.

"What the . . . fuck . . . er . . . flipping heck is this?" sneered Justin. He was at the stage of trying very hard, but unsuccessfully, to moderate his language in front of the children, who were apt to parrot the choicest phrases. "The French can't do pop songs. They all sound as if they were written in the 1970s."

"I can't disagree with you there," said Penelope. "But it's part of the French experience and I think that's the charm, isn't it?"

"It most definitely is not. Having your ears chewed off by howling sentimental ninnies trying to imitate the worst of British and American commercial pap is very far from my idea of charming."

Penelope sighed and deliberately left the radio tuned to the offending station. An hour of Claude François hits from the seventies had just begun. Let them suffer.

"What the fuck is this?" wailed Zack from the rear. The journey was completed to an accompaniment from the little boys of "What the fuck, what the fuck, what the fuck is this?"

⚶

AT THE lavender museum at Coustellet, Penelope urged them all in but said she needed to make a phone call before joining them inside.

On a bench by an old field-distilling machine, she rang the number she had once called regularly.

"List Office," said a voice that took her back immediately.

"Hello, Jim. This is Penelope Kite."

"Penny! It's been a while. How are you, m'dear?"

"I'm well, thanks. And you?"

"Not so bad. Same as ever in the old place."

She pictured Jim Perkins in his panelled room at London's Central Criminal Court, otherwise known as the Old Bailey, remembering his alert expression and dark, dapper suits. It seemed bizarre to be talking to him from a garden of lavender and olive trees.

"What can I do for you?"

She came straight to the point in the shorthand speech they had always used for professional matters. "Barrister. Roland Doncaster, recently deceased."

"I'm sorry to hear that, really I am, Penny."

"You knew him well?"

"Not socially, as it were, but he was a good sort. Eye for the ladies, but he didn't treat anyone badly. Rather the opposite, in fact."

"That's what I heard," said Penelope. If Jim liked him, he really must have been all right. "Any chance you could look up his case records to see if he ever tangled with a Barry Finch of Hackney?"

"I wouldn't do it for just anyone, but for you—and poor old Bonkaster . . . What happened to him?"

Penelope explained, to increasing consternation at the other end.

"Goodness me. He didn't deserve that. Leave it with me. Anything I can find, I'll email you," said Jim.

When Penelope checked her emails before going to bed that night, a message was waiting. Efficient as ever, he must have stayed late at the office.

❧

THE LAST trip that Penelope had planned was the Saturday-morning market in Apt. The aroma of roasting chestnuts and wood fires drew them into the narrow main street. Even the children seemed to enjoy the glorious symmetry of the fruit and vegetables laid out on the stalls, the piles of plump pumpkins, and the chickens roasting on spits. She tried to ignore Justin's unsuccessful attempts to barter with a French *paysan* for some truffles by pretending not to understand numbers in French.

The old man looked up again at Justin, shrugged, and stuck to his fifty-euro ticket price.

Penelope cringed. It was always embarrassing when one's fellow countrymen showed themselves up as prats. Worse still when they were family.

"Tell you what," she said to Lena and Hannah, "I'm going for a coffee at the café on the corner over there." She was bursting to call Clémence with the news from Jim Perkins. "You go off and enjoy yourselves and meet me back here in an hour or so."

She was about to turn away when her mobile rang. It was Clémence.

"You must be psychic! I was just about to—"

"Penny, we must speak. As soon as possible."

"What is it?"

"Scarpio. He was poisoned."

I knew it, thought Penelope.

"And Nina Chiroubles . . . she has been released by the police. Apparently, they had no proof of anything when they came to arrest her. That ridiculous man, Reyssens!"

"Who are you talking to?" Justin butted in.

"No one . . . just a friend," said Penelope.

"What?" asked Clémence. "Reyssens had her arrested—you were there! She did not go away with a friend."

"I *know* she was arrested." Penelope turned and started towards the café to find a more private spot but Justin followed her.

"Arrested!" he persisted. "Who's been arrested?"

"Sorry, Clémence," said Penelope. "Justin, do you mind?"

He backed away a little but stood there earwigging with a worried expression.

"We should meet," said Penelope into the phone. "I, too, have some extremely interesting new information."

"I have viewings in Gordes this afternoon and I am having lunch there. Would you like to join us?"

Lunch would be tricky with the family in tow, but she wasn't going to let that stop her. "Tell me where and I'll be there," she said.

"What was *that* all about?" asked Justin.

"Nothing to concern you," she said firmly.

"What isn't?" asked Lena, not wanting to miss out. Penelope was saved by an outbreak of savagery from Zack and Rory in which blood was drawn by an antique carving fork that was lying on a nearby stall. In the ensuing fight and the separation of the combatants, Penelope resolved to put her own interests first.

"I have just been invited to lunch."

"By whom?" asked Justin.

"By my former estate agent, if you must know. Who, I am sure you will be glad to hear, is female."

Justin looked unconvinced.

"Look, why don't I take the hire car, and you can drive the Range Rover back to St Merlot?" Then she had an idea. "Even better, you could all go off to Les Baux, to the art and light show."

She sold it to them as an exciting indoor activity. The children would be thrilled by the spectacle and the adults would be entranced by the giant images of famous artworks projected to music onto the cathedral-like walls of the old bauxite mine. Crucially, it was far enough away that she would have at least four or five hours to herself.

19

EVERY SLENDER CYPRESS TREE IN Gordes was perfectly shaped. The houses were all splendidly repointed. Penelope drove the hire car past terraces of immaculate gardens.

There was no problem parking in the centre, close to the château. She was opening the door when, out of nowhere, the red Mini Cooper screeched up beside her.

"Who's the other person coming to lunch?" asked Penelope as they got out of their cars. "You said 'we' . . ."

"You don't miss much, do you?"

"It's not M. Valencourt, is it?"

"Alas no, he is very busy at the moment, in Paris. But we have the next best thing!" She smiled and waved to a figure standing outside the restaurant just beyond the square. Laurent raised his hand, looking dashing in a black leather coat.

The trio was seated immediately next to a window with a dramatic view of a renovated farmhouse on a hill spur with the Petit Luberon in the background. It was like a magnificent landscape painting.

Gastronomic interests were attended to first, after a long, silent perusal of the menu.

Laurent leant forward, a twinkle in his eyes. "As they say, a jug of wine, a loaf of bread . . ."

"And thou," supplied Penelope without really thinking. Then she became self-conscious and embarrassed at her unintentionally flirtatious tone, and tried to change the subject quickly, whilst ignoring the hint of a smile on Laurent's face. "Omar Khayyám, the Rubáiyát."

Clémence got in first. "So Laurent, what do you think of recent developments?"

"Developments in what sense?" he asked, managing to sound positively seductive.

Penelope told herself to get a grip. It had only been a week incarcerated with the family and she was acting like she was on day release.

"Scarpio—poisoned. Who could have done it?" said Clémence firmly. "Nina—arrested and allowed to go. Was she released due to lack of evidence?"

Speculation on the poisoning was put on hold to focus on a bottle of Vacqueyras that suddenly appeared and was opened. The mayor swirled a little of the powerful red wine around his glass and held it up to the light. "You can always tell how old this wine is by its colour. The older it gets, the deeper red it becomes."

Also true of middle-aged Englishwomen, thought Penelope, hoping that her face was not showing similar roseate tendencies. Laurent nodded at the waiter to pour.

"You know, I was there with her when she was arrested?" Penelope said to Laurent. "Reyssens was none too pleased with my presence."

He grinned at her.

Clémence was determined to announce her news. "I have heard a rumour about Nina Chiroubles. This is incredible, but did you realise that she and Don . . ."

"Were secretly married." Penelope completed the sentence with some satisfaction. "Don and Fenella divorced back in July. Nina told me."

The other two were clearly impressed, though she had well and truly stolen Clémence's thunder.

"Phuket," added Penelope.

"Sorry?"

"Phuket, Laurent. That was where they got married."

"So Don and Nina were married, but they were not living together," said Clémence. "Don was on his own at his studio in Ménerbes while she was living in her gypsy caravan in the commune. Why was that?"

Blank faces all round.

"Don was still waiting for the house in Goult to be sold," went on Clémence, "but between ourselves, Fenella Doncaster had not been helping the sale. She made no effort to make it attractive to potential buyers."

"It wasn't in her interest to do so," Penelope pointed out. "The longer it took to sell, the longer she had a nice place to live. And her studio was there, don't forget. And, logically, that could have given Fenella a motive to want Don dead. Now she doesn't have to sell the house, or buy him out."

"But surely Don's marriage to Nina means that Fenella will have to sell after all," said Clémence.

"In that case, did Fenella know that Don and Nina were married?" asked Laurent. "Perhaps Don did not want Fenella to find out, at least not immediately."

"I can understand not wanting to get on the wrong side of that woman," said Clémence. "So then Don and Nina must have seen each other quietly at Ménerbes."

"Yes," said Penelope. "After all, he wouldn't have gone down well at Nina's all-woman encampment, would he!"

The food arrived: *terrine de foie gras de canard au melon de pays* all round.

Penelope seized the initiative. She'd been itching to tell them what Jim Perkins had unearthed. "I've found out something very interesting about Don and Scarpio."

She waited until she had their full attention.

"We know that Scarpio's real name is Barry Finch, and that he has served time in prison. We also know that Don Doncaster was once a criminal barrister. So it made sense for me to find out if there was a link between them. Well . . . listen to this.

"In 1998, more than ten million pounds was stolen, and the driver of a security van and a guard were killed in a security warehouse robbery just outside London. Afterwards, the gang used a number of petty criminals to cover their tracks and get the money laundered as quickly as possible—one of them was Barry Finch."

Clémence waved away the breadbasket and leaned in. Laurent put down his knife and fork.

"As the police gradually closed in on the gang, Barry fled to Fuengirola in southern Spain and lived there under an assumed name until 2003. The authorities caught up with him. He was extradited and stood trial.

"During the trial in 2004, Barry Finch turned Queen's evidence, which means that he gave evidence in court against his former partners in order to receive a less severe punishment. The prosecuting counsel—the lawyer who presents the case against the accused in court—was Don Doncaster."

"What?" chorused the other two.

Penelope nodded. "All absolutely true. No room for doubt. It comes from an old friend who works at the Central Criminal Court in London. Don Doncaster asked the judge to restart the trial and persuaded Barry Finch to be questioned again. Thanks to Don, Scarpio's confession secured long-term prison sentences for the gang. Finch also went to jail, but was given a shorter stint. He was out by 2010."

"Incredible!" Clémence raised her glass in a salute.

Penelope grinned. "The next part is mostly supposition. After leaving jail, Finch knew his life was in danger in the UK, so he moved to Provence and adopted his Spanish persona. At some point he must have met Don again. Gilles gave him carpentry and framing work. The question is whether that was by accident, or did he contact Don and ask him for help? Maybe he felt Don owed him one. How else did they both end up as artists represented by the same gallery?"

"Did he have a reason to kill Don?" asked Laurent.

"Who knows?" shrugged Penelope.

There was a lot to chew on. They addressed their starters in silence.

"Apparently, the police are still convinced Nina is the killer," said Clémence after a few minutes.

"In that case, do they think Nina had anything to do with Scarpio being poisoned?" asked Penelope. The new information about Scarpio seemed to have cast everything in a new light, opening up all kinds of confusing new possibilities. "Benoît told us that no one ever went to Scarpio's house—we were the first in months. It was hardly fit for visitors, what with the restoration and that vile-smelling insecticide he was daubing all over the oak beams."

Laurent got there first. "Insecticide? I'll bet that's another substance that contains arsenic."

"You're right. So we need to find out exactly where the arsenic that killed Don came from and keep this in perspective," said Penelope. "But Nina worked at the museum," she added thoughtfully.

"We can ask Claudine if she would have had access to poisonous substances," said Laurent.

Penelope sat back and took a sip of wine. "It's amazing in

how many places you can find arsenic, once you start looking for it. Normal garden weedkiller being the obvious one, along with certain rat poisons. Then there's tanning fluid. Are there any local artisans who use that? Forensics must be able to tell what residuals are also present, which should point the way."

"The police will not release details of Don's postmortem," said Clémence. "Not even to a contact of mine who is extremely highly placed. I am not sure whether they wish to keep the details of the poison secret to help their enquiries, or whether there is something else."

Penelope absent-mindedly took another piece of bread. "Do you think our friend Nina could be a little more calculating than she is letting on? All this crazy art and the women's camp near Avignon. Not living with Don. Did she really think Don could change? Maybe it was all an act?"

"Men don't change," said Clémence emphatically. "Some women think that they will, with a change of circumstances. But it does not usually work out like that."

"What do you mean, an act?" asked Laurent, slightly awkwardly.

"I don't really know," said Penelope. "Nothing more than intuition, but it all seemed . . . a bit staged, somehow."

Clémence sighed. "Like Don's artistic life for the magazines."

"Perhaps she'd learned a trick or two from him," said Penelope. She was beginning to feel mellow thanks to one glass of wine, carefully sipped. An exquisitely presented main course appeared: *dos de cabillaud rôti à l'huile d'olive, ragoût de petit pois, févettes, coquillages et menthe poivré, beurre blanc émulsionné*. It looked and tasted every bit as good as its lyrical description on the menu.

They ate, respectfully avoiding the subject of murder for a

while. Penelope regaled them with a few choice tales of the family's visit, making them laugh and recoil in mock horror in equal measure.

Afterwards Laurent and Penelope tackled a delicious *verrine crème mascarpone aux pêches, fruits rouges et crème glacée au lait d'amande douce*, while Clémence had a lime-leaf tea.

Despite the macabre subject of their discussion, it had been a very pleasant interlude.

20

THE FAMILY'S TRIP TO THE art and light show at Les Baux had been only a qualified success.

All had gone well until Zack had spotted the potential for an incredible game of hide-and-seek in the projected images of the Gauguin and Van Gogh paintings that swirled through the cavernous darkness. They had lost him for more than an hour. In the end, terrified he had wandered off into the darkest reaches of the old mine, Justin had alerted the management, and the lights had been switched on. There had nearly been a riot by furious spectators and strict French parents who could not understand how these idiotic foreigners could have allowed their child to misbehave and run off.

They had been asked to leave, and all of Justin's impassioned Franglais would not shift the management's line.

Penelope felt almost guilty about the enjoyable afternoon she had spent in Gordes. She had made a lemon drizzle cake by way of reparation. It had cooled enough to cut, and Hannah had taken a pot of tea into the sitting room when there was a thunderous knocking on the front door.

It was Georges Reyssens, accompanied by a young uniformed policeman.

Oh, God, thought Penelope, only now realising that she might not have been insured to drive the hire car. Who knew what trumped-up charges Reyssens would delight in bringing?

Reyssens pulled himself up to his full five foot five, and strode into the hall, puffing out his barrel chest.

"Mme Keet, I would like to speak to you."

He strutted into the kitchen.

"Tea? Cake?" offered Penelope, trying to make it sound as if she had been expecting him all along. The brittle tone in her voice gave her away.

Justin stood up and assessed the incomers. Lena looked terrified, and Hannah pulled Rory to her.

Reyssens flicked his hand to dismiss any suggestion that this was a social call.

"I think you had better leave us to it," said Penelope to Justin.

"I'm not so sure about that," he said. "Is this to do with the phone call about the person who was arrested?"

Penelope couldn't decide whether he was crosser with her or with these mysterious visitors. "Justin, please."

With a loaded glare, he withdrew into the sitting room, from where, Penelope knew full well, he would be able to hear every word. Reyssens refused her offer of a seat. He took a photograph from the inside pocket of his jacket and handed it over. "Have you ever seen this woman?" he asked.

Penelope took her time. "I think so," she said at last.

"Do you know who she is?"

"Her name is Anya. She works as an assistant to Fenella Doncaster."

"Are you sure about that?"

"Let me have another look."

The chief of police fidgeted, shifting his weight from foot to foot.

Penelope suppressed a private smile. He was so very easy to wind up. "I believe this is a photograph of Anya," she said after spinning it out as long as she dared. There were so many questions Penelope wanted to ask but knew she had to proceed with caution, probably for her own sake as much as Anya's. "Has something happened to her?"

Now it was Reyssens's turn to play the game. He took a wander over to the dresser where she had left an untidy mix of books, including *Managing the Menopause* and *Vitamin Therapy for the Over-Fifties*, and gave a dismissive snort.

Penelope waited, anxiety rising.

"Anya is fine."

"Thank goodness for that."

"Do you know her well?"

"Not at all. I have only met her once."

"Yet you were worried about her."

"I would worry about anyone, if the police seemed to be bringing bad news."

He paused, looking her squarely in the eye. "Where did you meet her?"

"At Fenella Doncaster's house."

"When?"

"About two weeks ago."

"How many times have you been to Fenella Doncaster's house?"

"Only once."

Reyssens sniffed, wrinkling his nose unpleasantly. "Does she also work for Nina Chiroubles?"

"I have no idea."

"Why would Don Doncaster's phone be full of messages and calls to and from her?"

"From whom?"

"From Anya," snarled Reyssens.

"You'll have to ask her. I only met her once."

"But you spoke for long enough to recognise her from this photograph."

Penelope allowed that.

"Did she say anything about her relationship with Don?"

"A little, yes."

"Mme Keet, would you care to expand on that?" His voice was dripping with false civility. "I would be extremely grateful if you would favour me with the benefit of your superior knowledge."

She decided it was best not to rise to it. "Anya admitted she and Don had had a . . . romantic relationship for a few months. I got the impression that she genuinely cared for him, but accepted that he was a man who moved on quickly to the next liaison."

"And?"

"That was all."

"Why has Anya been going to Nina Chiroubles's studio?"

"Again, I have no idea." Penelope wondered what this had to do with her. "Why are you asking me this?"

Reyssens came nearer. "Where does she come from?"

"I don't know. Eastern Europe, I think. She mentioned Prague."

He stood in front of her, too close, in a manner that might have been construed as threatening.

Then he nodded to his young officer and dismissed her. "*C'est tout.*"

❦

PENELOPE RETURNED from showing them out to find another interrogation party standing around the kitchen table.

Justin pounced first. "What the hell was all that about?"

"How does he know you, and what did he mean by you knowing more about a case than anyone?" asked Lena, rubbing her hands over her belly. Both she and Hannah looked appalled.

For once, the three little boys were the most acquiescent people in the house. Perhaps because, as she later discovered, they were dismantling Penelope's log pile next to the burner and trying to build a camp on the cream sofa.

"Georges Reyssens was the local chief of police when I had the . . . difficulties when I first moved in." Penelope sat down. "May I have my cup of tea now, please?"

"He was quite passive-aggressive," said Justin.

"He wasn't best pleased," admitted Penelope. Privately she was quite pleased at the amount of new information she had gleaned from his questions.

Justin's mouth was set in a line. "He was bloody rude to you."

"He doesn't like me much," said Penelope. Even though she had helped him solve two murders in her first weeks in St Merlot. She corrected herself. He seemed to hate her *because* she had found the solution to the mystery before he had.

"But *why?*" persisted Justin.

"Because I was right, last time, and he wasn't," she said bluntly.

"The business with the forensics." Lena had obviously paid attention to her stepmother's account of past events. "They should think themselves lucky that someone of your experience is here! Can you help this time?"

Penelope smiled gratefully. "I won't know till I try."

Justin shook his head. "Please, Mum, don't get involved." He seemed genuinely concerned. But then he spoiled it. "You're poking your nose into things that don't concern you. Please don't make a fool of yourself."

That really took the biscuit. She was going to solve the mystery of the Luberon poisoner if it was the last thing she did.

21

WITHOUT AN AUDIENCE PENELOPE SANG along to a George Michael retrospective on Radio Nostalgie as she drove the backcountry route to Nice. Perfect, she thought.

Joining in lustily with the chorus of *Wake me up before you go go*, she seemed to float down the mountain road to the valley. Nice lay to the southeast. On such a bright morning, the scenic option rather than the motorway was definitely the way to go.

The children and grandchildren had been safety dispatched back to England, the behaviour of the little boys markedly improved. Lena looked much less exhausted, and Justin and Hannah were considerably more relaxed. A heart-to-heart had taken place after dinner on their last night. Justin had apologised for his rudeness, confessing it was only out of concern for her.

"I know," Penelope had said, putting her hand over his. "But this is my time now. For the first time in decades I'm free to live my own life, without responsibilities. I'm sure I will make mistakes along the way, but I have to try."

The valley narrowed and the undulating folds of the mountains were heavily forested, as she turned towards the Southern Alps and the town of Digne-les-Bains. From there, she would follow the famous Route Napoléon, the road used by the ex-emperor on his short comeback tour of France that had ended at Waterloo. Penelope enjoyed the winding road to a swooping saxophone accompaniment and George's tuneful confession that he should have known better than to cheat a friend. He had moved into his more mature rehab phase by the time Penelope drew into Digne.

She pulled up in front of the cathedral. It was such bliss to be able to park so easily. A short stroll away, she found a promising small café with the usual blackboard outside. Inside, she was shown to a small round table by the window and ordered a Perrier.

Someone had left the local edition of *La Provence* on the next table. Penelope idly picked it up and started leafing through the pages. Most of the news in this agricultural area concerned food production and obscure crop pests and vegetable diseases. Truffles, flavour of the month, were well represented, with PR pieces about new restaurant recipes and outrage caused by fake truffles imported from China. A spate of thefts from rural churches. It transpired that wood panelling, some of it medieval, was in great demand; Penelope was reminded of her conversation with M. Bérenger at Viens. An anonymous churchgoer alleged that the panelling was being stolen to order for some rich Parisian restoring a second home. Parisians and the Marseillais were blamed for most of the misfortunes that befell Provence.

One very reasonable set menu later, of which the high point was the chocolate mousse (how *did* they make it so light yet so deliciously gooey?), Penelope downed her espresso and wandered slowly back towards the cathedral, looking up to its tall, rough-stone bell and clock tower. There was a magnificent rose window above the west entrance, where the grey and white horizontal stripes reminded her of the cathedral in Siena. She went inside briefly, and marvelled at the elegance of its vaulting and the pretty striped stonework of its mighty pillars with flower motifs.

The silence and contemplative mood turned her thoughts inward. Was she crazy for haring off to see Gilles like this? And did it really matter if she was? Having the family around had reminded her how happy she was on her own with a decent book and a glass of wine. Gilles's interest was flattering, but was it too good to be true? Alarms bells rang when she thought back to their lunch in Saignon and his suggestion that she quietly investigate Don's death. Could it be that he wanted to keep tabs on how much she knew, and what she was hearing from Laurent and Clémence? She was going to have to keep her wits about her.

оӾ╸

THE ROUTE Napoléon wound over the mountains of the Alpes Maritimes towards Grasse. Upon cresting a precipitous hill, Penelope found herself looking down on the coast and the deep blue sea beyond, the hazy red Esterel Mountains on one side and the conurbations of the Côte d'Azur on the other.

Penelope knew the area well. She had been coming here for most of her adult life, and every time she visited, the hills leading to the sea had grown a few more villas. She thought back to the villa her great-uncle had owned in Le Pré du Lac. The only other Englishmen there at the time were Dirk Bogarde and his partner. The three of them would run into each other at the local boulangerie and talk about cricket. In those days, between the towns, there were acres of pristine Mediterranean forest. Now the whole area was one sprawling Weybridge. As she coasted down the hill towards Grasse she could not help feeling a little bit smug about how unspoilt her selected corner of *la Provence authentique* was compared to all this.

The traffic was growing busier, louder, and more frenetic as she edged her way gingerly onto the dual carriageway and past Grasse and its perfume factories. She crawled towards the coast in a line of hooting traffic. Even though it was autumn, the temperature on the Riviera was still nudging a very pleasant sixty degrees.

It was past four o'clock when she finally passed the Nice airport and drove along the Promenade des Anglais. According to her map, Gilles's gallery was a few streets back from the Vieux Port. Penelope rounded the headland into the old port area of the city, where the wide boulevards and imperial architecture gave way to more traditional narrow, winding streets and Italianate houses in pastel variations of orange, pink, and yellow. The harbour stood between two hills, bristling with yacht masts. She parked and wandered happily along the quay, past restaurants and posters advertising trips along the coast. From there, she made her way through a square, where petals and leaves on the ground attested to a flower market held that morning. Finally, she turned into a cobbled lane and stood before the imposing façade of the Galerie Gilles de Bourdan. In the window hung a large canvas by Nicolas Versanne.

When she entered, Gilles himself was deep in conversation with a well-dressed man at the desk. Penelope caught enough of the conversation to assume he was a serious buyer. On every wall hung paintings that Penelope could genuinely enjoy: impressionistic landscapes and sensational still lifes and abstracts that might have been from the 1920s or '30s. Plenty of red stickers signified good sales.

"*Bonjour, madame.*"

The young man she'd seen at the Avignon gallery—the one who'd run to Don with the defibrillator—had exchanged the tweed suit for a vintage-look black flannel one, equally dapper. He had a broad, smooth face and brown hair cut in a retro style. "Alexis," he said, extending a hand. "Gilles's assistant. Let me show you around while he's tied up."

To the rear of the room a couple of instantly recognisable Doncasters were confined to a dark corner. A still life of a black cube, signed Scarpio, was actually not that bad. There was some justice in the world, she thought, as she spotted more of Nicolas's work, two of which boasted red stickers.

"Ah, Penny—sorry about that! How lovely to see you here!" Gilles swooped on her, bestowing the three kisses enthusiastically.

"Thank you for inviting me. Another fabulous gallery!"

He raised his hands modestly, as well he might, standing in front of a particularly nauseating Doncaster depicting a bug-eyed child in a beret holding a baguette.

Gilles followed her gaze. "I do wish someone would hurry up and buy that one. It gives me a headache every time I see it."

Penelope giggled. "If you can't sell it, no one can."

"Some artists improve with age, and some . . ."

"Just age? So death hasn't escalated the price of his work yet?"

"I can state with some certainty there is unlikely to be a retrospective at the Louvre."

"So why *did* you keep him on?"

Gilles smiled. "I will always support my artists, Penny. Now, come upstairs—I will give you a cup of tea! Alexis, will you make it, please? Use the English teapot."

❧

ON THE first floor, he showed her into an exquisite office. An antique desk and chairs stood at an oblique angle to the tall windows. A sofa and easy chairs were grouped around a coffee table. On the dark blue and smoky-grey walls, stunning paintings seemed to glow. A display cabinet contained delicate painted fans, silver items, a scorpion brooch, and a set of curious and macabre glass balls labelled "Nightingales' tongues" and "Ostrich brains" in faded ink. Over the mantelpiece was a frieze of a bull being sacrificed. In an alcove, statues of Roman gods offered stony reassurance.

"Venus, the goddess of love," explained Gilles, as he saw one of the idols pique her interest. "And Mercury, there on the right, the god who helps you get to places and succeed in business. Now, take a comfortable seat."

The tea was properly steeped and surprisingly good. Gilles took his with lemon, but Alexis brought in milk for her.

"This is the best tea I've had outside my own home since I arrived here," said Penelope. "Lovely."

"I am delighted to hear it."

They chatted easily, about everything from how long he had had this gallery (twenty-two years), its recent renovation (in which Scarpio had apparently shown a mastery of the art of carpentry which rather outshone his artistic skills), to the difference in clientele between the Riviera and inland Provence. Nice was where the seriously rich international buyers came, expecting top-quality works. They were all, dealers and clients alike, ever hopeful of finding an undiscovered Cézanne or Matisse, or failing that, of making a market in a second-tier artist with the right associations to the great names.

"The best deals are done here, in this room," said Gilles. "Mostly on work that has not been announced on the walls of the gallery. At a certain level, the market only works in secrecy."

"I'm intrigued."

"It's a question of security, mostly. For each side. We are talking extremely valuable art."

Penelope looked around. The comfortable, elegant room in no way resembled a fortress.

"I live here, too. On the upper floors. It takes twenty minutes to set all the alarms at night!" said Gilles as if reading her mind.

"You must have some reinforced doors, too."

"Plenty. And I have installed a new strong-room."

"But a good problem to have," said Penelope. "I mean, it's because you've done so well."

Gilles nodded, and allowed an engaging smile to light his eyes. He was passionate about his business, she thought. That was always attractive.

"Come!" He stood. "This I can show you."

Penelope followed him across the landing into a small back room. The shutters were firmly closed. When he flicked a switch, the only lights were above the paintings on the wall. Saints, angels, and the Virgin Mary and Child stared back at her from all sides of the room, their golden halos gleaming. The atmosphere was dim and religious, like that of an old church.

"That's so beautiful!" cried Penelope.

As her eyes adjusted to the darkness, she saw that more icons were stacked on the floor against the skirting board. "There are dozens of them!"

"Those are yet to be repaired or restored. The work has to be done by experts if the icons are to fetch the correct prices. I am a specialist in antique Russian icons, which is not unrelated to the numbers of very rich Russians who spend time—and plenty of money—here."

"Very clever. Where do you get them from?"

"Usually from old barns outside Moscow!" laughed Gilles. "You would be amazed what the old peasants spirited away during the Soviet days. I have contacts there, and I go over at least three times a year to negotiate for genuine antique pieces. Then I restore them. It began as a hobby, but it has become more and more lucrative."

"When you say you restore them, you mean you employ professional restorers?"

"Not in the beginning. I am actually a trained artist, though I never managed to make a living from it. I employ others now, but I very much enjoyed doing the work myself—still do, when I get the chance."

"Is it ever difficult to get art out of Russia?" said Penelope.

"It can be. But there are ways."

Penelope suspected there was probably a bit more to it than that.

"Now," said Gilles, "I will let you go to your hotel and check in. Shall I join you for an aperitif on the terrace at seven?"

Penelope walked back to the quayside car park. The sun was moving behind the hills and it had started to get a little colder. She found the signs for Monaco and the Grand Corniche and headed into the hills. On her right the dark blue Mediterranean shimmered as she wound upwards to the little speck that was Èze.

22

PERCHED PERILOUSLY ON A ROCKY outcrop overlooking Cap Ferrat, Èze was a perfect example of an ancient fortified village. Atop sheer cliffs, fifteen hundred feet up, stone houses leaned over the void.

Penelope had visited several times during her marriage, and knew exactly what to do. She parked at the foot of the hill, opposite the Fragonard perfume shop, then stepped up to greet the uniformed porter and handed him the keys to the Range Rover. Leaving her luggage in the car, she began the walk up through the twisty cobbled streets to the summit. The route to the hotel was like a long and winding staircase.

The Château Eza was an assortment of restored stone houses rather than a single edifice. Penelope checked in and was shown up a flight of outside stairs.

"You are in luck, madame," said a handsome young man in black. "It is low season, so we can upgrade you to the royal suite."

He opened the door to reveal opulent marble flooring and a truly huge bed upon which the crowned heads of Europe would be happy to repose. A huge stand-alone bath squatted in an alcove. Another bath in the bathroom had a control panel worthy of Mission Control at NASA to operate the Jacuzzi function. All in all, it was worth every penny she was going to blow.

The separate shower room looked over the sea and along the

coast back to Nice. The sun was beginning to set behind the hills. Down on Cap Ferrat, lights were coming on. Out to sea, cruise ships lit up along their length moved slowly to their next destination, like skyscrapers laid on their sides. Glimmers of silver on the sea indicated yachts and fishing boats setting out for the night. It was just as beautiful as she remembered it.

Since she had moved to France, Penelope had tried hard to look forward, not back. But here it was hard not to think of the past.

It had been a two-week driving holiday when she was still in her twenties. The children had been left with his parents. David had just taken possession of a new Golf convertible. Its square body and folded hood made it look like a large silver-grey pram. It had taken them south through France, roof down, cassette recorder (was it really that long ago?) on full, blaring out eighties' anthems. They had been two lobsters with terrible sunburn, but it didn't seem to matter. Staying at hotels picked from an upmarket guidebook, they had sampled haute cuisine for dinner and comfortable beds: a long way from the camping holidays of her youth. And the Château Eza was their destination: two days of luxury at mind-blowing cost to celebrate David's bonus. She remembered arriving hot, bothered, and windswept to be greeted by the gateman who needed some convincing that they really were guests. And then walking onto the balcony for dinner, totally speechless at the panorama that opened up before them. Their table was above a vertical drop to the sea. Then the luxurious room, the softest of pillows, the intimacy, the untroubled sleep.

So much had changed since then, she thought, but she still smiled at the happy memory. Since the divorce, they actually got on rather well, certainly better than the final years of their time together. David had moved in with a younger woman from the

City for a year or so, but as Penelope had expected, the novelty wore off and she acted as his agony aunt through the split.

She had stayed single, and the truth was she quite enjoyed being alone. But life in Provence had definitely opened up possibilities.

⚜

AT SEVEN o'clock, wearing her favourite blackberry silk dress, she walked down the stone steps and into the hotel. It was a dangerous descent in heels. At one point she had to make a lunge for the railing, hoping no one had spotted her staggering and drawn the wrong conclusions.

There were no longer tables on the terrace, but she braved the chill in the air in order to take in the glorious views of the Côte d'Azur once again, from pretty Beaulieu-sur-Mer to the smudges of the Esterel hills in the misty distance. She shook herself out of her reverie and went inside to the bar.

Gilles was waiting for her.

"Good evening, Penny, you are looking radiant! Cocktails? Or champagne?"

"Either would be lovely."

He ordered a bottle of Cristal.

"Are you celebrating?"

"Tonight, Penny, I shall enjoy the best food, the best champagne, and the best conversation with a wonderful woman. Who would not be celebrating?"

Penelope smiled broadly. She was going to enjoy this.

"I'm not a man to go for half measures."

Penelope thought they might get on very well indeed. Though her own ulterior motives and his undeniable attractiveness could well make it an unsettling experience.

❧

THE MEAL was as good as promised. Sitting at a large window, staring down at the black Mediterranean with only the lights defining the coastline, Penelope savoured every exquisite mouthful of scallops and sea bream as Gilles told her about his childhood not far away in Menton.

Sipping a glass of superlative Meursault, Penelope began telling Gilles about her return to music, and the bizarre circumstances of her first few months in Provence.

"You are a very brave woman, Penny. And to solve the crime . . . what a mind you have!"

He was laying it on a bit thick, thought Penelope, but who cared? The wine and food were working their magic. Time to prod a little more.

"And it seems I am doomed to repeat the cycle once more. Unfortunately, I had a visit from Georges Reyssens the other day. He was asking questions about Fenella Doncaster's assistant Anya—do you know her?"

"I do."

"Reyssens wanted to know if she also worked for Nina Chiroubles."

"What did you say?"

"That I had no idea."

Gilles frowned. "There's no reason why she shouldn't know Nina, I suppose."

"I'm sure she did. You know that Don and Nina were actually married?"

"I . . . no, I did not. I thought they were avoiding each other after a falling-out."

"I think they were trying to keep it a secret."

"Poor Don. From Fenella to Nina."

"It does seem he liked feisty women," said Penelope. "A good thing, too," she added, doing her bit for the sisterhood.

"When did this marriage take place?"

"A few months back, I believe."

Gilles hesitated. He looked out of the large window to the cruising yachts in the sea far below. "I knew Don well. I saw the way his health suddenly declined this summer. The redness in his face. The slowness in his reactions. He was unsteady. He had bursts of rage that was not the old Don. He complained of chest pains, shortness of breath. I saw the desperation as he tried to attack life with his old vigour. Now you tell me he was actually married at this time to Nina."

Penelope thought of the Don she had met at the gallery, the offputting way he had seemed to be trying too hard. "That's a big leap of logic," she said evenly. "The police released her without charge," Penelope pointed out. "Why would she murder Don?"

"Nina has always needed money. Now she is his beneficiary."

"Only if the marriage on the beach in Phuket is legal," said Penelope. "Remember Mick Jagger and Jerry Hall, and the wedding in Bali."

"Eh?" said Gilles. Clearly he didn't have the advantage of her shameful addiction to the *Daily Mail*'s gossipy insights.

"It wasn't binding. Jerry didn't have an automatic spousal claim on the money when they divorced—or rather, split up."

Gilles looked glum.

"You really did like Don, didn't you?" said Penelope.

"It's true, I did. Forget the bad pictures, he was good company. The more time you spent with him, the more you liked him."

"Someone else told me that, too."

Silence.

"At least Scarpio's recovering well," said Penelope. Clémence had called her with the news just before she left St Merlot. "It seems it was a reaction to the insecticide he was sloshing on all the beams at the mill, with no protection over his nose and mouth."

"Yes, he gave us all a scare. But he's out of hospital. I'm going to give him an advance on some more renovation I need him to do for me at Avignon."

"That's very good of you. Mind you, that won't get his mill done any quicker, will it?"

Gilles shook his head. "But it's the right thing to do and he can earn some money. He's a one-track artist and I fear his market in black is at saturation point right now." He twisted his wine-glass on the table. "You haven't found out any more about Don's death, then?"

"Not really, no." She hesitated. "It's not the same as last time, when I was personally involved and everything was happening on my doorstep. I couldn't help but get caught up in the investigation. But this . . ."

They fell silent for a moment as a delicate lemon mousse and parfait confection with white chocolate shards was placed in front of them. Penelope found she didn't really want to talk about matters related to murder in this fabulous setting with a handsome man across the candlelit table. Especially when she wasn't sure that any of what she'd found out was going anywhere.

Over coffee, she asked him about his career and he expanded on his life-changing discovery at twenty that art could be studied and taken as seriously as history or mathematics. He had taken a fine-art course in Paris and then completed a masters at Aix-en-Provence. Penelope countered with her love of music and the years of her youth that she had devoted to playing. They were beginning to find much in common.

Penelope had unconsciously leant in as she spoke about the

moment she drew the bow across the strings of her cello for the first time in many years. She felt their knees brush momentarily, and realised she liked it. Maybe, she thought, maybe.

But not yet.

The conversation paused naturally.

"Gilles, I have had the most lovely evening. Thank you so much."

"Penny, the pleasure has been all mine. You make the perfect companion . . ."

They got up and she kissed his cheek.

Gilles smiled. "Ah, the English! Always so polite. One day, Penny, you will find that the French way is much more fun." He gazed into her eyes, with that melting way he had. For a moment she thought he might kiss her on the lips, but after a delightfully anticipatory pause, he gave her shoulder an affectionate squeeze and drew away. "I hope that we can repeat this in the Luberon."

"That would be lovely."

"Let's do that."

※

PENELOPE HAD a long, luxurious lie-in the next morning, with breakfast in bed.

Propped up with the heaped pillows behind her head, she could see blue skies and the darker blue of the sea. This was certainly the life.

The day passed lazily with a spot of clothes shopping back in Nice, carefully avoiding the street where Gilles's gallery was—it wouldn't do to seem too keen. Sauntering along the shore on the Promenade des Anglais, it was impossible not to replay the evening with him. Could there be any more to it than two new friends having dinner?

Did she even believe in love anymore—romantic love? Was she so much older and wiser now that it could be dismissed as a rush of blood and hormones? No, she told herself firmly, she had to believe it was possible. The alternative didn't bear considering.

She skipped lunch, then went into the Hotel Negresco for a cup of tea and a delicious pâtisserie. It was heavenly not having to please anyone but herself. Nor to think about murder.

Back at the Château Eza, she sized up the instructions and managed to set the Jacuzzi bubbling. She was just about to get in when the roiling water gave her an idea. She went over to the minibar, extracted the half bottle of champagne, and popped the cork.

She raised her glass to the happy woman in the mirror.

⚜

THE NEXT day Penelope returned to St Merlot on the motorway. It was a quicker if less attractive route, and involved negotiating the tangled tentacles of Aix-en-Provence. But it was worth it for the view of Mont Sainte-Victoire ahead of her.

Back at Le Chant d'Eau she breathed a long sigh of relief at the absence of visitors.

In contrast to the coastal dazzle, the landscape was rendered in a muted palette of greys, misty blues, and golden brown. The leaves on the trees were shades of worn leather and the ground offered milky sable and chestnut tones. In the low-angled sunlight, roofs wet with dew or melted frost glistened silver.

The quiet was all-encompassing. Penelope had never known such rich, ripe silence; the countryside seemed to be turning in on itself and preparing for winter. Scents of the soil and wet stone had replaced the summer fragrances of thyme and rosemary and lavender. As she paused on the doorstep, she saw a deer on the track, and watched without moving, hardly breathing.

The grandchildren had left various trails of destruction in surprise locations round the house, but it was blissfully quiet as she sat gazing at the logs blazing mesmerically in the woodburner.

The next event would be the music group's concert at Roussillon. Rehearsals were scheduled at Viens over the next week, with a final one at the venue on the day of the performance. She was excited at the prospect, and a little nervous about playing in front of an audience after all these years. The piece by Robert Schumann was familiar and not overly difficult, but nevertheless required empathy and depth to carry it off. She adored Schumann and wanted to do him, as well as herself, justice.

All her friends had said they would be there. She so wanted to impress them, especially Laurent and Clémence. Well, to be honest, especially Laurent. It occurred to her that she might invite Gilles, too.

That afternoon and evening, she practised and practised, oblivious to the time, until the notes seemed to flow newly composed into the air.

23

ALL TOO SOON, IT WAS the day of the concert.

Since her return from Nice, Penelope had done little else but attend rehearsals and practise. She had also managed to stick to a six-day crash diet, by dint of seeing no one but M. Charpet. Clémence had rung; there was no news of any kind but Nicolas and Claudine had kindly suggested she use their house close to the museum to rest and change before the performance instead of driving back to St Merlot, and Penelope had gratefully accepted.

The task of choosing a black dress from the number she possessed proved a morning's work, with an array of clothes, tights, and various other accoutrements piled up on the bed where they had been tried and discarded in exasperation. How could it be so difficult, she raged at herself, to choose something black? After a few hours, the wardrobe was denuded and her bed resembled a funeral pyre.

In the end, she chose one she had bought in Nice with Gilles in mind, though he had sent regrets that he wouldn't be able to come due to a prior engagement. The dress was clingy enough to show off her curves and stretchy enough to play in. Women cellists always had to balance elegance with practicality.

❧

IN EARLY afternoon, she set off with butterflies in her stomach and her cello in the boot. The run-through in the village hall went well, and Penelope felt relaxed as she drew up at the substantial house opposite the ochre museum.

Claudine opened the door. "*Bonjour,* Penny."

Her greeting was a little brusque, and her face was blotchy.

"Are you all right?" asked Penelope.

Claudine stiffened. "Yes, of course. Coffee? Something stronger?"

"Best stick to coffee, thanks."

They went into a spacious kitchen with shiny red units and a splendid American fridge. Penelope couldn't imagine that the self-controlled Versannes would ever fill it.

"The police haven't been round again, have they?"

"Why do you ask?"

"Because I had a visit from the odious Reyssens the other week, and it was not pleasant."

"I'm sorry to hear that," said Claudine.

Penelope waited but Claudine did not ask what Reyssens had wanted. She was obviously preoccupied. Wary of pushing her for an explanation, Penelope said brightly, "I went to Gilles's gallery in Nice. Several of Nicolas's paintings had sold stickers."

"That's good."

"*Very* good, I'd say."

Again, Claudine showed no curiosity about what Penelope had been doing in Nice. She handed Penelope a small cup of black coffee from an espresso machine.

"Thank you. I thought his paintings there were even better than the ones in the Avignon exhibition."

"He works hard."

"Is he in his studio now?"

"I suppose so. I made him promise to be back in time to change for the concert though." Claudine visibly gathered herself. "Let me show you to a guest room. You can have a rest before you have to change."

In the generous spare room with en suite bathroom, Penelope lay on the bed with her eyes closed for a while, then took a bracing shower. She was pulling on her black dress when she thought she heard Nicolas return. Voices were raised and, indistinctly, she heard what sounded like a heated argument. He was shouting; Claudine screamed back. This went on for ten minutes or so, then a door slammed.

Penelope sat in front of a dressing table mirror and did her makeup carefully, diplomatically taking her time. Perhaps this was one of their rows about money. She gave it a good half hour before going downstairs.

"Oh, Penny, you look wonderful," cooed Claudine. "That dress suits you very well."

"Thank you—and for letting me change here. I really appreciate it. I think I should get myself to the hall now—shall I see you and Nicolas there?"

Claudine's face changed. "I am so sorry, Penny. I am not sure he will be joining us."

"Oh?" Penelope kept it light.

"He will try to get there for the second half," Claudine assured her.

She offered no explanation.

❦

PENELOPE DROVE the short distance from the house and parked in the village square. Evening had crept up on them, and the old lamps provided minimal illumination in the misty half-light. She was glad she had left her cello on the stage and was not lugging it up the street.

Inside the hall, though, the atmosphere was cosy. Two elderly ladies sat at a small table counting out piles of change. Another was placing programmes on all the wooden seats. The musicians were setting up.

Monique waved. Her short brown hair shone in the low light, and her eyes sparkled. "Are you ready, Penny? This will be a good one, I feel it."

"I hope so!"

She was setting up her music stand when she heard a familiar clickety-clack on the stone floor. Clémence teetered up, elegant as ever, on improbably high heels.

"*Bonsoir*, Penny. Are you ready for your entrée into the musical world of the Luberon?"

Penelope cleared her throat and nodded. "A bit nervous, but excited."

"I am sure you will play marvellously."

"Thank you. I hope so."

Clémence smiled. "So . . . it went well with Gilles, then?"

"I had a lovely time in Nice."

"And . . . ?"

Penelope was about to elaborate when she spotted Laurent behind Clémence. He bounded up, looking distractingly dashing in a dark blue suit and tieless white shirt. Her knees gave a minor tremble.

"Good luck, Penny. I am looking forward to this very much. I have heard that your touch is quite exquisite."

Penelope felt the warmth of a huge blush suffusing her face. She opted for rapid retreat. "Must go, last-minute checks . . . er . . . tuning . . . that sort of thing. Bye!" She turned smartly and rushed off to the haven of the music stand behind which to compose herself. She really did want to impress him, which made her all the more nervous.

The seats began to fill. She noticed with a thrill that M. Charpet, his sister Valentine, Pierre Louchard, and Mariette had dutifully arrived from St Merlot, along with the baker and his wife, and several of the pétanque team. A sudden rush of love for her new village threatened to overwhelm her.

Claudine came in alone and took a seat close to the back, keeping another free by her side. What was going on with Nicolas? No doubt she could find out later from Clémence, but for now she had to put these thoughts out of her mind. She tuned up with the rest of the group, and they awaited the conductor's entrance.

To gentle applause, Sylvain strode onto the rostrum, resplendent in a dinner jacket that was several sizes too large for him but which gave him room to swoop around extravagantly with his baton. He tapped it against his stand and the audience quieted. Penelope prepared to throw herself into the strange mindset of concentration and freedom that musical performance requires.

The first piece was a Mozart chamber piece that she knew fairly well. She always loved and hated Mozart in equal measure; the gorgeous music was tempered by the potential for disaster. Every mistake in this type of ensemble was instantly audible. But all went well, and she could see the appreciative smiles from the audience.

At the end there was enthusiastic applause, with a muscular contribution from the St Merlot pétanque players who, from their ruddy demeanour, looked to have prepared for this night of culture in the local bar.

In the interval, Penelope slipped out of a side door into the street. It was a beautiful clear, cold night, stars studding the black sky. Golden light spilled from the hall, and she could hear the muffled sounds of the audience chatting as they made their way over to the makeshift bar for a glass of wine. She breathed deeply, rolled her shoulders, and prayed the next piece would go as well.

After a few moments of quiet, she went back inside and shyly made her way to her group of friends. M. Charpet rushed up and planted three enormous kisses on her cheeks.

"Madame," his voice quivered in suppressed emotion. "Madame, your playing of the Mozart was very beautiful. It is one of my favourite pieces, yet I felt tonight that I had heard it for the first time."

Penelope marvelled once again at the man's hidden depths. As others gathered round to congratulate her, she suddenly found herself staring into Laurent's startlingly dark blue eyes. They had a strange, almost wistful look.

"Penny, my dear. You are a constant surprise. What will you do next? You have enchanted me."

She did her best not to show the intense pleasure this gave her. "Thank you. I just hope the next half goes as well when it's my turn in the spotlight."

Ever since Penelope had heard a recording of Jacqueline du Pré playing Schumann's Cello Concerto, she had been determined to master it. It was one of those works, she considered, that revealed the very soul of the instrument. The lyrical and romantic heights that it explored never failed to move her, and though she had performed it before on a number of occasions, she had never wanted to impress an audience more.

"I am sure you will delight us," said Laurent. With that he dissolved into the crowd, surrounded by people eager to talk to him. She was left slightly breathless and wondering when, or indeed whether, the promised dinner à deux would ever take place.

All too soon, they were all back in their seats. In the hushed silence of the church, Penelope heard the first soft chords drift up to the roof, and drew her bow. The plaintive melody sung out from her instrument. She felt the strange detachment that was part of performing; at the same time, the music filled her, washed over her, her fingers acting almost unconsciously to translate the black notes on the page to such a ravishing sound.

Her concentration was such that she scarcely noticed time passing. The music built to a climax and then a resolution. Joy and relief surged through her, so much so that at first she was unaware of the sound erupting from the audience. As she settled back into herself, she looked up to see the audience standing as one. Overcome, she stood and bowed. Sylvain jumped off his rostrum and clasped her warmly in an embrace. She returned the hug, and bowed. He led her off, and on again, to cheers.

The applause finally subsided.

"Mme Keet," Sylvain announced. "I think we have all witnessed something special this evening. I congratulate you and I hope fervently that you will continue to play with us."

It felt like a missing piece of her life, so long repressed, had finally fallen back into place.

"I cannot tell you how much I have enjoyed this," replied Penelope, feeling herself smiling uncontrollably. "I am honoured that you asked me to play with you, and I would love to continue doing so."

He kissed her hand theatrically and left her to the queue of people behind him all wishing to offer their congratulations. First in the line was Clémence.

"Penny, that was marvellous! I knew you were good, but that, that was . . . unbelievable. Congratulations!"

"Thank you, Clémence, I really appreciate that. And for introducing me to the music group in the first place. I hope Laurent enjoyed it, too."

"Oh, I am sorry, Penny, did he not tell you?"

"Tell me what?"

"He had to leave at the interval. Some urgent business to attend to."

Her elation drained abruptly. Under her breath she muttered "Bugger," and tried to disguise it with a fit of coughing. Clémence looked on embarrassed.

The feeling of let-down was temporary. It had gone so well, who cared if he didn't see her moment of glory? Well, I care, she thought in reply to herself. But not enough to let it ruin the evening. Her smile returned, and with it the warm glow of satisfaction. She let herself be shepherded around by her diminutive French friend, being introduced to the great and the good of the Luberon and accepting their praise. She even managed to grab a glass of rosé as she passed the bar. Never had it tasted better.

It was only when Claudine reminded her that it was the opening ceremony for the waterwheel the next day that Penelope realised Nicolas had not made the concert at all.

24

BY THE TIME PENELOPE ARRIVED back in Roussillon for the waterwheel ceremony, she was still buzzing from her triumph the previous night.

The mood at the museum was strained, though. Claudine was extremely jittery, even more so than the previous afternoon. It was quite unnerving; Penelope had always thought of her as someone completely in control. Clémence and Laurent were already there offering their support. Penelope wanted to ask Laurent why he'd missed the second half of the concert, but didn't get the chance. No sooner had he greeted her than he took off with Claudine to deal with a last-minute staff issue.

"What's happened, Clémence?" asked Penelope when they were alone.

"It's Nicolas. He didn't go home last night."

Penelope was taken aback. "No message from him? You've checked all the phones?"

"No, and yes."

"No sign of him at all? Did he go to his studio last night?"

"Nothing. I have checked his studio. It's close to the house, in the garden. Everything was locked up as normal."

"I think they had an argument before the concert," said Penelope.

"Why do you say that?"

"I heard them. I was upstairs getting changed. There was a lot of shouting."

Clémence sniffed and said nothing.

"Claudine didn't say anything about that to you?"

"Not much, no."

Understandably, Clémence was loath to discuss her friend's marital spat. "Did anything come out of Reyssens speaking to her again?" asked Penelope.

"I don't think so."

Conversation was awkward. Penelope tried several other gambits, but nothing seemed appropriate.

When Claudine reappeared, though her hair and makeup were immaculate as ever, she looked even more pinched. "Where *is* he?" she asked Clémence, apparently oblivious to Penelope's presence. She sounded on the verge of tears.

"Try not to panic. I'm sure there's a rational explanation," said Clémence. She looked up as Laurent joined them.

"Maybe he has a surprise for you, for this special day," he said.

That sounded pretty feeble to Penelope, but it was the best anyone could offer.

"The cameras haven't arrived, have they?" asked Claudine.

Clémence shook her head, "Not yet."

"They won't be long. I have so much to do before then!"

Penelope decided practicality was all. "What can I do to help?"

The museum director seemed to draw on her inner resources to gather herself. "That is very kind. If you are sure, you could tidy up the front of the museum by sweeping away the leaves. The groundsman has picked this week to be off sick, and I can't spare anyone else. I want the TV people to get a good shot of the entrance. First impressions are so important. There's a broom over there."

Clémence received instructions to get some coffee, and the two of them disappeared inside, deep in conversation. Laurent walked over to the car park and made a call on his mobile.

Broom in hand, Penelope set to work, trying not to fret too much about getting her new black trousers dirty. It made no sense. Why on earth would Nicolas choose last night, of all nights, to disappear—knowing that today was a big day for Claudine?

She had only just got the forecourt looking neat when a large van fitted with an impressive satellite dish pulled into the car park. The TV crew had arrived. Penelope hastily ran inside and knocked on the door to Claudine's office. When no response came, she opened it slowly, then stashed the broom there for want of anywhere else.

"Claudine!" she called.

Outside, a team of four with tripods and cameras was already assessing certain spots and camera angles for potential interviews.

Claudine came running from the direction of the café. Her face was a mask, and Penelope sensed that abject panic was close to the surface.

"Have you heard something?" asked Penelope, dreading the answer.

"No."

"The TV crew is here. You'd better go and greet them."

Claudine nodded, looking numb.

Unsure whether it was acceptable, as a new friend, to reach out, Penelope awkwardly patted the museum director's shoulder. "Try not to worry. I'm sure he'll be back soon—and then when the filming is over, you can be really cross with him."

Claudine made an effort to smile. "If he returns now I will kill him with my bare hands! I have not been able to do half the things I meant to this morning. And with the groundsman off . . . I just hope everything works like it did yesterday."

Penelope watched through the window as the Frenchwoman straightened her back, paused for just a moment, and went out to the crew. A short conversation ensued with a man dressed in an anorak and jeans and a girl holding a clipboard. Penelope walked past the open door and went to find Clémence.

The estate agent was alone, on her mobile by the coffee machine in the café. She finished the call and looked up.

"Does Nicolas often do this?" asked Penelope. With some effort, she refrained from saying anything more judgemental.

Clémence shrugged. "He has his moments."

Penelope wasn't sure what to say.

"Unless he gets back in the next half hour or so, he's going to miss the TV cameras," Clémence continued. "He's supposed to be doing a live interview."

Claudine reappeared, followed by the man in jeans who seemed to be in charge and a man carrying a camera.

"Still no word?" asked Clémence.

"No. We will have to do the filming without him. *Salaud!*"—

It was decided that the interview would be filmed in the shop where the colour swatches hung alongside the paint samples. Claudine obviously still had her commercial wits about her.

Clémence and Penelope sat helplessly in the café.

"Would it help if *you* called Nicolas's phone?" suggested Penelope.

"I already have. It went straight to voice mail."

"You said earlier that Nicolas 'had his moments'—what did you mean by that?"

Clémence hesitated.

"It's OK, you don't have to tell me. I shouldn't have asked." Penelope understood. Clémence's loyalties were to her friend.

"No, it's just—"

A thin, bearded young man in a black leather jacket knocked on the door and entered.

"I wanted to check—has M. Versanne returned yet?"

"I am afraid that M. Versanne has been unavoidably delayed," said Clémence smoothly.

"All right, thanks. We are going outside now to set up to film the watercourse. It would still be nice to have a few words with him, though, so if he makes it back, would you tell him to go straight out there, please?"

"Of course," said Clémence.

"What's Laurent doing?" asked Penelope.

"Coming this way."

The mayor brought a cup of coffee to their table and joined them.

"Anything?" Clemence asked.

"I've tried everyone. No one has heard from him."

Penelope shifted in her seat. "I heard them arguing before the concert," she blurted out, trying to flag it up again.

There was a charged pause before Laurent spoke. "So what?"

"What were they arguing about?" said Penelope. "Could it have been something serious? Could it have been connected to the visits from the police and all the rumours about the arsenic in the paint? Were either of them really under suspicion?"

The expression on her friends' faces told her she had gone too far. She should never have given voice to her speculation.

Laurent stood up. "I'm going outside to see what's happening."

"Me, too," said Clémence.

Penelope trailed after them, feeling dreadful. Her mouth had run away with her.

Behind the museum the restored waterwheel gleamed like a great unblinking eye. Frost still crusted the path under the shady pine trees. Penelope shivered. She hoped the demonstration would be over before both she and the water froze.

They walked uphill beside the watercourse, which would be

filled when water was released from above to set the wheel in motion.

A group of schoolchildren aged about ten and two teachers were gathered outside a small ochre-plastered pump house. One of the teachers was explaining how the great iron lever worked. It stood ready for the big moment, guarded by the museum's technical director, a burly man with a balding head and a compensatingly luxuriant moustache and beard.

As Penelope waited with Laurent and Clémence, they could see more people arriving from the direction of the car park to witness the spectacle and potentially appear on the local news.

The TV crew was ready. The producer called for quiet and the small crowd hushed. They began recording, and a blandly handsome male reporter asked Claudine a few questions that she answered with bravado and duly explained how the contraption worked. Finally, she gave the nod to her technical director, who grasped the lever in both hands and gave it a yank. There was a loud shriek of twisting metal against metal, and further up the valley, a thump from where a sluice was being opened.

"It usually takes about a minute before the water reaches the wheel," said Claudine to the interviewer, and pointed up at the sluice. "You can see it is open now."

They all stared expectantly. It was an awfully long minute.

God, it's cold, thought Penelope, why is it taking so long?

The crowd shuffled and the children started whispering to one another.

An edge of desperation crept into Claudine's fixed smile as the seconds ticked by. "Any time now!" she repeated.

But there was still no movement. The technical director moved off, presumably to investigate. There was obviously some blockage in the watercourse.

"Please stay here. I will be back in a moment," said Claudine, evidently deciding to follow him.

Clémence nodded to Laurent, and they both slipped away while the teachers tried to quiet the children and everyone tried to chat to the TV crew. Penelope strode off in pursuit.

They followed the path up beside the dry watercourse lined with a concrete half pipe, and caught up with Claudine. No one said anything.

The technical director had stopped up ahead. Penelope could see that water was spilling over the course and soaking the pine needles, turning the exposed russet soil brown. Clearly there was an obstruction of some kind.

Claudine went forward and looked down into the half pipe. Then she seemed to freeze. Her hand went to her mouth. She said nothing.

Clémence looked at Laurent, then at Penelope. Something was very wrong.

The camera crew arrived in a hurry, bumping and stumbling with their equipment. They were just in time to see Claudine slide limply to the ground.

Laurent and Clémence ran over to Claudine. Penelope hung back, not wanting to crowd the poor woman. But from her vantage point she could see what was causing the blockage in the watercourse above the wheel.

The black suit was crumpled, the hair matted. A lifeless body lay wedged like a cork in a bottle, face white. It was the artist formerly known as Barry Finch.

25

THE MUSEUM FORECOURT FILLED AGAIN with police cars and a van for the scene of crime forensic investigators. With a scoop on their hands, the TV crew hung around, filming, asking questions, and generally getting in the way.

Penelope watched helplessly as Claudine, aided by Clémence and Laurent, tried to deal with the fallout. The police had cordoned off the area and were demanding immediate interviews. Except for the schoolchildren, who were ushered away protesting furiously, the spectators who had gathered for the ceremony were determined to stick around for the drama. They stood in clumps, twittering in shock and excitement. The only mercy was that Georges Reyssens was nowhere in sight as yet. Nor had Nicolas returned.

A tent was rigged up over Scarpio's body. A lawyer arrived, smouldered for the TV camera, and was sequestered in Claudine's office with her and Clémence for ten minutes before the police were permitted another round of questions with the museum director.

"How is she bearing up?" asked Penelope when Clémence emerged, looking shattered.

The estate agent shivered as she lit a cigarette, then gazed into the distance and exhaled. "She is doing what she has to do. She's in shock. She doesn't know whether to be furious with Nicolas or worried to death. He had been in a strange mood for days, apparently. She says he was sitting in his studio, looking at his canvases, but not doing anything. Just staring at them for hours. He would not speak to her. He would not tell her what was wrong."

"An artistic crisis?" asked Penelope. "It does happen. People get a block and they can't think of anything else for weeks and months."

"It's not *im*possible. But she did not think so."

"It couldn't have been because the police had been to see him, could it?"

Clémence frowned. "But you can't think . . . they can't think . . . that he had anything to do with the poisonings, surely."

"I'm not thinking anything. Simply observing."

Clémence took a long drag.

Penelope closed her eyes, visualising Scarpio's matted hair—had that been ochre or dried blood in it? The ghastly blueish pallor of the dead man's face. The partial death mask of red earth. Was his death an accident, or was he another poison victim who had succumbed after an illusory recovery?

Or was this completely unrelated—a terrible coincidence? Penelope's gut feeling was that that was unlikely. These events were related. They had to be.

"I wish we knew some more about the poison, and what exactly the forensic analysis has shown," Penelope mused aloud.

"Penny, please! A little thoughtfulness," snapped Clémence.

"A couple of officers have gone into the display room, just like before. Why would they do that? What else do you think they are looking for?"

"I did not see that."

"And they haven't said anything more about who could have taken the arsenic paint?"

Clémence pulled a face.

Penelope took that as a "no." "You don't think Nicolas could possibly—?"

"Penny! Stop this!"

Chastened, Penelope backed away. "I am going to have a mooch around."

"What is this mooch?"

"You know . . . a casual wander, a look around without looking as if I'm looking around."

Clémence gave her a loaded look. Not only for her gaffe in questioning the cause of Nicolas's nonappearance but apparently because, in addition, she thought it unlikely that a largeish Englishwoman in flappy trousers and a reasonably priced Marks and Spencer suede jacket would pass unnoticed, even at a time of crisis.

❧

FROM A discreet distance, Penelope watched the scene of crime officers and forensic team carry out their grim tasks, going in and out of the tent covering the water chase where Scarpio lay. She presumed that the police would want to take statements from everyone who had been at the museum that morning, and that would be the reason she would give for not leaving, but even so, she took care to avoid encountering any of the officials.

A nasty thought occurred to her as she wandered towards the outhouses at the rear of the old factory. The police might want to speak to her about overhearing Nicolas and Claudine arguing. No doubt Reyssens was going to be thrilled about that.

The outbuildings running at a right angle behind the museum were mostly open to the elements. The front walls had been removed—if there ever had been any—to accommodate supersized display cases of the old life of the ochre factory. They contained steam-powered machinery and massive kilns built of red stone bricks. There were huge wooden dyeing barrels and stunning displays of patterned terra-cotta tiles.

At the far end were two brick sheds. Penelope peered through the single window of each, but could see very little inside. The door of the shed farthest from the museum was on its blind side. She pushed, then pulled it, and it opened. Leaving the door open wide to let the light in, she stepped in.

Unsurprisingly for an unlocked building, there was nothing of value inside, only rusty pieces of machinery. There were more barrels and more tiles stacked on shelves. Crates of old tools and wooden paddles stained orange-brown were fluffy with cobwebs.

She could barely get any further in for the heaps of hardware. She turned to leave, curiosity satisfied. As she did so, the sun came out, sharply delineating the wall to her right. She went over to have a closer look. Behind the skeleton of some metal apparatus was a stack of polished wooden panels. Unlike everything else, these were not dusty or covered in cobwebs.

"What are you doing in here?"

She jumped, and spun around.

Laurent's face was unreadable.

"Oh!" gasped Penelope. "You scared me."

"You haven't answered my question."

"I . . . nothing." Penelope decided to be honest. "I was being nosy."

"Why?"

"Because I didn't want to get in the way. I assumed I shouldn't leave until the police told me I could, and I didn't want to hang around too obviously when everyone is so upset and trying to process what's just happened."

A pause.

"Where did you disappear to last night after the concert interval?" Penelope blurted out before she could stop herself.

Laurent stared at her in disbelief.

"Sorry, I didn't mean . . . I shouldn't have—"

Laurent looked at her wearily. All he said was, "Come back inside."

❧

IT WAS several long hours before Penelope was called to give her statement to a police officer and then allowed to leave. Too much coffee in the café while she waited on her own had her nerves jangling, as she fretted about whether she would be able to account for every minute she had spent here, and whether the others would remember when she had been with them. Could anyone vouch for the twenty minutes she spent sweeping up leaves at the entrance, for instance?

She walked out to the car park without having seen Claudine or, indeed, Clémence again. Laurent had disappeared. On the drive home, she felt a sudden exhaustion. Everything felt unreal: as if she was going through the motions without being fully present. As if the wonderful concert and the trip to Nice had all been a dream.

26

IN THE DAYS THAT FOLLOWED, Penelope naturally assumed that she would receive news from Clémence and Laurent. Or that she might hear from Gilles, come to that. But her phone did not ring, and there were no unscheduled arrivals. On the third day, she called Clémence at the Agence Hublot.

"Nicolas is still missing. Claudine is going crazy with worry. The police have finally started to search for him," said Clémence. "Sorry, I can't talk now."

But the estate agent did not call back the next day, or the next.

Penelope read reports of Scarpio's murder in *La Provence*. He had been killed by a blow to the head, though he had also sustained a nonfatal gunshot wound to his left leg. A wrench used in the pump house by the watercourse had been found with traces of the victim's blood. The gun was missing. The police had released no other details. There was nothing at all about Nicolas.

Winter hardened its grip. A chill wind blew, in all senses. The hills turned to brown velvet and grey clouds huddled on their slopes.

Feeling deflated, Penelope took to hunting halfheartedly for more furniture at the *brocante* warehouses, where secondhand chests of drawers, wardrobes, and bookshelves could be bought for a song, sanded down, and repainted in shabby-chic style. She practised some cello pieces, and went along to a meeting of the

string group to discuss the previous week's concert and possible
future events. She roamed her garden, planning its landscaping
and planting. A builder came to assess the work needed on the
outbuildings. But nothing filled the void.

After three more days of radio silence, she rang Clémence
again. "Any news?"

"Nicolas is still missing."

"Should we meet to put our heads together?"

"I regret it is a little inconvenient at the moment."

Penelope put the phone down feeling worse than ever. Had
she been completely insensitive to this close-knit band of friends
at the museum that morning? She had a horrible feeling that she
might have been.

Yet she still felt it was a question that had to be asked, if only
to discount it. Could Nicolas possibly have killed Don? *Was* it
unthinkable? What if he had disposed of Don because his success was a threat, or an artistic injustice? It seemed far-fetched.
And why kill Scarpio? Unless the small-time crook had found
out what he had done . . .

Penelope did not seriously think Nicolas had anything to do
with the deaths. At the museum, she had been thinking as an
ex-professional, not a friend. She thought that Clémence would
know that—she always seemed extremely perceptive about everything that was going on. But maybe not in this case.

Actually, she mused, Clémence had dodged the question. Was
it too far-fetched to imagine that the mayor and his on-again,
off-again mistress knew more than they were letting on? They
were all so loyal to one another.

When had the watercourse last been checked before the pump
was turned on? Surely Claudine and her team would have made
sure there were no obstructions before the ceremony? It defied
belief that no one checked it that morning. But the groundsman

had been off sick. Maybe, in the confusion, everyone had thought someone else had taken responsibility.

She paced up and down her kitchen. She put in a call to Fenella Doncaster, under the guise of asking about art classes, but it went through to voice mail. She didn't leave a message.

≈

PENELOPE NEEDED something tangible to get her teeth into. Something other than one of France's finest croissants or *pains au chocolat*.

She sat quietly at her kitchen table, trying to free her thoughts to make new connections. They might mean nothing, of course, but that hardly mattered. Penelope had always enjoyed researching arcane details even if they didn't bear fruit in the end. That had been her favourite part of working with Camrose for the Home Office. On the occasions when she had hit upon some vital yet overlooked aspect of a case, she felt as if she had won a great prize along with the warmth of Camrose's genuine admiration. Over time, he had come to trust her judgement, and her instinct.

He always had a calming quotation from Wordsworth's *Lyrical Ballads* at hand. She could hear him now. " 'Emotion recollected in tranquility,' that's what old Bill W said about poetry, and it's how I think of an autopsy after a violent crime. We proceed calmly and sensitively in order to read the emotions that inflicted the wounds. What does your intuition tell you, Penny?"

She closed her eyes and concentrated, allowing pictures and snatches of conversation to come to her. Tentative links formed and then broke up. She had to let her thoughts run free.

The clean wood panels in the outbuilding at the museum.

The run on the old wood from the chapel outside Viens.

The article she read in Digne about the thefts of medieval wood.

The panels in Scarpio's studio. What if he hadn't been daubing them in black but stripping off the polish and patina of years? As a carpenter, he might have been.

Were there any connections, or was she grasping at straws?

If only she could find some links to crack the cases, or even to point the police in the right direction, she might be able to make amends with her French friends, but this really was a wild-goose chase.

❧

PENELOPE BOUNCED the Range Rover down the track towards the main road with no destination in mind, only a change of scenery. She just avoided a nose-to-nose bump with a silver Clio outside Mariette Avore's house when the other car swerved sharply and pulled up. Penelope muttered under her breath but the driver waved in friendly fashion and got out of the car.

It was Monique from the string ensemble. "*Bonjour,* Penny!"

"Ah . . . *bonjour*! You haven't come to see me, have you?"

"No, my friend Mariette."

"I didn't know you knew—" began Penelope, then stopped herself. There were lots of connections throughout the local villages she could have no idea about.

"Hi!" Mariette emerged from the house and walked towards them. She kissed Monique three times, then greeted Penelope the same way after beckoning her out of the car.

"Are you rushing off somewhere? Why don't you join us for a little coffee?" asked Mariette. "I know you already know each other."

"Well . . . actually, that would be lovely, thank you." Penelope quickly parked on the verge and followed them inside.

The kitchen-snug room was bright and tidy. A smell of fresh paint hung in the air.

"You've done well," said Monique, looking around approvingly. "All your own work?"

"It is." Mariette filled the coffee percolator with water.

The wooden cupboards were pale sage green, and the walls were white. It was a lovely, restful room. Mariette must be a formidable cook, judging from the collection of copper pans and utensils on show.

"I'd wanted to brighten the place up for so long, but I never really had the motivation to do it while . . . you know, when my husband was still alive. And now I want to get it in good order to sell or rent out, I haven't decided which."

Penelope and Monique nodded. Mariette smiled, remaining coy about whether she had already moved into the farm along the track. She looked even younger and happier than when Penelope had last seen her.

Monique settled into a chair at the round pine table by the window. "How are the wedding preparations going?"

"Great! We've finally decided where to hold the wine reception after the ceremony at the mairie. The old Priory! A blessing in the chapel, followed by drinks. What do you think about that?"

"Not too cold in December?" asked Monique, again echoing Penelope's thoughts. "There can't be much in the way of heating there."

"Pierre's thought of that. He's rigging up a generator and electric heaters. Then we'll have lots of winter decorations so we'll feel the benefit but won't see too much of them. It will be fine for an hour or so of champagne and canapés."

"It sounds very romantic," said Penelope.

"It will be. I can't wait!"

Over coffee, they chatted about this and that: Monique's daughter, who was getting married the following spring to a nice man she had met at work as a local government administrator; the rearguard actions local producers, especially the lavender growers, were taking against interference from Brussels; the inexplicable dip in quality of the dried tomatoes on a certain market stall; the next pieces the music group might tackle.

It was all very pleasant. The sun shone on the table, and Penelope felt at ease. Her French was rapidly improving, helped by the excellence of her memory. Once she heard a phrase, she could file it away and reuse it at will.

"How did the lessons with Sylvain go?" Monique asked Mariette.

"Not bad. He's very patient, isn't he?"

"Mariette's taking up singing again," Monique told Penelope. "She has a beautiful voice but she hadn't used it for years."

"That's wonderful!" Penelope beamed. "Rather like me and my cello. When I wasn't very happy, I put it away and didn't even look at it."

"The only thing is, please don't mention it to Pierre," said Mariette, looking serious.

"Oh?"

"I want it to be a surprise. He used to come to hear me sing when we were young."

Penelope remembered that Mariette and Pierre Louchard were once teenage lovers, before their families intervened to stop the romance.

Mariette nodded. "I'm going to sing at the wedding reception. Monique is going to accompany me." She hesitated. "I don't suppose you would like to join us, would you?"

"Mariette, I would be honoured, truly."

"That's settled, then."

"We may have to rehearse at my house at Gargas, though," said Monique. "Obviously, it can't be here, just in case Pierre comes by. And I've just signed up for extra hours at work in December, so I won't have much spare time."

"What do you do?" Penelope suddenly realised she had never asked.

"I'm a nurse."

"A very good one," said Mariette. "She works in Critical Care, so working hours can be round the clock."

"Which hospital?" asked Penelope.

"The one in Avignon."

"That sounds like very hard work—but very worthwhile." It was a very long shot, but nevertheless, Penelope had to ask. "You weren't on duty, by any chance, when Don Doncaster was admitted?"

"The British artist?"

Penelope nodded.

"I wasn't on duty when he came in. But I did see him the following day. Had to turn quite a few visitors away, too."

"Really? Who were they?"

"One woman was very persistent. She said she was his wife, but we had already allowed his wife in."

"What did she look like?" asked Penelope.

"Rather bohemian, you know the type."

"What colour was her hair? Turquoise or shocking pink?"

Monique looked at her rather oddly.

"Penny is quite the detective," said Mariette.

"Impossible to say," said Monique. "She was wearing a scarf wound around her head and tied over one ear. Arty kind of clothes."

"Did she come back the next day?" asked Penelope.

"That, I can't say."

"Did the patient have any other visitors you can recall?"

"A couple of men, one of them very tall. Don't ask me what they looked like. We were battling to keep the patient stable and that was what I was concentrating on. Did you know the deceased?"

"I was at the gallery in Avignon when he collapsed."

"The whole thing was a strange episode," said Monique. "Alas," she looked at her watch. "I must be off. Mariette, it has been lovely as always, thank you."

Penelope left at the same time. She limited her drive out to a quick trip to Intermarché and headed back.

⚜

PENELOPE LOOKED long and hard at the phone that had been so quiet, then picked it up.

If only for a few moments, as she listened to the familiar British double ringtone, Penelope was back in the book-lined study in Manchester Square. The ringing continued.

No answer.

Penelope decided not to leave a message and called his mobile instead. He answered it almost immediately, as if he was still working. "Camrose Fletcher."

After a minimum of social niceties, she came straight to the point.

"How would you like a trip to France?"

"Penny, my dear, I am so sorry."

"What—what is it?" Penelope was immediately anxious. She could tell from the tone of his voice that something was off.

"I've broken my ankle. Idiotic decision to press on up Scafell Pike after a rain shower. Should have known better, but we all think we're invincible, don't we."

"Oh, no! Are you all right, where are you, how did it happen?"

"I'm fine. A stupid slip. I'm in hospital in Ambleside."

"Poor you! Is it very painful?"

"Not too bad. I am so sorry, Penny. I would have loved to come over to see you. What a shame. I really am immensely cross with myself."

Penelope swallowed her disappointment. "There will be other times, don't worry about that. The most important thing is that you're all right—and hopefully no lasting damage."

"I think I'll make a full recovery. It was a fairly simple break. The worst was having to call out the mountain rescue team. Embarrassing, really, as I know several of them from the pub quiz team at the Lamb and Fell, and I should have known better than to go skittering up wet rocks. Trouble is, I still think I'm forty."

Penelope could see him now, tall and broad and limber, in the jeans and chunky sweaters he wore in the Lake District.

"So tell me, Penelope. What do you need my advice about?"

He only ever called her Penelope as a tease. She could visualise the crinkling of the laughter lines around those bright blue eyes.

"Recovery from arsenic poisoning," she said, getting to the point as if they were still working together. "You remember I told you about Don Doncaster who seemed to be making a good recovery, but suddenly suffered a relapse and died?"

"Yes."

"Does recovery from poison often involve a relapse?"

"Rarely, I would say."

"But if it did, and the relapse resulted in death?"

"My first reaction would be to look at another cause of death, perhaps related to the first poisoning. Has another dose been administered?"

"Unlikely," said Penelope. "The victim was recovering in hospital."

"Do you recall the sad case of the wealthy old lady killed by her sons while she was ill in bed?"

"I do. That was exactly what I've started thinking about."

"Killed by air that induced an embolism," said Camrose.

"Just when it seemed she was getting better. Apart from air, what else would leave no chemical trace?"

"A pillow over the face, though suffocation would be evident."

"Anything else?"

"Water. Injected into the patient's veins, for example, could induce death yet leave no trace apart from a needle mark. I don't suppose you have the autopsy report?"

"Not exactly, and the police are hardly likely to let me see it either. The police chief in charge is what you might call an old adversary."

"How long have you been in France, Penny?"

"I know! It doesn't seem possible to have a Moriarty already, but there we are. He was not best pleased to see me sail into view, I can tell you."

They both laughed.

On a more serious note, she found herself telling him all about Scarpio/Barry and the ghastly discovery of his body, Nicolas's disappearance, and the lack of information since. With no concrete information to go on but her suspicions, all Camrose could offer was sympathetic advice.

"I agree that Nicolas is a suspect, but you should be sensitive about whom you mention that to, Penny."

"I know. I think I may have overdone it a bit."

There was a short pause. "You know I'm always at the end of the phone. Even more so over the next six weeks. Keep me in the loop, won't you?"

"I wish you were here," sighed Penelope. "But here's wishing you a speedy recovery."

She was disappointed, she realised. Not only that Camrose wouldn't be flying in for the weekend, but the acknowledgement that she was feeling lonely. Perhaps life in Provence for a single woman of a certain age was not going to prove as delightfully easy as the first few months had promised.

Oh, pull yourself together, woman, she told herself sternly.

She put the kettle on. The sun was setting with wisps of pink cloud. The oaks and beeches were losing their leaves. They stood out in stark black outline against the milky air. Below, the valley was silent.

She sat sipping her tea and trying to make sense of the latest death. With Nicolas still missing, every day that went by without news was more worrying. Did he have enemies? It seemed unlikely. Some professional enmity maybe, but little that could be serious enough to be a motive for murder. On the other hand, was it at all possible he could be the killer?

Penelope picked up her phone again.

"Frankie? How do you fancy a trip out here? You can even have your own bathroom."

27

ONE OF FRANKIE'S MOST ENDEARING attributes was her impulsiveness. Two days later, Penelope was on her way to collect her.

The leaves in the vineyards on either side of the road glowed like copper under the grey sky. What would her oldest friend make of the other changes since her last visit at the end of the summer?

At the Marseille airport, Penelope treated herself to a croissant in the coffee shop. She would need to keep up her blood sugar level with Frankie around.

She was ruminating on the reasons for her lamentable lack of sustained self-control when the arrivals board changed to show that the plane from London had landed. There was no hurry to finish off her coffee, though. Frankie never travelled light and there would be a substantial suitcase to wait for.

When the sliding doors began to disgorge an unmistakably British cargo, drab in their anoraks and raincoats with crumpled bags from Boots and WHSmith, Penelope walked towards Arrivals.

An abrupt movement caught her attention. Next second it was gone. Then a tall, dark man of distinguished bearing appeared from behind a pillar. At first she didn't recognise him in the long dark coat with astrakhan collar.

"Hello, Gilles," she said, feeling faintly embarrassed. Gilles had been conspicuously absent since their dinner at Èze had ended on what she had read as a romantic note. Had he been trying to avoid her just now, then thought better of it? They hadn't spoken since she called to invite him to the concert.

But his smile reached his eyes as he strode up to her.

"Penny, what a pleasant surprise!"

"And you!"

"Where are you going?"

"Nowhere. I'm waiting for a friend from England. She should be coming through at any moment."

"Ah, yes," said Gilles gravely, as he surveyed a chubby young couple in sports leisurewear. "The British have arrived."

They stood in slightly awkward silence for a few moments.

"Are you?" asked Penelope, "Going somewhere, I mean?"

"Russia. A business trip."

"When does your plane leave?" asked Penelope, feeling as soon as she said it that she was making it worse. How awful if he thought she was keen on him, when he had obviously lost what little interest he may have ever had. She glanced involuntarily at the departures board.

"Not for hours. I have a shameful phobia of being late, especially for planes. The flight to St Petersburg isn't even open yet."

"I was terribly sorry to hear about Scarpio," she said, suddenly realising that he was probably still trying to recover from the death of another of his artists, and feeling ashamed of herself. No wonder he hadn't called her.

"Dreadful business."

"Any news of Nicolas? Are the police still searching for him?"

Gilles shook his head, looking drained. "No news at all. No one has seen him since that night."

"How is Claudine?"

"Not too good."

Penelope was about to ask him how he was bearing up when she was knocked sideways.

"THERE YOU ARE, PEN, DARLING! And who's this you're making a move on, eh?"

Frankie was wearing an orange coat that managed the unlikely fashion feat of combining both glitter and fur. Her embrace was like being smothered in a sequinned avalanche. Penelope dug herself out.

"Frankie, this is Gilles de Bourdan, a friend of mine. Gilles . . . Frankie."

The man extended a gloved hand to Frankie.

"Madame, I am delighted to meet you." He gave a little bow.

Frankie took his hand and shook it vigorously. Her moon face shone. She was a big woman, both in height and girth, and took no steps to downplay it. "Any friend of Penny is a friend of mine. Love your coat!"

There was a small pause as Gilles smiled, slightly bemused, taking in the false eyelashes, the enthusiastic use of scarlet lipstick, and the sheer breadth and presence of Penelope's larger-than-life friend. It was abundantly clear she had not received the memo for the over-fifties from Inès de la Fressange.

"I wish you a happy time here," he said to Frankie, and then to Penelope, "I can see that you are in a hurry to get back to your home. Please, do not let me delay you. I have a few matters to attend to before my flight. Madame . . . ?"

"Call me Frankie, you know you want to!"

"Madame . . . Frankie, a pleasure to meet you, briefly. I am sure we will have a chance to get acquainted when I return. Good day to you both!"

He gave a second little bow and faded into the crowd.

"Well, that wasn't awkward at all," muttered Penelope.

Frankie goggled. "Ding dong! Penny, what else have you got to tell me, eh? Is he a little something you've been hiding from your best friend?"

"Oh, please. Absolutely not, Frankie! Honestly, what are you like!"

"Protesting too much, Pen?"

"Shut up, Frankie."

"Dresses well, too. Does he loosen up when you get to know him? Quite a smooth talker, and those lovely hands. I'd definitely have high hopes of a decent bod there!"

"Frankie!"

There was a pause. Frankie rearranged a flowing orange and pink scarf, and laughed.

"Don't suppose there's a chance of a drink? A glass of something cold and bubbly would hit the spot."

"We'll have a drink when we get home."

❧

HAVING HER old friend with her in St Merlot was a kind of happy madness. Penelope had readied herself with a two-day detox but she knew it was nowhere near long enough for the onslaught. Frankie was always a thirsty visitor, and her enthusiasm was hard to resist.

Her housegift to Penelope was a pair of high-powered self-focusing binoculars. From the terrace at Le Chant d'Eau, the view down the Luberon Valley was now sharpened into farmsteads and fields of wintering lavender and orchards, and villages sprinkled over the hills. In the distance, Roussillon was a striking red cliff adjacent to a smaller hill on which sat the village. Behind it was Gordes, grey and majestic.

"These are perfect, Frank. Thank you!"

"Cheers, Pen." Frankie hoisted her second glass of champagne.

In the end, Penelope had accidentally on purpose not passed any enticing café-bars on the way home, assuring her pal that a special bottle of pink fizz was chilling in the fridge for her arrival.

"By the way," said Frankie, "what *are* you wearing?"

That was usually Clémence's line. Penelope wondered if the only effect of being in France was to have made whatever she wore vaguely ridiculous to both sides of the cultural divide.

"It isn't one of those dresses you've been buying from the markets, is it?" said Frankie, giving Penelope's blue-grey knit dress a very critical appraisal. "It's very flouncy."

"Well . . ."

"Oh, Pen!"

"What's wrong with it? I quite like the bo-bo look."

"Bo-bo?"

"Bourgeois-bohème. Slightly playing at being bohemian, self-consciously artistic. Though not starving, obviously. No tiny frozen hands *pour nous*."

Frankie stared, and shook her head. "More like a slightly scary, superannuated Bo-Peep. Sorry, Pen."

"Around these parts, women of all ages can get away with wearing lacy layers and looped-up shirts and harem pants," she added, when Frankie's expression didn't change.

Her friend opted for a swerve of subject. "How's that gorgeous hunk of local mayoral-ness?"

"I wouldn't know. What's it got to do with him?"

"Don't be coy now."

"Really. Haven't seen him much."

"But you were getting on so well. I don't understand. What aren't you telling me?"

Silence.

"Pen?"

"Frankie, just leave it! I do not want to talk about Laurent. I'm just not interested."

"But who knew?"

"Who knew what?"

"See, I knew you were interested."

"Oh, please!" Penelope sighed. "All *right*. If you must know, I think he's upset with me because I may have seemed to suggest that his good friends Claudine and Nicolas could—theoretically— have had something to do with the poisonings. And now Nicolas is missing . . . so, yes, it was a pretty insensitive thing to say, but I was only thinking aloud. I didn't mean it. But—"

"Crikey, Pen—what did you expect?"

"I know, I know."

"I imagine that Clémence isn't that interested in putting your case to him either."

"Nope. She's been awfully quiet, too."

"Fat, fifty, and friendless, then," deadpanned Frankie.

"Charming," said Penelope, wincing inwardly.

"He might be jealous of your outings with that Gilles chap, have you thought of that?"

"Highly unlikely, I would have thought."

THE TEASING and bickering continued in this vein through- out lunch and into the afternoon. The woodburning stove was lit, scenting the house with a subtle aroma of green, spicy fig. Frankie was a brilliant sounding board, on all sorts of matters, fiercely clever and perceptive. She found Scarpio's untimely death fascinating, his real-life identity as Barry Finch hilarious, and suggested that her husband, Johnny, might have ways and means of finding out more about him.

She insisted on seeing the repairs and renovations that had been carried out since her last visit, then on checking the plans for the next phase of the project, the outhouses, one of which was earmarked for Penelope's music studio.

"Right, Penny," she said, bottle poised in one hand and an exceptionally full glass of rosé in the other. "As I see it, there's good news and bad news."

"Let's do the good news, then have another drink, then do the bad news," replied Penelope, all too aware that her good intentions were already being corrupted. Frankie upended the bottle of rosé. Penelope couldn't work out how the contents had disappeared so quickly.

"Right," said Frankie. "The good news is that all the house stuff looks good. No corners cut in those bathrooms, good-quality stone, and nice neat plumbing. I'll take a proper look around the outhouses and find out the state of play there. Make sure nothing gets missed."

"I knew I could rely on you. What's the bad news?"

"That chap, Gilles. I'll eat my hat if he's not hiding something."

"And I am not as green as I'm cabbage-looking!" said Penelope. "I did work that out."

They sat quietly for a few moments.

"Laurent will come round, you'll see."

"I keep thinking that if only I can find a way to crack these murders, or at least come up with an insight that could point everything in the right direction, then I could make amends."

"We'll do everything we can," said Frankie. "Now I'm here, we're in it together."

"Right in it together," chuckled Penelope.

28

THE NEXT MORNING, FRANKIE WAS up with the lark and with no ill effects from the bibulous day before. Penelope, on the other hand, gingerly assessed the state of her hangover. The best that could be said was that it wasn't quite as bad as she'd feared.

Downstairs the kitchen table groaned under a comprehensive selection of pastries.

"I walked up to the bakery," said Frankie, unnecessarily. "Got to have our treats, as we're in France."

"A dangerous philosophy for those of us who live here."

Frankie was one of those irritating people who hit the ground running at the crack of dawn, energy brimming, ready and optimistic about the day before them. Whereas before her infusion of caffeine, Penelope could scarcely get out of bed without a rest.

Frankie would not be put off.

"It's a lovely sunny day. Where shall we go? What shall we do?"

"How about staying entirely silent until the end of breakfast, Frankie. At least, that's what I'm going to do."

Frankie bit into a croissant, ignored this sound advice, and carried on regardless.

"When a woman is tired of rosé, she is tired of life, Pen," said Frankie. "And we both need to relax. Let's go on a little *dégustation* tour! Wine tasting is always much better done in the winter rather than in the heat and bright sunshine."

Penelope pursed her lips. "Has your HRT dose been upped again?"

"Might have been. But I feel great!"

Not for the first time, Penelope gave fleeting consideration to finding something stronger than Menopace vitamins and deep breathing to help her through this tricky time of life. She reached for a divinely buttery breakfast croissant.

"I've been thinking about Claudine and Nicolas," said Frankie. "When I met them, last time I was here, they seemed perfectly happily married, though one never can tell, of course. They may have had rows, but would he just run away? You know, Pen, I can't see it. And I certainly can't see him killing anyone."

"Neither can I! And I never said he did."

"But Laurent thinks you still suspect Nicolas."

"The problem was that Clémence and Laurent assumed that was where I was going with the questions I asked. They didn't give me a chance to explain. There's one huge piece of circumstantial evidence that says he couldn't have killed Scarpio."

"Which is?"

"Scarpio was shot in the leg, hit over the head, and bundled, unconscious or dead, into the watercourse at the museum. Why on earth would he put the body in the watercourse? He knew that Claudine was going to turn the water on the next day in front of a load of press and TV cameras. No, whoever did it cannot have known about the official opening."

"Unless that's exactly what he wanted—a dramatic unveiling of the crime," said Frankie. "But I take your point. It's very unlikely to be anyone connected with the museum."

"Most of Roussillon knew about the opening, too," said Penelope. "According to Claudine, they'd been drumming up publicity for weeks."

"When exactly was the argument between Nicolas and Claudine?" Frankie was good at logistics.

Penelope paused for a moment, thinking back to the evening of the concert. "It must have been between five-thirty and six. I can still hear that slammed door."

"You didn't hear any of what was said, though? Not even a few words?"

Penelope concentrated. "Not really. It was downstairs, and I was upstairs behind a closed door."

"You weren't tempted to open the door and have a listen?"

"No, Frankie, I was not."

"I suppose you weren't to know it was going to be important."

"Quite."

"When you say, 'not really,' though . . . ?"

"The problem is that I don't know now if I really heard it," said Penelope. "I've gone over that evening so many times and it might be partly my imagination, or what I thought I heard."

"Go on."

"Nicolas was yelling. It sounded like 'control.'"

"That's it?"

"That's it."

"Was Claudine a controlling sort of wife?" Frankie wanted to know.

"I couldn't tell you. I didn't know them well enough. Appearances can often be deceptive, but I wouldn't have thought so. If anything, it would have been the other way round. I got the impression that Nicolas had most of the power. They used to argue about how much money she spent."

Penelope thought back to the night of the concert. Her friends in the audience. Her disappointment at discovering Laurent had missed her performance of the Schumann. She still didn't know exactly where he had disappeared to. Her blood ran cold for a second before she told herself how ridiculous it was to suspect Laurent of anything.

"So when exactly was Scarpio killed?" Frankie reached for another almond croissant.

"I don't think the police have released a precise time of death."

"You couldn't make an educated guess from what you saw of his body?"

Penelope shook her head. "Very difficult. If I had to . . . I'd say around twelve hours. It looked as if rigor mortis was still set firm. His arms were up. As if he was trying to protect himself from an attacker."

"So it is reasonable to assume it happened during the night. The killer could even have been someone at the concert."

"Unlikely, I'd have thought. Why advertise your presence in the location?"

They chewed on that for a while.

"And we still have no idea *why* Nicolas disappeared. Did Claudine vouchsafe anything that might explain it?"

"Nothing specific. The night of the concert, she was clearly upset. But she didn't want to talk to me about it. Clémence said she was worried about him. He had been in an odd state of mind for a few weeks, apparently. Claudine put it down to Don's murder, but there must have been more. He didn't even like Don that much. Gilles told me that Nicolas thought Don lowered the tone—and Gilles's reputation, which in turn impacted on him."

"Interesting," said Frankie, through a mouthful of pâtisserie. "Has Clémence heard anything from her vast network?"

Penelope shrugged. "She hasn't returned my calls. I don't think she is very pleased with me at the moment."

"Right, that's it," said Frankie, dabbing the crumbs off her lips. "I'm going to ring her now. Sort this silly business out."

"And say what?"

"I don't know. Come right out with it, I expect."

"And what if she knows exactly why you're calling and doesn't want to speak to you?"

"I'll tell her I want to buy a house if I have to," said Frankie, getting out her phone.

❦

IN THE end, they went to one winery near Bonnieux, bought a single case of rosé, and found a promising restaurant for lunch. The scent of truffles and roasting meat pervaded the rustic dining room. They plumped for the three-course set menu, knowing there would be a memorable dessert it would be a crying shame to miss. A jug of red wine was automatically brought to the table along with one of water.

Penelope deliberately pushed her wineglass away and poured water into a tumbler. Frankie got stuck into the red with a gurgle of unalloyed pleasure. The set menu was a quiet triumph, starting with a rich truffle-infused omelette, followed by guinea fowl with roasted celeriac and braised lettuce, and a pear tart with whipped vanilla cream.

It was like being on holiday. All the more so because by unspoken agreement no mention was made of dead bodies.

❦

THAT EVENING at six, the aperitifs ready, they waited for the estate agent to appear at Le Chant d'Eau. Penelope felt awkward.

Ten minutes later, the Mini Cooper took the track with none of its driver's usual flamboyance, which was ominous in itself.

Frankie leapt for the front door when they heard the knock.

Penelope heard her greeting the Frenchwoman noisily in the
hall. They had established quite a rapport during Frankie's previous visits. It was a minute or so before they both appeared in
the kitchen.

"Hello, Penny. How are you?"

Was it Penelope's imagination, or was Clémence still distant?

"I'm fine, thanks. You?"

Clémence nodded. It was quite possible that she did not realise that for an Englishwoman, "I'm fine" meant her whole
world had fallen in.

"Pen's in a bit of a pickle," said Frankie, straight to the point,
as ever. "She knows she's upset you, and she doesn't know why."

Penelope glared daggers at her, but Frankie merely put her
head on one side and widened her eyes, as if to say that being
upfront was the only way to deal with misunderstandings.

"Whatever it is, I am truly sorry," said Penelope, taking the
bull by the horns. "Especially if you thought I was being insensitive on the day that Nicolas disappeared . . . that day at the
museum. It wasn't intended."

They both turned to Clémence.

The Frenchwoman nodded slowly, several times. "I think . . .
that we were *all* in shock," she said eventually.

"How's Claudine?" Penelope asked when they were seated
around the kitchen table and a bottle of sparkling Crémant de
Bourgogne had been opened. "Any news of Nicolas?"

"Not so good, and no."

"What are the police *doing*? Any progress at *all* with the
search—or with Scarpio's death?" It was odd how no one seemed
to call the late Barry Finch by his real name.

"Not that I have heard."

"One thing puzzles me," said Penelope. "Why didn't someone
check the water system before the TV crew arrived?"

Clémence nodded. "I had been thinking the same. I asked Claudine. It had been checked the night before, and Claudine was going to give it a final test on the morning of the official opening. But then, with all the worry about Nicolas, and the groundsman being off sick, it didn't happen. Everyone thought someone else had done it."

Penelope remembered the state she had found Claudine in.

"You were right about them arguing the night before." Clémence ran a hand through her hair. "Claudine had been worried about him for weeks. He wouldn't tell her why, but he hadn't been himself. At first, she thought it was to do with Don's murder, and it may have been. But Nicolas never liked Don, so that didn't really make sense. It must have been on a more existential level."

"Or for another reason entirely," chipped in Frankie. "Tell her what you told me about 'control,' Pen."

Penelope sighed, wishing her friend hadn't mentioned it. "I'm not sure it means anything, or even that I'm remembering it correctly. But I thought I heard Nicolas shouting about 'control.'"

"Only that?"

"Yep."

"Was she a control freak, or was he?" bludgeoned Frankie.

"Neither," said Clémence.

"Unless . . . wait a minute." Frankie clenched her fists. "*Contrôler* . . . it doesn't necessarily mean 'to control,' does it, Clémence? It can mean 'to check,' can't it? Perhaps he was reminding her to check something, or he had checked and found something wasn't right."

"That would make more sense," said Clémence.

Penelope wasn't convinced. "A hell of a row to have over checking something."

"Checking the watercourse?" prompted Frankie.

"Not his responsibility," said Clémence.

"Any possibility that Scarpio's death was an accident after all?" said Frankie.

"Unlikely. There was a gunshot wound."

"Have the police found marks in the earth from the top of the cliff? He must have been dragged to the watercourse."

"According to Claudine, the killer—or killers—were very careful to sweep away any disturbances in the soil. The police spent a long time on a fingertip search, taking photos and speaking to the groundsman at the museum. They haven't found anything."

"Did Scarpio meet someone up there? What was he doing there in the first place?" Frankie drummed her fingernails on the table.

"So far, no one knows," replied Clémence.

It seemed she was as stumped as they were.

"I made a horrible faux pas with Laurent that day," said Penelope. "I might even have implied that I thought he could have been up to no good on the night of the concert."

Clémence frowned. "What did you say?"

"I asked him where he disappeared to after the interval." While I was playing and hubristically wanted him to hear me, she thought. "I didn't mean what he thought it did."

"And what was his answer?"

"He didn't give an answer."

The Frenchwoman nodded. "I should have told you. His younger daughter—she's nineteen, a student—was knocked off her bicycle, dislocated her shoulder, and broke her arm. She wanted to speak to him from the hospital before she went under the anaesthetic for the operation."

"Oh," said Penelope. "She's OK now, though?"

"She won't be cycling in Paris traffic again, but yes. And Laurent has been up to see her. That is probably why you haven't been able to get hold of him."

❧

THEY HAD another glass of wine and tackled some tiny tapenade toasts.

"Gilles . . . what tickles his fancy, then?" asked Frankie, mock-innocently.

Penelope shuddered. "I really wouldn't know, Frankie. And do you have to use that vulgar expression?"

But it was water off a duck's back.

"When are you going to see him again?"

"Well, he's away at the moment, isn't he?"

"What's this?" Clémence wanted in. "You and Gilles de Bourdan? Is it serious?"

"No! I've only been out with him once. Well, twice if you count a surprise lunch in Saignon."

Frankie turned to Clémence. "Not gay, is he?"

The estate agent shook her head. "I don't think so, but who knows?"

"You'll have to find out, won't you, Pen. I got the distinct impression you really like him. A bit like that time you decided to chase after Keith Simmons, remember? The captain of the swimming team at the boys' school. You were distinctly captivated by his form in *and* out of the pool, *especially* out of the water, in those racing Speedos."

"That's not quite how I remember it, Frankie."

"Course you do, with that huge—"

"Moving swiftly on," said Penelope sharply.

"And you pretended to be Mark Imrie's sister to go to that swimming gala and took your mum's camera in order to . . ."

This was the downside of having old friends. They never let you forget.

"Stop now, Frankie! It was a very long time ago, Clémence. And I think it says more about my friend here, who remembers it so well, than it does about me, who had completely forgotten this shameful episode."

But Clémence was enjoying herself hugely. Any awkwardness had well and truly disappeared, along with the second bottle of sparkling white as Frankie went into even more mortifying detail.

"Kill me now," groaned Penelope.

Though that was a dangerous thing to say in the current circumstances.

29

PENELOPE WAS FEELING A LOT happier after mending bridges with Clémence. She suggested going to the market at Lourmarin, a pretty village nestling on the southern flanks of the Luberon with a very smart market on Friday mornings.

Frankie was enthusiastic. "Any good clothes stalls for the generous of waistline?" she chortled.

Penelope assured her that all shapes and sizes were catered to, both in the fashion and gastronomic departments.

"Marvellous," cried Frankie. "We can look at some clothes, have a jolly good lunch, then go back and buy them a size larger." Penelope envied her friend the apparent lack of concern about her figure.

The only drawback to going to Lourmarin market, in Penelope's mind, lay in the journey there and back. A thin canyon split the Luberon ridge at Apt, and a road wound down through the high cliffs on either side to Lourmarin and the south. The Combe de Lourmarin was vertiginous at the top, then the road zigzagged all the way down, at times through walls of sheer rock, providing a motoring challenge for local racers of all ages and abilities. Penelope's nerves were always shredded by the time she reached the end. But all the other ways to Lourmarin involved going three times the distance, around the Luberon Mountains.

Frankie was not scared of much, but even she looked a little grey around the gills when they staggered out of the car at Lour-marin, having just missed an overtaking lorry on the final bend.

"No wonder you call it the Canyon of Death, Pen! There were moments there when my life passed before my eyes. And at our age, they were bloody long moments . . ."

"Provençal driving. It's either racetrack speed, or four-miles-a-fortnight behind a tractor. Provençal-*vite*, or Provençal-*glaciale*, not much in between. So, to market?"

"We may need a tiny stiffener first. We are in France, after all."

Shaking her head, Penelope led her friend along the stall-lined streets to the centre of the village where three cafés vied for busi-ness. If she didn't know Frankie as well as she did, she might be starting to wonder if Frankie had an alcohol problem. But she knew this was simply exuberant release, and making the most of a carefree week away from home. Frankie worked hard six days a week for the family construction company. She was only conforming to the British holiday norm of drinking like camels arriving at an oasis.

It was early, around eleven o'clock, but many of the outside tables were full. They ordered two coffees, a carafe of rosé, and a plate of vividly coloured macaroons.

⚜

ABOUT AN hour later, two merry Englishwomen could be seen laughing their way down the narrow streets, arm in arm, stopping at various clothes stalls, and selecting various woollen dresses and long, flouncy cardigans. One would pose with the garment held against her, the other would look her up and down in a stern fashion, then make some remark that would set the two off laughing again. The stallholders often joined in. There was no sign of offence being taken, but there again, little evidence of purchase.

After the abortive attempt at finding Haute Provençal couture, Frankie decided that she needed some higher culture.

"Let's see if the spirit of Don Doncaster inhabits the galleries of Lourmarin or whether that outbreak was contained in the Luberon Valley," she announced, stopping in front of a smart shop selling pictures. She plunged in and immediately picked out an exhibit on the wall.

"Look, Pen!" she exclaimed. "It's a Dufy. Who would have thought?"

The owner did not seem to catch the sarcastic tone.

"*Oui, madame*, Raoul Dufy . . . friend of the great post-impressionists." He paused, and added in broken English, "Four thousand euros. A verrry goooood price. Not so much money."

"Very cheap!" agreed Frankie. She turned to Penelope. "Very, very reasonable . . . by about two million quid."

"You are quite right, madame."

Penelope started. Beside her a small man in black had materialised, holding a notepad and shaking his head.

"Unfortunately not many have your knowledge. There will always be some tourist with more money than taste who will buy this and leave thinking he has made a great discovery. And then, the next day, there will be another 'Dufy' on the gallery wall, probably with the paint still wet on the canvas."

Penelope recognised him immediately. It was Emile Sablon, the lugubrious art critic she had seen at the Bourdan Gallery.

"It is the scourge of Provence, *mesdames*," he carried on gravely. "All this money, the famed history of artists who lived here, and some unscrupulous forgers. Imitation. Everywhere there is imitation!"

He sighed.

"And do you know what the real problem is?"

"I am sure you will enlighten us," said Frankie.

"When you look at the new original paintings, they are even worse! When I was in Paris, these canvases would not have even made it onto the railings along the Seine."

"You must miss Paris, monsieur," said Penelope insincerely.

"Alas, yes. I try to bring the power of my taste and experience to *La Provence*, but they are more interested in grapes and boules." He sighed again and walked off to look at the other paintings. Penelope could hear him muttering "*mon dieu*" and "*quel horreur*" followed by long, lamenting moans.

The two friends looked at each other and tried to contain their giggles.

Sablon was writing furiously in his notebook in front of a smaller picture. He looked up. "See! This is what I mean! Even for M. Doncaster, this plumbs new depths! Enough. I can bear no more." He turned and exited the shop like a dark rain cloud on its way to the beach. Penelope and Frankie were left staring at the canvas.

A dog with malicious eyes and dripping maw stared back. Penelope spotted the signature DD in the bottom corner.

"That's amazing! It's Perky to the life!" cried Frankie. As with so many dog owners, she was blindly besotted by her pet. "I'm having that!"

"You can't buy it!" Penelope was horrified. It was quite a scary painting. Mind you, so was her friend's Rottweiler.

"I can, and I will."

"You should always go easy on the rosé before you buy art, Frank."

But Frankie haggled the man down from a hundred to sixty

euros, and was delighted with her purchase. "I'll hang it in the corner of the kitchen back home in Perky's special place."

"I hope he takes it in the spirit it's meant, and doesn't try to fight it," said Penelope.

"He might eat it, I suppose . . . but I can't resist."

As sobriety beckoned, the pair purchased provisions for a late lunch and supper and, both staggering slightly under the weight and size of the carrier bags needed for this modest supply, returned to the car.

"Half a league, half a league, half a league onward. Into the Valley of Death rode the four by four hundred," chanted Penelope as she rammed the car slightly carelessly into first and took off back to Apt. "Belt up, Frankie, this is a rollercoaster."

❧

THEY WENT for a walk after their late lunch back at St Merlot. A path led downhill into a wooded area where the ground was softened by a carpet of pine needles, and the gin scent of juniper bushes tickled their senses.

"Returning to the dead artists conundrum," said Penelope. "We're missing something. The question is, what?"

"The deaths of Don and this Scarpio, and the poisonings before they died, *must* be linked, surely," said Frankie. "Both in the same circle. It's not a coincidence, is it?"

"Maybe that's what everyone is supposed to think. But in fact, there are different perpetrators, and different motives. The last murder is done by someone who had nothing to do with the first, or the attempted murder, but makes it look as if it's linked in order to push suspicion elsewhere."

"That makes it all very complicated."

"That's the point," said Penelope.

"I may like a bit of blue sky thinking, but I'm no conspiracy theorist."

"I seem to recall you thought there was something in the story about the royal family being aliens," said Penelope slyly.

"It was in the *National Enquirer*. The evidence was very compelling."

"I know I shouldn't be thinking this, but I've still got the strangest feeling that Claudine knew more than she let on," said Penelope, trying to get them back on track. "Nothing more than a gut feeling. But maybe . . . oh, I don't know. There's something not right about Nicolas's disappearance coinciding with Scarpio's death." She looked up, trying to marshal her thoughts. A bird of prey hovered high above them, silently riding the thermals in the air.

They marched on in silence as the spongy path descended. They came to a halt by a stream.

"OK, facts only, no supposition," said Frankie. "Don Doncaster. He was an accomplished womaniser. He must have been a master at ducking and diving and covering his tracks. What else was he hiding?"

"He happily allowed himself to be written about and portrayed as a bohemian. Any woman he was involved with knew what he was like and seemingly didn't care. He didn't have to hide anything," said Penelope.

"Except his marriage to Nina," Frankie reminded her.

"If it was actually valid," said Penelope.

She told Frankie about the feminist encampment outside Avignon, uncomfortably aware that she was revealing her own suburban middle-class prejudices in turn. She had hoped she had left most of those behind in Esher, but it seemed not. "It was a wimmin's mothership. All idiotic graffiti, and harem trousers where the crotch hangs down around the knees." Penelope put those in the same category as mung beans and wild lentils. Worthy but not advisable in company.

"Load of old nonsense," said Frankie crossly. "If any of them want to talk to me about equality, I'll tell 'em how it's done—by knowing as much about building as any man and working just as hard to earn respect from everyone."

"Gilles thinks Nina is the one who's hiding something. That she was making Don ill."

"Possibility she's guilty, then," said Frankie. "Of crimes against common sense, if nothing else. We should go and see her."

Penelope was unconvinced. "The police released her without charge."

"Where's her studio in Avignon?"

"In the building opposite Gilles's gallery."

"We need to go there, then." Frankie had the bit between her teeth now.

"We can't."

"Why not?"

Penelope didn't answer.

"It would be a very good excuse to visit the scene of the first crime, wouldn't it? If we see Nina, we say we're just there to look in at Gilles's gallery. I'd genuinely like to see it."

"Might be awkward with Gilles," said Penelope.

"Gilles is in Russia, remember?"

❧

"AWW, NO! Will you look at that?"

Frankie held out the painting she had bought in Lourmarin.

The ghastly dog had a long, deep scratch running across its mean little eyes and part of the nose was missing where the paint had been scraped off.

Penelope winced. "Where did you leave it—outside?"

"No, in the hall. I propped it up on the table under the mirror when we came in."

"You didn't see any damage then?"

"Well, it's a bit dark in the hall, isn't it, when the shutters are closed."

"It could have happened in the boot of the car. Maybe during that last emergency braking manoeuvre on the Combe de Lourmarin," said Penelope. "Sorry, Frankie. Perhaps we can repair it."

By the light flooding in from the large kitchen windows, it looked as if the paint was still tacky. Where the long scratch was, it had peeled off like skin.

"That's not wood showing through, though," said Penelope. "It's more like dark oil paint. There's something underneath."

They looked at each other.

"How much do you really like this picture?" asked Penelope. It had been a bad painting to start with, and now it was ruined anyway.

"Not as much as I'm curious to know," said Frankie. "Have you got a scraper?"

Ten minutes later, they could just make out a face and a beard.

"A man standing in front of a sun," said Frankie. "Even I can see it's better than what was on top, though it could do with a good clean."

"Not a sun," said Penelope. "A halo."

"Really?"

"That's an icon you've got there. This could be a find! Now we really do need to go to Gilles's gallery."

In the excitement Penelope put aside her qualms about coming over as a man-chaser. "We know he won't be there, but there must be some assistant or other we can pump for a bit of info. You can see the gallery and then we could potentially look in on Nina. She'll either be in the studio working or at her encampment."

Frankie looked at her friend. "I devoutly hope it's the former, Penny. Feminists don't usually take kindly to my style. And I'm not just talking about the bling."

30

❧

"*'SUR LE PONT D'AVIGNON, L'ON y danse, l'on y danse. Sur le pont d'Avignon, l'on y danse tous en rond!'*" carolled Frankie as they skirted the bank of the River Durance, the city ahead of them.

Penelope felt anxious without knowing quite why. "I suppose he must be in St Petersburg now."

"Gilles?"

"Yes. I was just wondering how long he will be away for. It must take most of the day to get to St Petersburg from here. Then he has to see his contacts and everything. Another day for the return trip. I'm sure he won't be back, which is probably just as well. I'd hate him to think I was chasing him."

"Though we do want him to look at the icon," Frankie pointed out.

"True. But all in good time."

They found a car park just by the city walls.

Walking briskly through the quiet cold streets to the gallery on the Rue des Teinturiers, Penelope thought back to her last visit, with Laurent, and what fun it had been, despite having to see Reyssens. It seemed a long time ago.

They rounded a corner.

"Here we are, the Rue des Teinturiers. The gallery is further up."

Frankie wobbled on the cobblestones. "Shouldn't have worn quite such high heels," she said. "But I wanted to make a good impression."

"One way of putting it," said Penelope absently. Her friend's outfit was even more eye-catching than normal: a coral pink dress topped off with a leopard-print faux-fur coat, burgundy felt hat and matching shoes, and an orange bag for contrast.

"Rude."

Against the grey grandeur of the eighteenth-century street, Frankie was a gaudy bird of paradise. "Ooh, look at those beautifully constructed waterwheels!" she gushed, the insult immediately forgotten. "The street of the dyers. You can just imagine, can't you! Crystal-clear water running from the hills outside the town into this tiny canal. The workers would be shaded in summer by all these trees. A hive of activity, water splashing as the wheels turned . . ."

Penelope gazed into the water at the rippled reflections of bare trees against a smoky grey sky. Skeins of ivy reached into the canal, and pigeons pecked at the moss on the old stones.

"That's how it worked, can you see?" Frankie's enthusiasm was infectious. "Hydraulic wheels. There's only the axle left on this one. No paddles, probably rotted away. But if you lean over, there are the old supports—and the cylinder that protected the lubricator. Maybe there were dyers here in the Middle Ages, but by the industrial age, the water course and wheels would have been powering machines, I should think."

They continued along, past a small monastery, the Brotherhood of the Pénitents Gris, Frankie still offering engineering insights.

Penelope came to a stop.

Beyond another waterwheel was a sight with which she was all too grimly familiar. Police tape sealed off a damaged door and signs forbade the public to enter. The building across the street from the Gilles de Bourdan Gallery was charred and smelled of smoke. Black soot streaked the stucco above glass-less windows. Firefighters were still damping down.

"What the——?" Penelope's heart sank as an all-too-recognisable figure emerged from under the tape at the entrance without much need to duck.

He seemed almost as nonplussed to see her.

"*Ça alors!* Mme Keet!"

Chef de Police Georges Reyssens's face indicated anything but pleasant surprise. "And may I ask what you are doing here?"

Penelope pulled back her shoulders. "*Bonjour, monsieur.* I am here with my friend from England. We came to see Gilles de Bourdan's art gallery. Is everything all right?"

Reyssens curled his lip. "You didn't come to see Nina Chiroubles?"

"No."

He clearly didn't believe that for a moment.

"As you can perfectly well see, madame, everything is not all right. And though it gives me pain to say it, I think it might be helpful if we had a little discussion."

With a sickening lurch, Penelope understood. "Nina's studio was in that building, wasn't it!"

The policeman did not deny it. "It is owned by Gilles de Bourdan."

Frankie spotted her opportunity and seized it. "Lunch is on me." She held her arm out to the stunned policeman, half her size thanks to the high heels and the enormous coat. Before Penelope could say anything, Reyssens was marched off down the street like a child being abducted by a giant leopard. As she followed them to a brasserie on the corner, she overheard Frankie laying on a charm offensive in fluent French that better men than Reyssens had found impossible to resist.

"Did I ever tell you about my time in Paris . . . I was a dancer at the Moulin Rouge, you know?"

"Madame, I beg you, please . . ."

"Of course, I was only nineteen then. Nineteen! With a tiny waist, too. Imagine it, this innocent young girl in corsets and stockings in the middle of naughty Montmartre . . ."

For once Reyssens seemed to be struck dumb. One up for Frankie, thought Penelope. She watched with certain dread of the consequences as her friend pulled the policeman through the door into the steamy interior.

The restaurant that spread under the trees by the waterway in summer had retreated indoors into a dark-panelled room. A log fire burned in the grate and all but one table was taken.

Frankie called for drinks.

Penelope sat back and wondered again at the sheer chutzpah of her friend. She judged it best to sit quietly and allow Reyssens to talk. Unfortunately, Frankie was steaming ahead with questions and unsought opinions. Penelope feared it could only end badly.

When the drinks and the menus had been promptly provided and Frankie had stopped talking to take a long slurp of red wine, Reyssens narrowed his eyes across the table at Penelope.

"You can deduce what has happened, I am sure. We were called to the fire early this morning. The firemen have found a body in the ruins."

"Oh, no!" Penelope and Frankie reacted simultaneously.

"Oh, yes."

"How dreadful. Was it an accident—or . . . ?"

"We are making our investigation."

Penelope straightened up in her chair. A fleeting suspicion hardened into something more unpleasant. She had known that Reyssens wouldn't have let himself be press-ganged into speaking to her unless he had the upper hand. She took a deep breath. "The body . . ."

"*Oui, madame?*"

"Whose body is it?" Frankie butted in impatiently.

"The deceased has not been formally identified, you understand. But I strongly suspect it is . . ." Reyssens paused for dramatic effect, "the artist, Nina Chiroubles."

Penelope couldn't believe it. Another of the artists dead.

"I thought you suspected her of killing Don Doncaster . . ."

"She had been released pending further enquiries."

"Did she—I mean—was she killed, or does it look as if she took her own life?" asked Penelope.

Reyssens glowered at her. "Did she have a reason to take her own life?"

"I don't know. I hardly knew the woman. But it's unwise to take anything for granted."

"You hardly knew her, and yet you were there when she was arrested," he reminded her.

"I'm interested in art."

It never took long before they were at loggerheads.

"Tell me again everything that you know about Nina Chiroubles."

It didn't amount to much. Penelope sipped some water and risked a question of her own. "Do you know yet if she died in the fire or before?"

"The smoke in the lungs should confirm that."

"Estimated time of death?" asked Penelope automatically.

"Really, Mme Keet. You cannot expect me to tell you that. I am the person charged with asking the questions, remember? And of course we will perform the postmortem, as we always do."

"And you'd get better answers if you showed some respect," cut in Frankie. "My friend is a woman of considerable experience—"

"Frank, please!"

"Well, honestly . . ."

"Not helping," said Penelope firmly.

A dark stare from the policeman. "I will tell you one thing. The doors were locked."

"Are you treating it as an accident?" she went on.

"I cannot tell you that. We have to follow protocol. I am sure you understand."

"Of course, Inspector. Very commendable."

Did Reyssens lack the necessary experience of British sangfroid to detect the vein of sarcasm running through Penelope's voice?

He settled back in his chair and took a sip of wine. "Madame, when it comes to solving crimes, it is all about protocol! If it were not, I would not be where I am today." A closer look at the deep red of his glass of Châteauneuf-du-Pape was followed by a larger swig. "Mme Keet, can you tell me precisely what you were doing yesterday evening?"

Penelope gave an involuntary splutter. It was as well she was drinking water and not red wine, else she would have sprayed an angry rash across Reyssens's pristine white shirt. "What on earth do you mean, Inspector? Do you suspect me?"

"I suspect every-bod-y, madame. I do not say I suspect him and then I suspect her, and then I suspect somebody else. I keep myself quiet, and I compute it in my head. And then I have the answer."

"I think you've been reading too many Hercule Poirot detective novels."

"It is very interesting, madame, that you have not answered my question. Such a simple question."

"Please don't take that tone of voice with me," said Penelope. "If you must know, I was at home after going to Lourmarin, for the market. With Frankie, here."

"But the market is finished by the afternoon."

"Yes. Then we went out for a walk. We were together all day and all evening." Penelope was in no mood to be interrogated.

"Can anyone confirm this?"

The diminutive policeman with a distinctly comic toupee was clearly not a person to let bygones be bygones.

"No."

"And you, madame." Frankie was now in his sights. "Did you know Nina Chiroubles?"

"No," she said. "I never met her."

Reyssens seemed to be about to speak, then to think better of it. He pushed the menu away. "I regret I am unable to take lunch with you, ladies."

"Because we're suspects?" asked Frankie, incredulously.

"Because I have important work to do." But he did not get up to leave. "Have you seen Gilles de Bourdan recently, Mme Keet?"

"Fairly recently."

"Where—and when—was that?"

Penelope looked at Frankie. "We ran into him at the Marseille airport three days ago."

"Really?" That was clearly not what Reyssens had expected to hear. He was distinctly interested.

"I was meeting Frankie, and Gilles was taking an afternoon flight."

"Where to?"

Something stopped Penelope. She looked Reyssens straight in the eyes and replied. "I've really no idea. He said it was business, I think."

"And did he say how long he was going for?" Reyssens seemed to sink back into his seat, as if this new information had crushed another theory.

"I'm not sure he said, did he, Frankie?"

"Search me. I'd just come off the plane. I wasn't taking notes."

Reyssens moistened his thick lips in a decidedly revolting way. "We are still building the case against the killer of Don Doncaster. He was poisoned. He was linked with Nina. And we also have Scarpio, another artist in the group who suffered poisoning and has been murdered. One must be sure before proceeding to the next stage."

"Indeed one must," said Penelope. "I assume you have interviewed all the nurses who were on duty when Don was in hospital?"

The chief narrowed his eyes. "Why do you ask?"

"Because I know one of them, and she told me that before he died, Don was visited by a number of women and two men. Are you sure that it was poison that killed him, and not some intervention from one of his visitors?"

A pause.

"Rest assured, our investigations are continuing. But I am more interested at present to discuss Nina Chiroubles."

"What do you want to know?" asked Penelope. "Not that I know very much about her."

"What exactly was the status of her relationship with Don Doncaster?"

"I understand that they were married."

"So what was she doing living in the women's collective?"

"Labia painting," said Frankie, "or so I heard."

"Please, madame!" Reyssens was beginning to look haunted.

"When did the fire break out?" Penelope turned his disgust to her advantage. "Some time yesterday evening, most likely late last night. Am I right, Inspector?"

Reyssens sighed. "You are correct, madame. The fire appears to have started in the early hours of this morning. It was reported about two a.m. With all the chemicals and materials in the studio, the firemen had to be very careful. She had gas canisters as well. It took over six hours to control the blaze and make it safe to enter."

"So you only found the body this morning, Inspector. Presumably very badly burnt."

"Almost beyond recognition. We will need to access her dental records to be sure."

He suddenly looked harassed and tired, and Penelope felt a momentary wave of sympathy.

"We are speaking to all those who knew her. If you could add anything helpful, especially about the new Mme Doncaster, I would be grateful."

❧

"WHAT DO we do now?" asked Frankie, after lunch. Penelope was still feeling sickened by the latest death she had blundered into.

Frankie and Reyssens had done justice to the bottle of wine, then eaten a game terrine starter with a basket of bread before he bustled off, claiming he really didn't have time to eat lunch. Penelope fervently hoped their discussion at the restaurant would not have unforeseen consequences.

"Exactly what we came to do," said Penelope grimly. "We go to Gilles's gallery. If for no other reason than we told Reyssens that's what we were here to do."

"I think you're right. Someone will be at the gallery that we can talk to. They'll have heard about Nina and be as discombobulated as we are. People often want to talk when the unexpected happens. Now is the perfect time."

They walked back up the street towards the police tent, trying not to be too obvious about rubber-necking. But when they reached the gallery, it was closed, presumably as a mark of respect for the gruesome fates that had befallen three of its artists.

❦

BACK AT St Merlot, even Frankie wanted a quiet afternoon. She read a book while Penelope played her cello for a while. Then they joined forces to make an easy casserole for supper. While it was cooking, Penelope picked up Frankie's damaged picture. She turned it over to examine the back, but there was nothing to give her a clue as to the artist or provenance. Why on earth would such a potentially lovely painting be covered over by a Don-style abomination?

She went to her desk to see if the Internet could offer any insights, but before she could switch on her computer, there was a knock at the door. Hoping against hope that the chat with Clémence had worked its magic and it might be Laurent, Penelope smoothed her hair as she passed through the hall. She pulled the big oak door open with a welcoming smile.

"Oh, my goodness!" Penelope reeled back. "You! I thought you were dead!"

31

NINA CHIROUBLES SHIVERED, GAUNT IN her thin harem pants and sagging leather belt. Her turquoise hair was matted, as if it had not been washed for many days.

"Can I come in?" she pleaded.

Penelope led her through to the warmth of the kitchen. "I thought you were a ghost! I think you'd better tell me what on earth has been going on. But let me get you a drink first."

This was a job for M. Louchard's plum brandy, with its miraculously relaxing properties.

"How did you find me, Nina?" asked Penelope.

"Easy. Everyone knows you solved the St Merlot murders. All I had to do was ask anyone in the village. I went into the *boulangerie* earlier. They seem to know you very well there."

Penelope was momentarily floored as Frankie began to chortle.

"Go and get Nina something to warm herself," she snapped at her.

Frankie obeyed.

"Why have you come here, Nina?"

"I saw you in Avignon with that policeman. I need to know what's been going on, and what he's told you."

Frankie returned with a large white fluffy towel and draped it over Nina's thin shoulders. "Why?" she asked, blunt as ever.

Nina looked astonished, then her features twisted into fury. "Because my life has become a fucking nightmare. Because I have to find a way through this and I have to know what I'm dealing with!"

"No point in speaking to our friendly neighbourhood chief of police then?" Penelope made her scorn regarding Reyssens obvious, realising that they needed to establish a rapport quickly.

"You fucking kidding me?"

"I understand, believe me," said Penelope.

She was working out where to begin when Nina seemed to crumple. "I didn't mean for any of this to happen," she croaked as tears threatened to sweep away her bravado.

The two Englishwomen looked at each other.

"For what to happen?" asked Penelope. "Maybe you should start right from the beginning, and then we might be able to help."

Nina took a gulp of plum brandy. Almost immediately, she regained some colour. "It all started with the olives."

"The olives?"

"Yes, those special ones that he loved, from Goult."

"We're talking about Don, yes?"

A nod. "He was crazy for a particular kind of olive stuffed with almond. From a shop in Goult." Nina hunched over, as if she was trying to make herself as small as possible.

"Go on, Nina."

She started rocking.

"Did you do anything to the olives before giving them to Don?" asked Penelope gently.

In a tiny voice, she whispered, "Yes."

Another silence.

"Did you paint them green?"

Nina stared up at Penelope, eyes brimming. A tear finally popped and ran down her cheek.

"Scheele's Green, from the museum?" Penelope pressed home her advantage.

"What? No! That's what the police kept asking. I only used tiny bits of crushed-up sleeping tablet, pushed under the almonds. To make him too tired to go chasing after other women."

"So did you take the olives to the gallery that night?"

"No, I didn't! I even checked at Don's place in Ménerbes after he died. The olives I bought were still there—until the police came and took them away for analysis."

"So, you didn't use arsenic from the museum and you didn't take the olives to the party at the gallery," recapped Frankie, determined to get in on the act.

"No, I didn't." Nina put her hands over her face and began to sob. "It was only sleeping pills, but I thought I had . . . had killed him . . ."

Penelope shooed her friend off to make some coffee and readdressed herself to Nina.

"Nina, did you see Don when he was in hospital?"

She nodded. "He was getting better. I was so relieved! Why did he die?"

"I don't know," said Penelope.

"I saw him the day after he was brought in. He was still very ill, but improving, the hospital staff told me. Then the next day, he was . . ."

She could not finish the sentence.

Frankie brought her a mug of coffee.

"Did you tell the police about the sleeping pills?"

A vigorous nod of the head. "I had to. And I told the medics who took Don into hospital that he should be checked for an accidental overdose."

"Was that why the police arrested you?"

"Maybe. They said they had found my fingerprints on some bottle of old ink or something in the ochre museum. I said I guessed it was possible because I had been working there."

"And they believed you."

"They must have done. I was released."

"Where have you been since your release?"

"In my caravan, mainly. The police took my passport and told me to stay there while they continued their investigation into Don's death. But yesterday I wanted to collect something from my studio."

"What was that?"

"A sketchbook. Nothing important to anyone but me. But I wanted to start work again, to find something to take my mind off the grief. So I waited until it was late and went over there. I let myself into the studio, found the sketchbook, and was about to leave when I thought I heard someone come in."

"How did they get in?"

"I must have left the door unlocked. But the studio has been used by many artists over the years. Some of them still have keys—perhaps it was one of them. I didn't want to be seen there. I thought it might have been the police, and I was supposed to stay in the commune. I left quickly by the back door."

"Did you lock the back door, Nina?"

"Yes."

"And then went back to the commune."

"Yes."

"So what happened this morning?" asked Frankie.

"I had a bad feeling about whoever had come to the studio. I couldn't shake it, so much bad shit has happened. So I came back about eleven-thirty and saw the smoking ruins and Reyssens talking to you outside. Then I overheard someone saying that a body had been found. I didn't know what to do. I tried to call Gilles but got no answer. What did the police say to you?" Nina pleaded. "Do they think I killed someone else now?"

"They think it was you. The body," said Penelope.

"What?"

"It's true. You're going to have to tell the police that you're still alive, you know."

Nina took a gulp of plum brandy and closed her eyes tightly. "I know. I will. But I need to work some stuff out."

"What kind of stuff?"

"You have to trust me on this. Please."

"You should go to the police," said Penelope.

"I know. But there are things going on you have no idea about. This is bigger than you know. It's all connected, I'm sure of it. You have to believe me—why else would I have come here?" Nina stared glumly at her empty glass. Frankie put a plate of bread and cheese in front of her.

"Tell us, then," urged Penelope.

But Nina had fallen on the bread and cheese as if she was starving. Penelope refilled her glass with plum brandy. Nina swigged, then stared intently over Penelope's shoulder.

Penelope followed her gaze. Behind her on the kitchen sideboard stood the partially exposed icon.

"What the hell is that doing here?" asked Nina. She scraped her chair back and walked over to the painting. Her hands were trembling as she picked it up.

Penelope and Frankie exchanged glances.

"Have you seen it before?" Penelope tried to keep the excitement from her voice. "Do you know anything about it?"

They heard the kitchen clock ticking down the silence as Nina examined it. Long seconds passed. "Yep. I think so."

"The remains of the acrylic make it hard to be certain?" suggested Penelope.

"It's the acrylic that makes me certain."

"I don't under—"

"It's the same icon. There's a beautiful crackle on the gilding of the halo. It's the kind of thing I never forget."

"Can you remember where you saw it?" asked Penelope.

Nina picked it up for a closer look. "In the ochre museum."

"The ochre museum?" butted in Frankie.

"In the workshop Nicolas used there. He had become an expert on the authenticity of paintings. He would often be asked to look at pictures on behalf of buyers and sellers. There's quite a market in fakes, especially icons."

"Was Nicolas an icon specialist?" Penelope watched Nina's face as she ran a finger over the brown acrylic smears, all that remained of the dog over the original saint. She was nodding to herself as if satisfied she was right.

"I don't think so. I once overheard him and Gilles having a furious argument about an icon and Gilles telling him that he should be very careful about setting himself up as an expert. That he, Gilles, was the expert and Nicolas should stick to what he knew best."

"When was this?"

"A while back. Scarpio was also there. The three of them were going crazy, all shouting at each other."

"What was Scarpio's beef?" said Penelope.

"I didn't hear. But he was often hanging around the workshop. I suspect he used to steal things from the outhouses. He was always light-fingered."

"Interesting. What else can you remember?"

But Nina's attention was focused on the damaged icon. "Where did you find this?"

"In a shop in Lourmarin," said Frankie. "It was a painting of a dog."

"By Don Doncaster," added Penelope.

"We only discovered the icon when some of the new paint got accidentally scraped off," added Frankie.

"Didn't it occur to you there must have been a reason it was painted over?" asked Nina. "And the way it came off so easily?"

"Of course," said Penelope. "But why?"

"I'll tell you for nothing," said Nina. "To hide it from the authorities. Maybe from import duties, maybe from wealth tax. It would have been sent to Lourmarin for the real buyer to pick up incognito."

"How do you know all this?"

"I don't know it for sure. But Don knew something wasn't right. It was after one of Gilles's exhibitions in Moscow. Gilles had told Don all his pictures had sold, but not long afterwards, Don saw one of them in a shop in Ansouis. He was a very intelligent man. He worked out there was some kind of scam going on."

"Overpainting valuable icons with Doncaster-style—" Penelope had been going to say "rubbish" but stopped herself just in time. "Art? To get them through customs without paying extortionate duty?"

"And some very angry Russians will be trying to trace this one. I wouldn't like to be holding it when they arrive. They aren't known for their subtlety when it comes to dealing with a breakdown in the supply chain. Not the kind of dealers you want to mess with. Don was on the case. Maybe they were the guys who killed him."

"Wha-a-t? What are you talking about? Not all poisonings are done by the Russians." Penelope was highly sceptical.

Nina fixed them with a warning look.

Penelope felt a cold sweat breaking out.

"Gilles was worried about some of the Russian criminals in Nice," Nina went on. "Since Scarpio was killed, he'd got very edgy. He's even closed the Nice Gallery early for Christmas and moved most of his icon stock up here. Take my advice and get it to him as soon as you can."

Penelope crossed her arms as her mind made unwelcome connections. "Hang on, what if Gilles is *part* of the scam? You said the painting Don saw was supposed to have been sold in Russia—so Gilles must have brought it back."

"That's why I want you to take it to him. I want to see what he does next."

"Gilles might not be there. He's been away—in Russia."

"If he's not there, so much the better," said Nina. "See if you can find anything at the gallery, take photos of any Doncasters you can see. The icon business is the key to the murders, and to Nicolas's disappearance, I'm sure of it."

"I've been a complete idiot!" cried Penelope.

Frankie shrugged. "Don't beat yourself up Pen—we all have our moments."

"But it was under my nose and I didn't spot it."

"Spot what?"

"At the airport, did you notice anything odd?"

"Well, your shoes didn't quite go with your dress."

"No, no! Not about me—about Gilles."

Frankie looked perplexed.

"Well I did, but I didn't think any more about it, more's the pity."

"Go on."

"Gilles was on his way to St Petersburg, but hadn't yet checked in because he was so early."

"Yes . . . and?"

"He had no luggage, Frankie. Not even a briefcase."

Her friend's face lit up. Nina was wide-eyed, as if she had been given an enormous present.

Penelope whipped her phone out, and made impatient noises as it found the Wi-Fi signal. "There you go." She held it out.

"Marseille airport destinations. What do you see, Frank?"

"Look, they go to Marrakesh—I've always wanted to go to Marrakesh! Do you know . . ."

"For goodness' sake! It's not where they go, it's where they don't go."

Frankie read down the list.

"No direct flights to St Petersburg."

"Exactly, Frankie. Gilles was lying. He wasn't going to Russia."

They looked at each other.

"So he had to change planes," said Frankie. "Most likely in Paris."

Penelope shook her head. " 'My flight to St Petersburg,' that's what he said."

⋈

HALF AN hour later, Nina stood at the door, ready to leave. She refused to tell them where she was going so that she did not incriminate them further. Penelope knew it was very wrong, but she agreed. For all she knew, Reyssens and his men had already realised that the body in the burnt-out studio was not Nina, after all. Which begged the question: Whose was it?

The friends watched as Nina started up her motorcycle. They heard its throaty roar take the track and turn up towards St Merlot.

"Rock and a hard place," said Penelope. "Reyssens and the Russians involved in the illicit art market. But I've got an idea."

32

PENELOPE FELT PROFOUNDLY UNCOMFORTABLE ABOUT agreeing to keep Nina's visit a secret from the authorities, even for a short time. Had anyone but Georges Reyssens been in charge, she would never have even considered Nina's request. But if she was right about the Russian threat, her apparent death would allow her to gather more evidence whilst remaining beyond suspicion.

Frankie had googled the Bourdan Gallery and found out that at least once a year Gilles would take some of his artists' more portable output to Russia for an exhibition. The works of Scarpio and Doncaster featured heavily in the list. Dangerous as the game was, Penelope knew they should follow through. She needed to see Gilles's reaction to the icon Frankie had inadvertently purchased.

"It's high risk," said Frankie, stiffening her resolve, "but it's the only way we have of finding out what the scam is—and whether it's linked to Don and Scarpio. The gallery's open today, even though it's Sunday. People are in a relaxed mood, perfect for buying art."

"We don't have much choice," agreed Penelope reluctantly. "We also told Reyssens we wanted to go to the gallery. But if the police see us, we'll have to say that we've come to make sure they realise it wasn't Nina who died in the fire."

"OK. At the gallery, if Gilles isn't there I reckon we should find a place to leave the icon without telling anyone. The fewer people know about this the better."

"How will we do that?"

"I'll create a diversion," said Frankie.

Penelope knew it was a dangerous move to have Frankie take the lead, but it was hard to argue against her logic.

Half an hour later, fuelled by two almond croissants each, they were on the road to Avignon again. The icon was in a bag from a dress shop, wrapped in tissue paper.

※

THEY WENT straight to the gallery. Across the street, a couple of police officers were packing away the tent and tape from around Nina's studio. To Penelope's great relief, there was no sign of Reyssens.

They passed a number of black canvases stacked on the floor in the entrance. A couple of browsers wandered around quietly. Gilles's foppish young assistant, Alexis, today wearing tortoiseshell glasses and a tweed jacket with burgundy corduroy trousers, was on the phone behind a sleek black desk. "He's due back tomorrow. Paris. I'm not sure. Check with Sergei. Speak soon." He looked up as he replaced the handset. "*Bonjour.* How can I help you? Ah, Mme Kee—"

Frankie parked her not inconsiderable behind on the desk. "Good morning! I have come to buy lots of lovely paintings for my new house in Gordes. Do you actually sell them here or just dream about it?"

She had his full attention.

"Of course, madame, allow me . . . what exactly was it that you were looking for?"

"Big paintings. Very, very big. With subtlety and intensity and an understanding of form and history. And good investments!"

"My good friend, Mme Turner-Blake," said Penelope by way of introduction.

The assistant assumed an obsequious manner. He got to his feet, almost bowing in front of the light-refracting blouse that faced him, and smiled ingratiatingly.

"In that case, madame, I am sure you have made the right decision to come here . . ."

Frankie was into her stride. "I must say, as a British woman with Scottish ancestry, that is a most elegant Harris tweed jacket you are wearing, extremely good quality and in perfect taste— not always easy for the young to achieve."

It was the first Penelope had heard of any Scottish antecedents.

"Now," Frankie schmoozed, "I want you to come and help me select some pictures. I have an extremely large house, with plenty of wall space." She avoided catching Penelope's eye as she steered the assistant towards the largest of Nicolas Versanne's paintings.

While Frankie tied him in knots of art history and modern technique and provenance and started to haggle over prices in a teasing kind of way, Penelope wandered to the back of the gallery, where the Doncaster collection splashed crude colour on the walls. None of them were on wood. All had a shiny acrylic quality, but when she touched one, the paint was hard. It would have been difficult to scratch the surface off any of these.

From the back of the room, unobserved, Penelope made sure she located the closed-circuit TV cameras she knew would be mounted on the walls.

When Frankie linked arms with the diminutive assistant and towed him into the next room, Penelope made her way casually

back to the desk. She cast an eye over the few papers and cata-
logues strewn across the top, but these didn't yield much of interest.

Laughter from her friend pinpointed her location out of sight,
and allowed Penelope to nose around undisturbed. Having seen
the layout of his Nice gallery, she reckoned Gilles might well
have a locked room here for art he was storing and dealing below
the line. Ideally, that was where she would leave Frankie's icon,
hidden in plain sight among the others.

She sat down on the chair next to the desk. That shouldn't
appear too odd, if she was caught on film, as there was no other
seat available. Just under the lip of the desk hung two keys on a
ring. Penelope resisted the temptation to grab them. She got up
and searched for the door to the staff office. There had to be one.
Frankie's chatter echoed through the gallery. The browsers had
left. They were the only people there.

The walls of the foyer exhibition space were filled with paintings, including a spectacular abstract Versanne that made Penelope think of a storm-filled valley. She could not find any lock
or piece of furniture that the key would open. She went into the
second room. It was more promising: on the right was the outline of a door that presumably opened with a sharp push. The
video security cameras were trained on the art on display, not a
staff door. If Frankie kept the assistant out of the way for a while
in the back of the gallery, she might be able to try it.

On cue, they reappeared. The assistant was holding a sheet
of red sticky dots, some of which had clearly been used. He was
smiling broadly.

"And now, we're going to go and have a little drinkie and discuss prices," said Frankie, winking at Penelope. "I'm sure that
some satisfying compromises can be found, on both sides, over a
bottle of champagne, don't you?"

"But madame," said the young man, "I regret I cannot leave the gallery! M. de Bourdan is not here. I am in sole charge."

"Would he want you to miss making a spectacular bulk sale, young monsieur? Think how your star will rise when he returns to find you have sold a number of Versannes and a Scarpio! It's a habit I've developed, when I make a major purchase, to drink champagne while the filthy business of money is settled."

Disappointment and frustration crushed his pretty features. "Is there any chance you could come back tomorrow when he should have returned?"

"Sadly not. I fly to Malaga for a party, and then on to Paris for a business meeting with my interior designers. It's now or never."

A battle waged on the assistant's face.

"I tell you what. Penny here can mind the shop whilst you take me to that nice bar at the end of the street. Have you been very busy this morning?"

"Well, not really."

"There you are, then."

The ambitious youth pushed out his chest and unhunched his shoulders. "I would be honoured, madame."

As they exited, Penelope simultaneously put her bag on the desk and reached down for the keys hanging there, hoping her sleight of hand would fool the video security system. She reckoned she had a minimum of twenty minutes.

She locked the front door, turned the sign to read "Closed," and hurried through to the second room. A strong push, and the staff door opened.

Penelope found herself in a small lobby. As expected, one door led to a bathroom, and another to a kitchenette. In a third was the keyhole she was seeking. Penelope tried the key. It turned with a well-oiled click, and the door swung open to reveal a small, dark room.

She stood in the doorway and fumbled for the light switch. Suddenly she was in a jewelled cavern. Angelic faces, saints, and the haloed Christ with the Virgin Mary gazed back at her, offering her the benediction of their smiles. On the floor more paintings were stacked, both icons and a number of black canvases that looked like they were by Scarpio.

Quickly, Penelope removed the icon smeared with the remains of its acrylic overpainting from the dress shop bag and slotted it into the stack.

Against one wall, under overflowing bookshelves holding loose papers and rows of box files, was a working desk. It was a lot less sleek than the one out front, with two columns of well-scuffed drawers. She pulled open the first drawer. She would scribble a private note for Gilles, "innocently" letting him know what she had done. He had to find the picture.

None of the drawers was locked.

The top two were filled with the usual invoices, letters, and catalogue drafts. No stationery. She would have to write on the back of one of the invoices. But at the bottom of the third drawer she found a sheaf of writing paper and a packet of envelopes, wedged in tight at the back. With a bit of gentle pulling Penelope managed to free the envelopes. The drawer was only half as deep as the others; she knew exactly what it was. Sure enough, running her fingers against the back of the drawer, she found the catch.

Curiosity had often been Penelope's undoing. But just as often, it had proved invaluable. She opened the hidden compartment and extracted some paper. The first was an invoice for a large quantity of wood panelling. Specifically, antique wood panelling. From a church in Manosque. The delivery address was Scarpio's mill near Reillane.

Had Gilles bought the wood panelling for Scarpio? Was it an

investment in an artist he believed in, who was poor as a church mouse? She took a photo of the invoice and replaced it.

The second piece of paperwork was a letter about an icon. The French was too complicated to puzzle over and time was of the essence. So she took a shot of that, too. She replaced everything carefully, wrote the note to Gilles, and left it prominently on the desk.

Checking that all the drawers were tightly closed, she eased herself out from behind the desk. She jumped when her phone pinged with an incoming text.

"On our way back."

Penelope moved quickly, reaching the black desk out front and placing the key back in its hiding place not a moment too soon. Through the glass frontage she could see Frankie and the assistant walking down the street. Frankie stopped and pointed upwards, forcing the assistant to take note of a roof or some architectural detailing. Penelope made it to the door and unlocked it just in time. Frankie sailed through the entrance like a battleship, threw off her coat, and plonked herself down on the chair. "I thought I drank fast, but I met my match there," she hissed to Penelope.

"You know, I am being rather naughty, Alexis darling. I ought to check with my wealth manager before I settle up for my wonderful purchases. I'll email him. Do you mind if I use your computer? Don't suppose there's any chance of a cup of coffee?"

"You'll go too far, one day," whispered Penelope.

But the youth had clearly fallen under Frankie's spell. He left the room through the door Penelope had recently exited, presumably to start the coffee machine.

"Did you find anything?" whispered Frankie. "Gilles is on his way back. Alexis got a text from him after the first glass. That's why we had to hurry back. I was rather enjoying myself. I've still got it, Pen, if you know what I mean."

"Thank God for that," said Penelope. "That Gilles is on his way, I mean. When's he expected?"

"Any moment now. Gosh, this is quite exciting," said Frankie. "I'm going to have to do a runner. Don't *really* want to have to buy twenty-five thousand euros worth of Versannes with an option on a Scarpio. You'll have to make my excuses."

"What? Frankie!"

But Frankie was already striding out of the gallery. She turned left and disappeared.

As if on cue, the assistant arrived back in the room bearing two cups of coffee.

"I am sorry, Alexis, isn't it? Madame has been called away. Urgent business matter. She'll be back shortly. In the meantime I would love to hear about your experience working here at the gallery with Gilles. Have you been here long?"

"About a year," said Alexis.

"Do you enjoy it?"

"Very much."

"Do you get involved with the artists at all?"

"How do you mean?" He seemed a bit nervous, as if he was finally working out that two eccentric middle-aged Englishwomen were taking him for a ride. "Please don't tell Gilles that I left the gallery," he begged her.

"Don't worry, I won't."

He clearly wasn't convinced.

"I think Gilles has more important issues to deal with," she said. "Did he say why he was coming back earlier than planned?" She assumed it was because the police had called him after Nina—or rather, the body—was found in the burnt-out studio, but she wanted to hear it spoken out loud.

Alexis shook his head. He looked worried.

"Terrible business with Nina Chiroubles," Penelope volunteered.

"Indeed."

"Have the police spoken to you about her?"

The door buzzed as it opened.

Penelope felt a burst of quiet annoyance as Alexis straightened his posture and turned away to greet the potential customer.

Then she saw who it was, and caught her breath.

Gilles de Bourdan looked haggard, as if he had been travelling without sleep for several days and nights. Deep hollows and shadows accentuated the momentary look of horror that crossed his face as he registered Penelope's presence.

33

FRANKIE'S ICON WAS PROPPED UP on the desk. Under the saint's serene scrutiny, Penelope sat with Gilles in the small back room. He seemed to have aged ten years, and it was clear that he had more important matters on his mind than a hidden icon and its peculiar provenance. She had so many questions, but she knew she couldn't rush them.

For now, Gilles was the one who wanted answers.

"Have you heard about Nina? Do they know how the fire started? Was it arson?"

Penelope tried to remain comforting and calm. "I was here yesterday, and saw the aftermath. They don't know yet how it started. The police told me Nina had been trapped inside, but . . ."

Gilles put his head in his hands. The latest blow seemed to have brought him close to breaking. She felt for him, then reminded herself of all the reasons not to trust him. But he was not faking this exhaustion and horror. Whatever he was involved in, he was no threat to her—not in this state.

"I don't know whether we can talk here," said Penelope, thinking of the security devices. "But there's something you should know about Nina."

He straightened up with a jolt. "What have you found out now?"

"Not here."

"No, you're right. I need some air. Come with me."

Alexis shot Penelope a plea for discretion as Gilles informed his assistant that they were popping out. Gilles took a long, hard look at the burnt-out building across the street before they walked slowly away from the gallery.

After a while, he offered her his arm and she took it. Penelope felt she was almost supporting him as they negotiated the spider-web of streets leading into the centre of the city, past towers and churches and defensive walls, windowless cliffs of stone. Penelope noticed the iron bars on railings and balconies and ground-floor windows, the sense of secrets enclosed and centuries of hard lives. And then the sun caught a façade unexpectedly, and its beauty dazzled. Avignon was a cruel and unusual city, Penelope remembered reading somewhere.

Something cruel and unusual had happened to Gilles, she was sure of it. Was it because he thought Nina was dead, or did he know something else? Was Nina right about Russian criminals—was he in fear of them? He certainly seemed scared enough. She started to say something, and he shook his head. "Wait."

So they walked on, saying nothing, through hidden court-yards, half in shadow, to corners that concealed the narrow access through an archway into another square as they went deeper into the maze. The biting wind strengthened, whipping up the leaves fallen from the plane trees.

"Where are we going, Gilles?"

"Not far now."

They came out into the huge empty square. On one side the Palais des Papes, sheer and rock-solid, reared up into the heavens from the cobbles.

"Up here."

They were climbing towards the top of the city walls. Penelope was surprised he had the energy. He opened an iron gate into a garden of trees and shrubs. "You first," he said.

A sign announced the Rocher des Doms.

Gilles seemed to relax fractionally as they took a path through the park. Penelope dug her hands into her coat pockets and took a deep breath. She still wasn't sure she should risk trusting him. "You cannot ask me how I know this. But the body in the studio was not Nina."

He stopped abruptly and turned to her. "Not Nina? Are you sure? There's no mistake about that?"

"I am sure."

He took a few moments to process this, then gave a strange choking sigh. Was it relief, or something infinitely more complicated? "But then why are the police saying it was Nina who died in the fire?"

Penelope shook her head. "I cannot say."

"If it wasn't Nina, who was it?"

"I don't know," she said.

A loaded pause.

"Why did you come today, Penny?"

"I told you. The picture. The icon underneath."

"You didn't know I would be here."

"I was hoping you would be," said Penelope, businesslike.

"Tell me again, where did you get it from?"

"A shop in Lourmarin. I'd like to say it was a great spot by Frankie, but she was actually drawn by the dog. It looked like a substandard Doncaster. Which took some doing. Then I saw it was signed DD. Which was strange because the Doncasters I saw at the exhibition were signed RD, Roland Doncaster."

Gilles hunched further inside his coat.

"So it was an obvious imitation Doncaster, to someone who knew what they were looking at." She was prodding him, trying to gauge his reaction. She had to know whether Nina was credible about the icon business and its fallout.

Still he said nothing.

Penelope took a flyer. "The Russians don't mess about when something goes wrong, do they?"

A jolt seemed to pass through Gilles. "You are a brave woman, Penelope Kite," he said.

Their eyes met.

"You push on, don't you, even though you have doubts about me."

She nodded weakly.

"I have done some bad things, and I will pay for those," said Gilles. "But you must believe me when I say that you have to trust me now."

How uncomfortably close these words were to Nina's the previous night. "I am sorry you had to find out about the Russian icons. I wish I had never got involved in the first place. I did not appreciate until it was too late that it was not a pastime that could be enjoyed, then put aside and forgotten."

She had no idea what he was talking about, only that she ought to look as if she did.

Gilles began walking again. "I went to Moscow for the first time in the early nineties to finish my studies. That's when I began buying icons. After glasnost, everything was for sale—everyone needed money. At first I bought them to study, then their values increased. I began dealing in these works. It was simple enough to find the icons in Russia. The problem has always been getting them out of the country."

"By painting over them."

"Exactly. We would take an 'exhibition' of Scarpio and Doncaster to Russia, dispose of the originals somewhere and then come back with icons painted in the style of Scarpio and Doncaster."

"Why those two?"

"Well, Scarpio's paintings aren't exactly difficult to copy, as long as you have enough black paint. And Doncaster was easy to replicate—his style was so dreadful." He started laughing. "It's quite funny, *non*? The terrible art hiding the masterpiece!"

"But you didn't let Don in on this little secret."

"No. He was an honourable man. He would never have sanctioned it. We told him his paintings had been sold." Gilles paused. "When supplies of icons dried up, I produced some of my own. Most people never knew the difference."

She tried to make sense of it all without interrupting. Was Frankie's icon real or fake?

"I was good. I used authentic period paint and centuries-old wood."

Penelope shivered. Another piece of the puzzle dropped into place. "And Scarpio helped you get the wood, didn't he."

"He used to buy it from reclamation. It was working well until the idiot got greedy and branched out on his own."

"What, the thefts from churches?"

Gilles grimaced and swallowed some French swearword.

"I should have known from his record that he was not to be trusted. But Don didn't tell me that when he introduced us, at least not at first. Scarpio was a thief. He stole a couple of genuine icons and sold them himself, claiming to be an associate of mine. Trouble is, he stole fakes, too—he couldn't tell the difference."

"And you don't mess with the Russians . . . could they have killed Scarpio?"

They reached a point where they could see the Rhône and the famous half-bridge below. Gilles seemed to focus on the water. "I wouldn't be surprised."

A pause.

"So Don didn't know about your other business," said Penelope.

"Not until fairly recently."

"You mean, shortly before he died?"

Silence.

Gilles abruptly marched on in the direction of a large pond from which a bronze statue of Venus rose, attended by swans, ducks, and carp. Penelope skittered after him.

"This is dangerous. You do understand that?"

"The Russians?"

"You can leave the Russians to me," said Gilles grimly. "I know how to deal with them."

Penelope hesitated, but knew she had to ask. "At the Marseille airport. You said you were taking a flight to St Petersburg, but where were you really going?"

Gilles exhaled. "I wasn't going anywhere. I was hoping to meet a Russian contact who was flying in from Paris. I was going to try to enlist his support. But the guy never showed up."

Two bars of electronic samba music burst from the depths of Penelope's bag.

"My phone, sorry." She dug out her phone. "Hi, Frankie."

"Where are you, darling? I've been hanging around for ages in the bar where we went with Reyssens."

"I'm with Gilles, in a park above the bridge."

"How long are you going to be?"

"Not long. Bear with me, this is important." She stuffed the phone back in her bag and turned back towards Gilles. "I should get back. Frankie is waiting."

"I'll take you on a short cut."

They descended to the battlements of the old city walls. From this vantage point, the slate-grey expanse of the Rhône moved magisterially.

"You must listen to me, Penny. Go home and stay there."

"But why?"

"You ask too many questions."

"But—"

"So did Don."

Penelope's mind fizzed. "Nina is scared they are coming for her now," she said. It was beginning to make sense, though all the connections were still tenuous. And dependent on whether Gilles was telling the whole truth.

"Well, she would say that," he said quietly. "If Nina is still alive, she's the dangerous one." He seemed almost to be speaking to himself.

"Why do you say that?"

He didn't reply.

Was he still convinced that Nina had killed Don? She wondered whether she should tell him about the sleeping pills Nina had admitted to administering. But she buttoned her lip. Gilles could be lying. Or was Nina the liar?

"It's Nicolas I'm worried about," said Gilles. "And Claudine, of course."

"Why?"

But they had reached the brasserie where Frankie was waiting. She loomed colourfully behind the glass.

"Go home, Penny," repeated Gilles, quickly taking his leave.

34

"GILLES THINKS NINA IS DANGEROUS." Penelope exhaled deeply. "But I still don't know . . ."

She and Frankie were back at Le Chant d'Eau. As a measure of the seriousness of the situation, lunch had been forgotten.

"You should have called the police last night, Pen. Who knows where Nina is now, and what she's up to."

"But who is telling the truth?"

"Nina convinced you she was, last night," said Frankie. "She almost had me convinced, too."

"What d'you mean, almost?"

"She's a very odd mixture, that one. She gives off an aggressive strong-woman vibe, then she crumples into a weepy one. Seems a bit contradictory."

Penelope had to admit that was exactly what Nina was like, thinking of the time they'd talked at the encampment.

"Nina might just be a bit dippy, of course," Frankie went on. "Doesn't necessarily mean anything."

Penelope ran her hands over her face. "Gilles has always thought that Nina killed Don. She was at the hospital not long before Don died. She told me herself. Monique, the nurse, all but confirmed it, too. Two women in arty clothes, she said. One of them must have been Nina."

"What's wrong with that?"

Frankie whistled after Penelope explained what Camrose had said about how water or air could kill if injected, mimicking death from natural causes, or an existing malady.

"So why did Gilles say that the people he was most worried about were Nicolas and Claudine?"

"He didn't say. Hang on a minute! At the gallery. Before Gilles came back. I found something in his back office. It clean went out of my mind."

"Told you you should get HRT, you'd be amazed how——"

But Penelope wasn't listening. She pulled out her phone and found the photos she had taken. "This is an invoice." She held it out. "Wood panels . . . from a church in Manosque. The delivery address is Scarpio's mill near Reillane."

"So what?"

"I think Gilles used the panels to paint fake icons. But this is the important one."

The other photo she'd taken was rather blurred. Penelope couldn't immediately read the tiny font, but as she enlarged it, bit by bit, the letter and its subject matter became clearer. She handed it to Frankie, who read it out, translating as she went.

Dear Sir,

I am writing to advise you that I expect immediate recompense for the Madonna and Child purchased from you in Nice on 23 March 2018. I was advised to check the authenticity of the work for the company that insures the works for my buyers in Russia. I sent it for analysis to M. N Versanne, an expert in historic paints. He has recently replied, stating that certain of the pigments in the painting are of a type more modern than the suggested date of the picture. It is in his view extremely unlikely to be an original. I do not wish to know if this was an error on your part or fraud by your associate

M. Scarpio with whom the deal was concluded, but I require compensation immediately, or this matter will be referred to my lawyers.

They locked stares.

"Nicolas was working on official authentications, using his knowledge of historic paints to prove suspicions about fake icons . . . he will have papers in his office, or perhaps kept at the museum . . . perhaps that's what Gilles meant," said Penelope.

"So he was telling the truth about that, then." Frankie tapped her magenta-coloured fingernails on the table. "That's it," she said. "You *have* to tell the police about Nina."

"I know." Penelope leapt up. "I need to go and see Claudine now to warn her."

"I'm coming with you."

"No. I want you to call the police in Avignon and tell them about Nina coming here. Say whatever you have to say to get me off the hook, that you're calling because your French is so much better than mine, that . . . I don't know . . . you'll think of something brilliant."

"It's bloody well going to have to be," grumbled Frankie.

"I know you will rise to the challenge."

Penelope raced out of the door to the Range Rover. She pulled out her mobile whilst steering the car out the front gate, veering to the left and right as she tried to push the right buttons. The phone started ringing and a voice answered.

"Bonjour, this is Claudine Versanne. I cannot answer your call at the . . ."

"Bugger!" shouted Penelope as she steered onto the main road. "Claudine. Call the police immediately. You are in danger. Don't let anyone in. I'm on my way. It's Penny."

She threw the phone onto the passenger seat and addressed herself to the road.

❧

PENELOPE'S DRIVING was positively Provençal-*vite* as she sped along the valley road to Roussillon. The sky was monochrome, heavy with the threat of snow. The red cliffs of Roussillon hove into view, duller and more forbidding now in the flat winter light, less a ruby in a sea of green than a rocky island buffeted by stormy waves. She took the bend before the museum too fast and almost came off the road. She decelerated and turned, shaking, into the car park. The path down to the watercourse was still barred by police tape and no-entry signs. There were few other cars. She walked briskly to the main building.

"I'd like to see Mme Versanne, please," she told the woman at the ticket desk. "It's a personal matter."

The assistant reacted with insouciance. Madame was in a meeting, and might be some time.

"I'll wait," said Penelope firmly.

"As you like."

There was nowhere to sit, so Penelope wandered into the shop. Ten minutes later, feeling ever more anxious, she went back to the foyer. There was no one at the desk.

Penelope made her way over to the door of Claudine's office. She listened, and when she heard nothing, she pushed it open.

The room was dark. There was a PowerPoint presentation on the screen at the end of a table. Of Claudine there was no sign. As Penelope's eyes adjusted to the dark, she realised that someone else was already there. A figure rose from the far end of the darkness.

"Penny!"

"Gilles!"

"I told you to stay at home . . . but it seems we both had the same thought."

"Where is she?"

"Claudine has been called away to deal with some problem. They said she could be a while, but at least she's safe."

Penelope sat down, feeling the wind drop from her sails. If Gilles was already here to warn Claudine about Nina, or the Russians, then there was no point in her interference. But she wanted to see this through.

"I had a quick look at the icon you left at the gallery," said Gilles. He looked even more drawn than before.

"You didn't need to do that. There was no urgency."

"It's very interesting," he said. "All the indications are that it is eighteenth century, in the Minsk style."

"There must have been some reason why it was covered in acrylic paint."

Gilles's face was in shadow so she couldn't see the haunted resignation on it. But she heard it in his voice. "It must have been stolen. By Scarpio, I would guess."

"Nicolas's expertise in analysing and verifying old pictures was often used by insurance companies, wasn't it?" Penelope was grasping the nettle, not even sure herself where she was going with it.

"That's true."

Gilles shifted in his seat. It was hard to see his expression in the dim light. "Did you show him that picture you brought for me to examine?"

"No. Frankie only bought it last Friday."

A light was blinking on the phone on the desk. Had Claudine actually heard her message? Where *was* Claudine?

Penelope felt the temperature drop. What if Gilles had heard it? Sickeningly, she was now certain she could not trust him.

"Why don't you go home, Penny?"

"I must see Claudine first."

"I am worried about her, too. Let's go see if we can find her."

The reception area was deserted.

"Claudine?" shouted Penelope.

No answer.

They went outside into the chill. All her instincts were screaming that she had to prevent another dreadful event from occurring. She looked up the hillside. At the top of the watercourse stood a slim figure in silhouette.

"Claudine!" Penelope shouted.

Penelope followed Gilles as he ran along the path. The figure was no longer in view.

Then Gilles pulled up abruptly where the land dropped away to a red ochre void. Heart in mouth, she scurried over to see for herself what had stopped him in his tracks.

35

SHE DID NOT SEE THE blow coming. A sharp pain erupted on the side of her head, and she was stumbling with flashes of light in her vision. Dazed, she felt her cheek. It was wet and warm. There was blood on her hand. Then she was hit again, and the world started to drain away into darkness.

The next moment—or was it longer?—she was being dragged roughly by her arms, heels scraping across the ground. Her shoulders hurt. Then the back of her head hit something hard as her attacker let go.

She saw red earth and pine trees overhead, and panicked. Then, as she came round fully, she realised, terrified, where she was. Far too close, the land dropped away. Gilles was standing a few metres in front of her. She cursed herself for misjudging him.

"What's going on?" The ground seemed to tilt as Penelope cried out.

"Get up!"

She winced as she lifted her head towards Gilles. What could she say to him to make him see reason? Her arms were leaden as she tried to push herself into a sitting position.

"I said, get up!" The same voice came from behind her.

"No, Alexis!" cried Gilles.

Penelope managed to wrench her head round far enough to see Gilles's assistant standing over her. In his raised arm was a heavy metal wrench. If he brought it down with enough force, he could smash her skull in an instant.

Alexis seemed to weigh his next move, and then slowly and a little reluctantly he lowered the wrench to the ground. "You are right, Bourdan. Far better to make it look like an accident, an unlucky fall from the cliffs in the dark."

Penelope saw Gilles move towards her. Instinctively she curled into a ball.

"Stay away from her, Alexis. She's not part of this. You will just make more trouble if you do anything to her."

Gilles continued slowly towards Penelope, his hands out-stretched.

"Penny, I did not know—"

He was only a pace away when a muffled shot exploded from the shadows. Gilles staggered back, one hand rising to his shoulder.

"Nobody move!"

Penelope froze. This was a woman's voice. With an accent she recognised.

A slight, black-clad figure emerged from the shadows of the pine trees. Gilles turned away, still gripping his shoulder with one hand. Penelope saw the other hand move to the inside of his jacket.

"I said, nobody move!" Anya stepped out of the gloom. "Alexis, take his gun."

Alexis moved round to Gilles and extracted a small revolver from his boss's breast pocket.

Penelope watched dumbstruck as Fenella Doncaster's young assistant coolly asserted her authority. Gilles did not seem sur-prised. His reaction was one of resignation mingled with con-tempt.

"On your knees—over there, with her!" commanded Anya.

Gilles slowly obeyed. "What have you done with Claudine?"

he rasped as he sank down awkwardly, still clutching his right shoulder. Blood was seeping through his fingers.

Penelope instinctively put her hand out to steady him.

The pistol Anya held was pointed directly at Gilles. It had a silencer attached. Very professional, thought Penelope, as she struggled to sit up.

"Claudine knows where Nicolas is, doesn't she?" said Anya.

Silence.

"She doesn't," said Gilles. "No one knows where Nicolas is."

"But that's not true is it, Gilles? You know exactly where Nicolas is." Anya's pretty face was set and utterly ruthless. "Tell me where he is."

Gilles was sweating profusely. Beads of perspiration stood out on his forehead, and his hair was damp. "How should I know where Nicolas is?"

Penelope's legs felt as if they were made of cotton wool. She closed her eyes as she tried again to raise herself up. She felt a weight on her shoulder and almost screamed with pain as she was pushed back down on the ground.

"You stay where you are," ordered Alexis.

"Because you were there when Scarpio was killed," said Anya to Gilles. "When you and Nicolas killed Scarpio."

Gilles's breathing was heavy. It filled the still air.

"Scarpio was told to deal with the Nicolas problem. What were you doing there?" Anya demanded coldly.

Penelope tried to read Gilles's expression as, piece by piece, fragments of events aligned. He gave nothing away.

"Instead, Scarpio is found dead. Nicolas vanishes," Anya went on impatiently when he did not reply. Perhaps she was more nervous than she looked, thought Penelope. "And you go to Paris to see our Russian friends. Over our heads. But you've left a mess, haven't you? Your so-called protectors are no longer as powerful as they were. New blood has taken over, like me and—" she glanced at Alexis. "And you didn't even realise—none of you did."

"Don realised." Gilles finally spoke. "And he told Nina."

"Poor Nina, such a silly girl," sneered Anya. "The amateur poisoner. I saw her in the act, crushing up sleeping pills at the studio in Ménerbes. My brief was always to watch Don Doncaster, to make sure he didn't know what his paintings were being used for, wasn't it? But in the end, Nina was extremely useful. Weakening Don with the pills was a great help. I had hoped to administer the final coup de grâce with the arsenic on the olives, but Don was always a bit more energetic than I gave him credit for."

"You'd know that, wouldn't you!"

Anya did not smile. "Try not to anger me. It will not make much difference to your end, but it might hasten it."

Another ratchet in Penelope's mind clicked into place. Despite her aching head, she had a sudden burst of clarity. Or rather, she knew something for certain, if she could only be sure what it was.

Don. The hospital. It was Anya who finished Don off in the hospital. Disguised with a headscarf so as to pass for Nina or Fenella. What did she use—water or air? Penelope was not daft enough to ask the question out loud. While all the attention was on Gilles, in the gathering darkness Penelope managed to push herself up. She thought about trying to activate her phone but there was no way to do it where she was without being seen. She had to find the strength to get to her feet again. She was almost there.

Alexis was too quick for her. He grabbed her and lurched towards the edge of the cliff. It occurred to Penelope, in a distant, depersonalised way, that the only reason they were discussing murder in front of her was that they did not expect her to be able to tell anyone afterwards. No one knew exactly where they were.

Not Claudine. Not Frankie. Her legs trembled. She couldn't have run, even if there had been anywhere to run to.

"Was it you two who set the fire at the studio?" asked Gilles in a weakening voice. He had to have medical help soon.

No response.

"But you didn't manage to get Nina, did you?" said Gilles. Was he playing his only ace?

Alexis's grip tightened; he was holding her like a vice. It might have been all that was keeping her upright.

"What do you mean?" Anya's poker face cracked. "Who was inside, then?" She brought up her other hand to steady the revolver.

"You don't even know, do you?" said Gilles. "It wasn't Nina."

He looked to Penelope for corroboration.

"Don't play games with me, Gilles," said Anya.

"If it wasn't Nina, who was it then?" asked Alexis, mockingly.

From the trees behind them came a new voice.

"It was Fenella. She wears the same kind of clothes that I do. I can see why you might confuse us."

Nina stepped out of the shadows. "She had just found out about the wedding in Thailand and knew what that would mean financially for her. I think she came to the studio to confront me. I had slipped out the back, but you didn't know that." She squared up to Anya. "You thought she was me."

Anya gave a thin laugh. "Try proving that!"

"I'm right, aren't I!" cried Nina. She looked as if she had barely slept since the previous evening. "The icon scam . . . the only part Don got wrong was that he never suspected *you* were involved. But it was your rotten art crimes"—she shouted at Gilles—"That's what got him killed! We were just your cover story, weren't we? You didn't have to believe in our work. It was better you didn't! The real business was your trade in

Russian icons. You took Scarpio and Don's paintings to Russia
for exhibitions, you junked them when they didn't sell, and then
painted over valuable icons with imitations of what had been
in the show to bring back to France. Scarpio's were even easier than Don's—all you had to do was splash black paint over
them! Couldn't get much easier, but then when Don started asking questions—"

Anya extended her gun with the silencer. Penelope's heart
lurched as she saw that Nina hadn't counted on that.

The girl cocked her revolver and looked at it almost apolo-
getically. "Such is the way of the world that I can't do business
without one. Now walk, that's right, over to her, the inquisitive
Englishwoman, by the edge. You, too, Bourdan."

The vertiginous drop where the roots of the vegetation lost
their hold was dizzying. Pillars and twisted funnels rose above
them. Below, the hollowed red cliff face was an open wound on
the landscape.

Penelope was hardly more than a metre from the edge. She
could go no further.

"Stunning, don't you think?" said Alexis.

"Penelope, I'm sorry. This is all my fault," said Gilles next to
her. "I should have chucked it in much earlier, but stopping
becomes more and more difficult . . ."

Penelope didn't speak.

"It was all fine as a sideline with Scarpio until this lot got
involved. I lost control. I didn't want to do it anymore. I had no
idea until a few days ago that Alexis had been planted on me to
hold me to my commitments."

"You killed Scarpio," spat Alexis.

Gilles did not deny it. "He was going to kill Nicolas. I had no
choice."

Anya stepped up to him. "I ask you again, where is Nicolas?"

"He is safe," said Gilles. "No matter what you do, I will never—"

One shot. Then another.

All of a sudden the sun came out. Or so it seemed. Hands flailing above his head, Gilles stood for a second, haloed like one of the saints in his icons, then fell backwards into the brightness. For a split second he seemed to hang in the air. Then he was gone.

Penelope was bathed in light. It was all around her. Of course, it's not the sun, she thought groggily, I am about to meet my maker. It's celestial.

The light intensified. The ground began to throb.

It was only then that she registered the pulsing clatter of rotor blades. A helicopter rounded a column in the sandstone and hovered, spotlight fixed on the quartet standing so precariously close to the edge of the cliff.

They froze, blinded by the light, as a voice issued from a megaphone.

"Step away from the edge now!"

"She's got a gun!" cried Nina.

"We have you covered. Put down the gun and lie on the ground, Mlle Kulikova."

There were more figures in the wood now, creeping towards the group. Dark-clothed and stealthy, they moved with purpose.

Anya and Alexis looked around wildly, searching for an escape route. But they were surrounded. Moments later, Claudine ran towards Nina, and Penelope was wrestled flat on the ground as two strong, sequin-encrusted arms flung themselves around her. "Thank God you're OK, Pen!"

36

IN THE MORNING SUN, THE roofs of the outbuildings at Le Chant d'Eau shimmered silver-white. The hillside was covered in coarse frost. It was Penelope's first winter scene, and it was beautiful. Standing by her bedroom window, she did some star jumps to warm herself up. Perhaps Swedish army exercises would prove the answer to survival until March in a cold stone house. Then she stopped abruptly.

Gilles was dead. Remembering the long night talking to the police, the hours of explaining to Chief of Police Reyssens exactly what she had found out, who had told her what and when, and accounting for every action she had taken in the previous weeks, she felt for the dressings on her head and her swollen black eye. Perhaps the bump on her head had affected her short-term memory.

Penelope slunk back into bed. The painkillers she'd been given must have been strong. Her head was numb. Gradually she recalled being taken to the hospital in Apt, Frankie loudly accusing Reyssens of being more interested in interrogating her than her well-being.

Frankie was here to look after her. She had talked of extending her stay. Penelope wasn't sure she would be able to take the pace of the kind of recuperation her friend had in mind. She closed her eyes and slept again until eleven.

When Penelope eventually went downstairs, the woodburner emitted a cheerful, well-fed heat and a sumptuous brunch was arrayed on the kitchen table. Her best friend had been shopping again, having walked up to the village in an old pair of M. Charpet's gardening boots.

The branches of the trees in the courtyard dripped pearls as the frost melted. They were just discussing thermal underwear— were French thermals any sexier than British ones?—when there was a knock at the door.

It was Laurent, with an enormous bunch of flowers. He was full of apologies, asking how she was, hoping she was not too badly hurt or shaken up. If Penelope hadn't known better, she might have thought the supremely confident mayor of St Merlot was a little flustered.

"I'm fine, really," said Penelope. She buried her face in the bouquet of amaryllis, camellias, and casablanca lilies, to avoid showing how touched she was.

"I can still hardly believe what happened, how brave you were—if a little reckless!" went on Laurent. "And Gilles de Bourdan . . . what a terrible thing to happen, a terrible thing for you to see . . ."

Penelope nodded. There was nothing she could say to that. She still hadn't processed what she felt about Gilles, the shock of seeing him shot in front of her, the uncomfortable sorrow bound up in the feeling that he was not quite the irredeemable villain he had been painted.

"Why didn't you call me?" asked Laurent.

But they both knew why.

Her eye had puffed up into a real shiner, and the ache when the painkillers wore off was excrutiating. She turned her head to the side so she could hide the worst of the bruise from him. "I'm sorry if I was insensitive when Nicolas went missing. Everything seemed completely unreal that morning at the museum. I didn't know about your daughter's accident."

Laurent nodded, then smiled broadly. "Reyssens did tell you, didn't he?"

"Tell me what?"

"That the police found Nicolas!"

"What? No!" chorused Penelope and Frankie.

"Yes! He was in Gilles's strongroom at the Nice gallery. He'd been there for weeks—for his own safety. It was Gilles's way of protecting him."

"Oh, my giddy aunt," said Penelope, feeling rather giddy herself. "That is good news."

Laurent sat down at the table next to her. "I spoke to him this morning. Gilles saved him from Scarpio, the night of the concert in Roussillon."

"Gilles killed Scarpio," said Penelope. "But only to save Nicolas. He said so last night. How is Nicolas now, is he all right?"

"He's OK. Exhausted and shaken up, but physically fine. Relieved it's all over. It was like being in a cell for three weeks but he had food, water, even wine."

Penelope pushed away her plate, on which sat the remains of a croissant.

"You found out about Scarpio first," Laurent said. "Everyone else had accepted him at face value."

"Scarpio starts as Gilles's framer and carpenter," said Penelope, thinking aloud. "He helps Gilles get the old wood he needs for his forgeries. But he overreaches himself. He steals a couple of icons and sells them on. Some of them, unfortunately, are Gilles's fakes. Scarpio doesn't know the subtleties. He mucks up the whole business by trying to pass on the wrong icons to the wrong people. He also resorts to stolen antique wood instead of acquiring it discreetly and legitimately.

"Gilles wanted out of the fake icon con," she continued. Her head hurt, but she was determined to wrap it all up. "But Scarpio had cut himself in and was making too much money out of it to consider stopping. And then Nicolas stirred the hornet's nest by calling out the fakes."

"How do *you* know that?" asked Laurent.

"I may have inadvertently found myself in a back room at Gilles's Avignon gallery, and, er, found myself riffling through the drawers of a desk there," she confessed. "I came across a letter that said Nicolas had been unable to authenticate an icon Scarpio had sold."

Laurent was incredulous.

"It's a long story," chirped Frankie. "Beginning with Nina returning from the dead."

Luckily he did not enquire about the chronology of that aspect.

"But we *knew* Gilles wasn't on the level before that!" Frankie blazed as urgently as her pink and orange sparkly sweater. "When I arrived at the airport he was behaving suspiciously, lying about where he was going."

"At that stage it looked as if he was keeping tabs on me," explained Penelope. "He'd already asked me to find out what I could about the circumstances around Don's death. Now I realise that he was genuine in wanting to know exactly who the murderer was—and he also needed to know whether anyone understood *why* Don had died. I'd said no, I wouldn't do any amateur detection for him, though I would pass on anything I heard. We had dinner together and we talked about the case, but we hadn't seen each other since."

"Actually, Gilles was at the airport hoping to meet a Russian contact who might have been able to help him," added Frankie.

Laurent listened thoughtfully.

"Go on, tell us what happened the night of the concert," Penelope urged him.

But a rattle of stones outside announced another car and more visitors. Frankie glittered off to the door and returned with Clémence and Claudine. Behind them, hanging back self-consciously, was Nicolas.

Penelope rose from her chair to greet them and instantly wished she had not. Her head swam and she slumped back down.

Laurent rushed over to Nicolas and clapped his arms around him.

Claudine handed Penelope an elegant box of chocolate truffles.

"You should only eat one a day!" cautioned Clémence.

"Thank you!" Penelope looked from Claudine to Nicolas. "I am very pleased indeed to see you."

Nicolas was pale and perhaps a little thinner, but otherwise looked remarkably normal. He took Penelope's hand. "Thank you. For everything."

"I didn't do much," she said.

"But you did. You kept asking questions, making connections. If you hadn't gone to see Gilles, perhaps I would still be in Nice. And if Anya and Alexis had managed to kill Gilles before your intervention, then I might still be there, unknown to anyone. It would only have been a matter of time before either they, or their associates in Nice, got to me."

They all solemnly considered that.

Claudine put her hand on his arm. "And I thank you, too, Penny. From my heart."

"Hear, hear!" cheered Frankie. "Laurent was just telling us what happened to you," she said, clearly keen to get on with the story.

They all sat down and accepted black coffees.

Laurent turned to Nicolas. "I was telling how you went to meet Gilles outside the museum the night of the concert and were ambushed by Scarpio."

Claudine shook her head. "I was so angry with him, going out again. He refused to tell me where he was going. I knew something wasn't right, but he insisted." She let out an exhausted sigh. "My poor Nicolas. And all the time I thought he had run away."

"It was dark," said Nicolas. His voice trembled slightly. "I set off for the museum car park where Gilles had insisted I meet him. He wouldn't tell me what it was about, only that it was urgent, perhaps the most important thing we would ever talk about. He told me not to tell Claudine where I was going or who I was seeing. It sounded serious, so I did what he asked.

"I arrived at the car park to find it empty. I couldn't see Gilles or his car or the gallery van. Then suddenly I was stopped—by Scarpio. He had a gun. He was going to shoot me. But first, he said, he wanted me to write a letter of authentication for an icon. He knew that I would do it, if only to give myself a chance of survival. I had no choice. We were walking towards my workshop, when there were footsteps behind us.

"It was Gilles. He brought something hard down on Scarpio. It was one of the winches from the watercourse machinery. Scarpio twisted round, and Gilles saw the gun. Gilles hit him again. The gun went off. Scarpio was wounded in the leg. Gilles hit him yet again, and Scarpio went down.

"I thought Scarpio was injured, nothing worse. I was shaken up by the fight, by the gun. Gilles told me to wait for him in the gallery van. That now I could see how serious this was. I did as I was told.

"Eventually Gilles reappeared. He was filthy and sweating. He told me he had patched up Scarpio—it was just a flesh wound—and told him either go to hospital and get himself checked over, taking the risk that questions would be asked about the fight, or to go home. Gilles had taken Scarpio's gun. He put it under his seat.

"Then Gilles told me he had a problem with 'the Russians' and admitted everything about the icon business. He was ashamed. Then he said they were coming for both of us. But he was going to buy us some time. I had to lie low—and no one, not even Claudine, for her own safety—could know where I was while Gilles went to Paris. He intended to speak to some powerful Russian contacts there who might be able to offer us protection.

"We drove to Nice that night. Gilles closed the gallery and I camped in the strongroom."

Murmurs went around the table as they let out their collective breath.

Clémence leaned forward towards the mayor. "Have you heard anything more from the police this morning? Are they satisfied that it was Gilles who killed Scarpio to save Nic?"

"I think so. Penny heard him confess to it last night, before . . ."

Penelope fought the image of Gilles falling backwards. "He didn't deserve that," she said at last.

"No, he didn't," said Laurent.

A silence freighted with mixed emotions took hold again.

Penelope frowned and addressed Nicolas. "By the way, did the wood panelling in one of the outhouses at the museum belong to you, or had someone else put it there?"

"It was mine," said Nicolas. "I bought it to conduct some experiments on when I became suspicious about the icons after seeing several that I couldn't authenticate. I wanted to see for myself how the wood would absorb a new application of old pigment."

"Now," said Clémence, looking very excited, "I have spoken to the police this morning, unofficially, to one of my contacts. The autopsy on Don Doncaster revealed an unexplained puncture mark in one of his veins."

"I knew it!" said Penelope.

They all looked at her.

"Anya killed Don," continued Penelope. "And I think I know how." She walked them through Cam's analysis of possible methods to kill someone without leaving a trace.

Laurent studied her in amazement. "Have you told the police this?"

"Last night. It was the only logical explanation—I was sure about it. I just didn't know who had actually done it."

"There's more," said Clémence. "Gilles de Bourdan's DNA was found on Scarpio's body. And Nicolas managed to pull out some of Scarpio's hair during the attack—before Gilles appeared and finished Scarpio off."

"That was clever," said Frankie.

"It was self-defence," said Nicolas. "And then Gilles did everything he could to keep me safe from Anya and that treacherous Alexis. He found out too late that Alexis was a plant. He worked for the Russians who were taking over from the old Russian mob in Nice. Anya had been a sleeper for some time, first for the old guard, keeping an eye on the art operation from close by, then switching to the new gang."

Penelope choked up as she thought of Gilles. His charm and his crimes. He had done wrong, but he had tried to redeem himself. Clémence noticed her shaking slightly and laid a kindly hand upon her shoulder.

"Do not blame yourself, *chérie*—we were all taken in by Gilles. Well, except for you, Laurent."

Penelope nodded carefully. "What's happened to Nina?" she asked. "Presumably the police have been speaking to her again."

"She's all right. Shocked after the events yesterday, as you are," said Laurent.

"She came to see me in the afternoon," said Claudine.

"I was going to ask you about that, how she suddenly appeared on the cliff," said Penelope.

"Nina is a funny one, that's for sure, but she means well—mostly." Claudine acknowledged what they were all thinking. "Anyway, she turned up at the museum around three-thirty saying she needed to speak to me urgently. But she wouldn't tell me anything until we were out of the building, out of my office, in particular. I suggested we go over to my house, but she didn't want to be there either. She wanted to go up into the museum grounds. That worried me, as you can imagine, given what happened to Scarpio. But she was quite happy for me to tell Aline on reception where we were going, and that if anyone wanted me I was 'in a meeting.' Nina even told me to make sure I had my mobile with me, and asked Aline to call my number at various intervals, so I was reassured that she wished me no harm."

"That sounds as if Nina was worried herself," said Penelope.

"Oh, she was. Terrified, I would say. And we were only just in time. We saw Gilles arrive in the museum car park and walk towards the building. If I had been in my office alone . . ." Claudine shuddered. "But as it was, the two of us, Nina and I, took the path through the trees, talking as we walked. Don had warned her months ago that Gilles and Scarpio were working together on some bad deals, though he didn't know exactly what. They—Don and Nina—owed Gilles so much that they decided to overlook his side deals. Don said it was nothing to do with them, and that the art world was full of exaggerations and bad faith."

"Well, he knew firsthand that it was, from his own financial success," pointed out Clémence.

"But then Nina's studio was burned down," resumed Claudine. "She knew she had been the target. She was caught between the police and the person who wanted her dead—and she did not have long before the police worked out that she was not the body in the burnt-out studio—but she wanted to do all she could to warn me. She also needed some proof about the fake paintings and the reason for them. To find out how guilty Gilles was."

"Gilles insisted to me that she was dangerous," said Penelope. "But now I think that must have been because he thought she was a loose cannon who might put the searchlight on his gallery in Nice and expose Nicolas's hiding place."

"That could well have been the case," said Claudine. "Because she made a breakthrough where she was least expecting it—right here in this house!"

"Blithering heck, my dog icon," interjected Frankie.

Claudine pulled a face. "I know nothing about a dog, but she saw an icon that had been painted over in acrylics. Then you told her it had been bought as a Doncaster. Nina told me that after seeing you she decided to go to Goult to the only other person who might be able to help."

"Fenella," said Clémence.

Penelope sat up. "But of course Fenella was not there."

"And we now know why," added Laurent grimly.

There was a pause, during which they all gave a thought to poor Fenella, the third victim who had almost been overlooked.

"But Anya *was* there," said Claudine. "And Anya had been trying to see Nina. She had been to the studio several times to look for her but she was never there. And as they spoke, in English, it suddenly occurred to Nina that Anya was not Czech at all, as she had always claimed, but Russian. It was there in her accent. And she didn't seem to have anything she wanted to discuss with Nina, certainly nothing pressing enough to have prompted her to come to the studio several times. Something wasn't right. Nina got out of there as quickly as she could.

"So, Nina and I are in the woods. We see Gilles arrive, then you, Penny. All we're doing is keeping safe. Then two more people arrive. It's Anya and Alexis from the galleries. At that point, Nina told me to call the police and tell them everything. She'd made sure I had my mobile, remember. Hers was long out of power.

"We were waiting until the police arrived to move from our spot." Claudine paused for effect. "We waited for some time. Then we heard voices. Gilles was coming up the same path, with someone else. A woman's voice, speaking in English. It is likely only to be one person!"

Penelope raised her palms.

"Nina told me to stay where I was, and she tracked you onto the cliff edge. She knew the police would soon arrive."

"I'd called them, too," put in Frankie. "As soon as Penny left for Roussillon. We had to tell the police that Nina was still alive and that it wasn't her body that was found after the fire. I told them where Pen had gone and that Claudine was in danger. That it was somehow all connected—"

"That would explain the helicopter, then," said Claudine. "They obviously thought it was a major incident."

"I may have exaggerated a little," admitted Frankie. "But when your oldest, closest, and most annoying friend is involved, you don't want to take any chances."

"Hey! I think you'll find that you're the annoying one," murmured Penelope, widening her eyes at Frankie.

"It was a very good call," said Claudine. "It ensured that the police took us seriously."

"How did they know to look for Nicolas in Nice?" asked Penelope. "Gilles refused to say where he was, right up to the end."

Laurent ran a hand through his hair. "It seems Gilles knew his part in these events might be coming to an end, that he might not survive a confrontation. An anonymous call was made to the police in Nice, telling them to check the strongroom in his gallery there. It was traced to the phone at the Bourdan Gallery in Avignon. The Nice gallery had closed early 'for Christmas.'"

They all reached for the comfort of almond croissants, even Clémence.

37

"HAVE YOU SEEN OUTSIDE, PEN? It's wonderful!"

The garden was carpeted in white and the Grand Luberon was dredged with icing sugar, the gullies and creases of the mountain highlighted by fresh snow fallen in the night.

"How exciting!" Penelope felt like giggling. "Nice day for a . . ."

"White wedding" sang Frankie, slightly off-key.

"Who'd have thought we'd still be quoting Billy Idol thirty years later in a farmhouse in Provence?" laughed Penelope.

"But it's so apt. The first snow of the year on the day that Pierre and Mariette are getting hitched. It's almost Hollywood!"

"Indeed, and there's a serious amount of work to do before we set forth to the mairie!"

Penelope did some light exercises (Frankie excused herself from Zumba class on the grounds of being on holiday), washed and blow-dried her hair, took the dress she was going to wear from the wardrobe—a cranberry "Bombshell" wrap dress in wool crepe that flattered her hourglass shape—and checked the black boots that the weather dictated. She then began the painful job of dealing with her face. It wasn't physically as sore as it had been, but more than a week later, the cut to her cheek and the greenish remains of the black eye were still visible. She cursed Alexis again as she tried to apply enough foundation to mask it.

"I still look like the elephant man, Frankie!"

Frankie was considering the ankle-length snakeskin lamé dress she had bought for the celebration. "Bit much for the morning at the mairie, even for me. But I'm bloody well wearing it this evening." She came over and scrutinised Penelope's face. "You'd have to get really close to see anything untoward, Pen. So unless you're planning something with Laurent, you'll be fine."

Penelope felt herself blush deeply underneath the layers of makeup.

Frankie was looking out of the window.

"Glad you've got a four-by-four. It's snowing again. Getting heavier."

The lazy flakes that had drifted down so elegantly that morning were now cottonwool balls.

"It's a shame in a way, Frankie. Pierre has been polishing his prize-winning tractor for weeks for today—he wanted to arrive at the mairie in it. Not sure if he will want to now."

She peered out of the clouded windows. It really did feel like Christmas was near.

❦

ST MERLOT'S square was full of parked cars. Most of the village had apparently been invited to the mairie for the civil ceremony.

The room was so packed that it was close to becoming tropical. They slipped into seats close to the back.

At that moment, Monique hurried in, giving the thumbs-up. Mariette had arrived, beautiful in a classic navy dress with matching jacket, and a white rose on her lapel. She and Pierre walked down the aisle to the table at the front where Laurent stood ready to officiate. After a rowdy cheer, the room fell silent.

The ceremony was mercifully short, and when the newlyweds

had left the room to resounding applause and backslapping, they all followed outside, where they posed for photographs and confetti mingled in the air with snowflakes.

"*Bonjour*, Penny. It's very romantic, is it not?"

She jumped and turned around to see Laurent smiling. She blushed, tried to pretend she was not blushing, then blushed a little more as she tried to present her unblackened eye to him. "It's perfectly lovely."

"By the way, have you seen *La Provence* this morning?"

"No, why?"

"Our friend Reyssens, *M. le Chef de Police*, has received an award. For single-handedly solving the case of the murdered artists along with exposing a network of Russian art crime. With no assistance whatsoever from anyone else!"

"What a remarkable man he is," said Penelope.

"I wondered if you would be interested in having dinner this evening—to celebrate his success . . . ?"

They both laughed.

"Well, it would be nice, finally!"

"Good. After the reception this evening, then, we'll go to—"

He was unable to finish as Pierre Louchard waved for attention and shushed the crowd.

"*Mesdames, messieurs.* Now we are married . . ." Some cheering and jokey heckling ensued. "Now we are married, my wife and I . . ." More cheering. "My wife and I look forward to seeing you at the Prieuré this evening at six o'clock for a blessing in the chapel, followed by the *vin d'honneur.*" A spectacularly loud cheer echoed around the square.

"So, if I made a reservation at Le Carillon at Goult, for around eight-thirty?" Laurent continued.

"That would be perfect," replied Penelope, "and now I must leave to prepare."

"Prepare, Penny? Surely it will not take you that long to get ready for dinner with me!"

Penelope laughed. "We have a surprise for Pierre, and for the first time ever, you don't know what it is and I do!" With that she turned and walked smartly back to her car, stopping only to remove Frankie from the centre of a raucous mob comprised mainly of the St Merlot pétanque team, with which she had clearly already formed a deep attachment.

"Hang on, Pen, I was just getting to the bit where the Saudi sheikh, you know, when the cucumber got lodged in . . ."

Penelope turned her friend in the direction of the car and gave her a small shove. "Not sure St Merlot is ready for your Moulin Rouge stories quite yet, Frankie."

❧

THEY TOOK it easy in the afternoon. Penelope sat down with her cello to practise the song that Mariette was going to sing.

She drew the bow across the strings of her cello, imagining the entwining counterpoint of Mariette's voice and Monique's violin, as she played through the piece. It was an adaptation of her favourite Fauré song, "Après un Rêve."

In a slumber which held your image spellbound, I dreamt of
*   happiness.*

The first lines of the poem by Bussine had always moved her, and this time, as she considered the long nightmare endured by Pierre and Mariette before fate had intervened to provide them with their dream, a tear dripped off her nose onto the mellow brown wood of the instrument.

From the sofa, Frankie applauded as the last notes disappeared into the air.

"You're a bit of a softy underneath aren't you, darling!"

A wave of sadness swept over Penelope. She thought of Don and Gilles, of Nicolas's ordeal, of Nina's bravery and how she had misjudged her. She felt Frankie's gentle hug as her head was pulled towards a not inconsiderable chest.

"As I said, a bit of a softy—but that's why we all love you."

Penelope let it all out, then sat up and wiped her eyes. She felt suddenly lighter.

❧

A RED sun hung just over the distant hills as dusk fell upon St Merlot. For a moment the snowy landscape was suffused with pink. Penelope put her cello and their shoes in the car, and then went upstairs to change into another berry-coloured dress, this time a silk crepe maxi with a wrap skirt.

Frankie appeared in the bronze snakeskin-patterned sheath that many a smaller woman would not have got away with, but on her was a monument to self-confidence at any size. She topped it off with the leopard faux-fur coat, and they both pulled on gumboots for the short journey to the Priory on the other side of St Merlot.

Through the lichen-encrusted gateposts of Prieuré des Gentilles Merlotiennes, brilliant white lights twinkled in the avenue of bare plane trees that reached skeletal hands to the sky. Next to the venerable Priory door stood an enormous Christmas tree, hung with lanterns and gold-meshed bags of lavender.

Frankie was entranced. "This way to Narnia!"

They giggled, and drove round the back as instructed by

Mariette. A teenage niece was there to collect the cello. Then they continued round to the parking area and walked up to the great door.

Altar candles illuminated the entrance hall and the way to the chapel on one side and to a room decked with pine branches and red roses on the other.

There was a tap on her shoulder.

"Monique! *Bonsoir!*" said Penelope. They all exchanged kisses for the second time that day.

"Your cello is hidden in that room over there," Monique whispered. "I will get it out and set it up behind the screen in the main room once Pierre has gone into the chapel."

Soon, the trickle of guests arriving became a deluge. The volume of excited conversation rose. Penelope and Frankie swiftly claimed two seats in the chapel. Apart from a display of red roses and fronds of fir, there were no wedding decorations here. The walls soared to join knotty stone hands in the vaulted ceiling.

"I do love a man in uniform, Pen!"

Penelope turned to see Pierre Louchard wearing the full ceremonial dress of a captain in the French Foreign Legion. He walked proudly square-shouldered up the aisle and took his place at the front.

Then, as she looked around for a first sight of the bride, her heart missed a beat. Clémence stood in the doorway on the arm of a distinguished-looking man with black and steel-grey hair in a dark suit and a row of medals on his chest. Could it possibly be the elusive M. Valencourt? She felt the delicious anticipation of another mystery about to be solved. But first, the blessing.

Mariette appeared in a stunning deep cream mid-calf dress with a sweetheart neckline, carrying a posy of red roses. She took Benoît's arm and they walked solemnly towards the groom.

❀

CHAMPAGNE CORKS popped. Filled glasses on silver trays greeted the guests as they entered the Christmas wonderland of the reception room. More candles danced in lanterns between red roses, pine branches, and trailing ivy. When everyone had a glass, Laurent rang a bell for silence. "And now, my friends, we salute our happy couple with a *coupe de champagne*. Every happiness, dear Mariette and Pierre!"

The villagers bellowed back the words of the toast as they raised their glasses.

"Thank you, dear friends," said Pierre, clearly emotional. "We thank you for being here and celebrating with us on this wonderful day, in this wonderful old building, in this wonderful village!"

He wiped a tear to roars of approval.

Frankie turned to Penelope. "Off you go, I'll save a *coupe* for you!"

Penelope winked at Monique, who was also quietly moving towards the screen. This time it was Mariette who waved for silence.

"Pierre. My husband Pierre."

More cheers.

Mariette looked down and had to stop for a moment, then resolutely raised her pretty face in the lamplight. "I never thought I would say that. But now my heart is so full of joy, and this is for you, Pierre."

She walked over to the screen. Two waiters removed it deftly to reveal Monique and Penelope sitting ready with their instruments. A murmur of surprise from the floor was quickly hushed. The two musicians drew their bows across the strings to introduce the melody, quietly at first then with more volume and urgency. All stood quiet as Mariette's rich, honeyed mezzo-soprano voice filled the hall.

> *Dans un sommeil que charmait ton image*
> *Je rêvais le bonheur, ardent mirage . . .*

It was not a long piece. But as the last chord rose and died away, leaving a charged stillness in the air, the only sound that could be heard was the rustle of tissues simultaneously extracted from bags and pockets. Even Frankie looked misty-eyed as Mariette walked over to give her new husband the most intimate of kisses.

Laurent raised his glass again. "To the happy couple."

"To the happy couple," repeated the crowd.

The bride and groom kissed at length.

Gentle laughter and chat filled the air. Penelope saw that Laurent was making his way towards her and felt another thrill. Let the countdown to dinner à deux finally commence, she thought. The restaurant he had chosen was quiet and romantic, the perfect choice after an emotional day.

"Penny, I must say hello to some of the other guests, but I hope that eight-thirty is still good for you."

Very good for me, she almost replied. She felt a tremble of anticipation. "That will be just right, I think." She was about to ask him whether they would make the drive together when she felt a hefty dig in the ribs.

"Hang about, Pen—what am I going to do for dinner?"

"I'd try the pétanque team, if I were you, Frankie!" said Penelope, distracted. Penelope had spotted the noble figure of M. Valencourt on a mobile on the other side of the room and was desperately trying to think of a way of getting over there without being too obvious.

"Penny! Another musical delight—what a moment, and how marvellous to hear Mariette sing again!" In the commotion, Clémence's stilettoed approach had been muffled. They exchanged kisses, and Penelope tried to engage her brain in some introductory small talk. But it was no good.

"Clémence, is that your husband over there?"

"*Oui*, Penny. Would you like to meet him?"

"I would be honoured!"

"Whoa, wait for me, Pen! Just need a little top-up and I'll be—"

But Penelope was off like a shot to the corner where M. Valencourt had been standing.

He was no longer there.

Penelope scanned the room and the hall from the doorway but there was no sign of him anywhere. Clémence stopped and pulled her phone from her Chanel handbag.

"*Zut, alors!*"

"What is the matter, Clémence?"

"It is a text from Thibault. He has had to leave immediately and has taken the car. What a shame. I was looking forward to introducing you. Now it will have to wait until he gets back."

"Will he be long?"

"Quite some time, I should think. It usually is."

"Where's he gone, then?"

"To Paris."

"Paris?" echoed Penelope. "That's a bit abrupt, isn't it?" Her actual thoughts were considerably less charitable than that, both on Clémence's behalf and her own thwarted curiosity's. But she could not stay grumpy for long. After all, soon she would be off into the night with Laurent.

As if on cue, the clock in the hall—working for the first time in many years, according to Pierre—chimed an elegant carillon signifying seven-thirty, and Laurent materialised next to her. He leaned forward and whispered in her ear.

"We will just need to listen to Pierre's speech, which will no doubt be too long and too full of his philosophical meanderings, then we can be off."

"I thought he'd already done that."

"No, that was just the welcome."

Penelope smiled and prepared herself as Pierre made his way through to stand at the doorway. Laurent and Benoît called again for silence.

"*Mesdames, messieurs*, I was going to make a speech this evening. But Mariette has said it all already in her wonderful surprise. But now I can surprise her! You are all invited to a wedding dinner in the refectory, the first time it has been used for more than sixty years."

He cast his arms wide, and as if by magic the large wooden doors across the hall to the grand refectory were opened.

"Dear God, we're at Hogwarts!" breathed Frankie.

The guests bundled out to see long lines of tables illuminated by candles. The walls had been adorned with red-berried holly and more pine branches and roses. At the end, on a table running across in the opposite direction, white-aproned cooks stood ready over steaming platters of food. The crowd needed little bidding to surge forward through the doors, leaving Pierre and his wife in another romantic clinch.

Penelope's heart seemed to stop.

She looked at Laurent, hundred-proof handsome in the candlelight, and as realisation turned to disappointment, let the pictures run through her mind one last time as if trying to prolong a lovely dream after waking: the fantasy of an intimate dinner at the restaurant in Goult, the chance for a closer understanding between them (she would dare to imagine no more than that). Laurent looked at her. It was definitely a moment.

A moment comprehensively ruined by Frankie's voice ringing through the room.

"Well, that's Pen's night buggered!"

Penelope felt heat rise in her face, but then started to laugh.

"Maybe next week, Penny," said Laurent, with a hint of a wink.

"It might have to be a New Year's resolution," she replied. "I'm going back to England for Christmas with the family."

"A New Year's *reservation*, then!" And then, he was gone, carried through in the tide that surged into the refectory.

"No dinner with Laurent, then. Bad luck." Clémence materialised at her side.

"*C'est la vie*," said Penelope, linking her arm through the Frenchwoman's. "I like a challenge."

Acknowledgments

꧁꧂

Croissants and rosé all round to all those whose faith in Penelope Kite has seen her back in a second adventure. The books started as a fun project with plenty of laughs right from the outset with literary agents Stephanie Cabot and Araminta Whitley in New York and London. We are incredibly lucky to have them.

It continues to be a joy to work with editor Jennifer Barth and her unerring appreciation of British humour, and to have the support of Harper president and publisher, Jonathan Burnham. Big thanks to all at Harper editorial, especially Sarah Ried, Yvette Grant, Jamie Kerner, and Joanne O'Neill. Emily VanDerwerken and Megan Looney have been fantastic in spreading the word in the media.

We'd also like to thank all the libraries who bought *Death in Avignon* for their lists and all the wonderful Instagrammers who have been so creative and enthusiastic in their posts about the book.

Deborah Lawrenson
Robert Rees

About the Author

SERENA KENT is the nom de plume of Deborah Lawrenson and her husband, Robert Rees. They met at Cambridge University and pursued completely different careers—she in journalism and fiction; he in banking and music. They live in England and an old hamlet in Provence, in houses full of books and in dire need of more bookshelves.

ALSO BY SERENA KENT

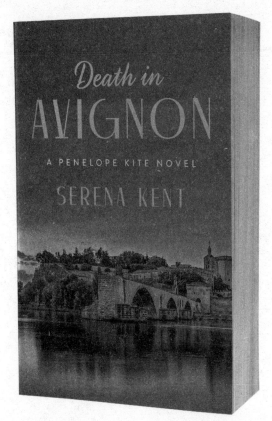

DEATH IN AVIGNON
A PENELOPE KITE NOVEL

Set amidst the gorgeous backdrop of Provence, Serena Kent's second book in the deliciously entertaining Penelope Kite series finds the amateur sleuth dashing to solve the murder of an expat artist—perfect for fans of Peter Mayle and Agatha Christie.

After an eventful first few months in Provence, it seems Penelope is finally settling into her delightful new life, complete with a gorgeous love interest in the mayor of St. Merlot. Set against the stunning vistas of Provence, Serena Kent returns with the second installment of her charming mystery series featuring the unflappable Penelope Kite.